Josh's Fake Fiancee

Shelley Munro

Munro Press

Josh's Fake Fiancee

Copyright © 2024 by Shelley Munro

Print ISBN: 978-1-99-106350-2
Digital ISBN: 978-0-473-49761-3

Editor: Evil Eye Editing

Cover: Kim Killion, The Killion Group, Inc.

This book is a work of fiction. The names, characters, places, and incidents are products of the writer's imagination or have been used fictitiously and are not to be construed as real. Any resemblance to persons, living or dead, actual events, locales, or organizations is entirely coincidental.

All rights reserved. No portion of this book may be reproduced, scanned, or distributed in any manner without prior written permission from the author, except in the case of a brief quotation embodied in critical articles and reviews.

Munro Press, New Zealand.

First Munro Press electronic publication November 2019

First Munro Press print publication April 2024

DEDICATION

For Paul, my fellow adventurer.

INTRODUCTION

A fiancée fabrication might just save her life...

Ever since she was a five-year-old with pigtails, Ashley Townsend has dreamed of becoming the prime minister of New Zealand. Now, with a career in politics, she's well on the way to achieving her goal until a stalker threatens her life.

Josh Williams is taking time off after retiring from the military. A favor for a soldier friend? No problem. A pretend engagement? Okay, it'll allow him to assess his future. Hands-off? Sure, he'll treat Ashley like a sister.

After his first glimpse of his temporary fiancée, Josh admits he's in trouble, and suddenly this easy assignment is a mite trickier. Soon Josh is dealing with the stalker, protecting his sexy and smart fiancée, and his heart is on the line. The press is asking nosy questions, the gap between pretense and reality is blurring, and Josh is wondering if granting his friend this favor is such a bright idea.

You'll love this romantic suspense because it features an intelligent heroine and a protective soldier determined to keep his lady safe. Oh, and a little of New Zealand politics for spice and seasoning.

NOTE TO READERS

Politics in New Zealand is different than in other countries. Please keep this in mind while reading this romance.

Our two main political parties are Labor and National. Labor is center-left and supports social equality, while National is center-right. In truth, there is not a huge difference in their policies and beliefs.

We do not have an ultra-conservative party with great power. Scandals or dirty politics are uncommon. If a person has made a mistake in the past and has admitted to and paid for it, most New Zealanders are fair-minded enough to give them the benefit of the doubt. We believe in second chances for those who have earned them.

Our current prime minister lived with her fiancé and had a baby during the first year of her three-year term in office. The public barely blinked at this while I believe this situation might cause huge upsets in other countries.

To date, we have had three female prime ministers, which is fitting since New Zealand was the first country to give women the right to vote.

One final thing—it's quite common for a group of friends to have different political affiliations yet still remain good friends. Differences in political opinions seldom cause problems or confrontational comments.

If you have any questions, please feel free to email me via my website.

>Happy reading,
>Shelley Munro

1

JOSH RECEIVES HIS FAKE FIANCÉE ASSIGNMENT

ASHLEY TOWNSEND PARKED HER car, switched off the ignition, and sucked in a shaky breath. Then she followed her soldier brother's curt reminder to take stock of her surroundings. Her gaze ran over the brick walls of her Labor party office in Manurewa, Auckland, and the pots of red and white petunias purchased to make the ugly building more welcoming. Three other cars sat near hers in the tiny parking lot behind the office, and she recognized each of them.

A light shone from the office reception area, piercing the early morning shadows with a welcome glow. Ashley's breath hissed out, and she peeled her fingers free of the steering wheel. An uneasy laugh filled her vehicle interior.

Those letters.

The sense of someone watching her...

After another quick scan of the vicinity, she gathered her laptop, a fat purple folder, and her black handbag.

Time to get her crazy-busy day started. The campaign trail waited for no one since the election loomed in four weeks. With the way the Labor party—her chosen political affiliation—trailed the incumbent National party in the polls, she required every day, every minute, every second to sway voters.

New Zealand used the mixed-member proportional method or MMP system, where each voter received two votes: one for a party—any of ten this election—and one for a politician who stood in the voter's region. This meant the smaller parties nipped at their heels too, jockeying to earn five percent or more of the votes. Any party reaching this milestone gained a parliamentary seat and, with it, influence for three years until the next election. She couldn't afford to slack or to take a break to deal with her personal life.

Ashley exited her vehicle, locked it, and darted to the rear entrance she and the staff used. As per Matt's lectures, after her mother and father had tattled, she kept focused. Two parked vehicles near the mini-mart across the road. One driving down the main road. Not stopping. Probably another worker starting their job at six-thirty in the morning. People lurking in the carpark. Nil.

Her pulse raced, faster than average, and didn't slow until her hand settled on the doorknob and she stepped into the coffee-tinged atmosphere of her constituent office.

"Good morning," she called out.

"Morning, boss," Robert, her right-hand man, returned in a rumbly bass. He was two years older than her twenty-eight. Solid and dependable. His black hair and well-trimmed beard gave him a scholarly-look, but he was a keen runner and played soccer for a local team during the weekend.

"Hi, Ashley," their young political hopeful chirped. With her restless fidgeting and bright-eyed enthusiasm, Carrie reminded Ashley of a young puppy, eager and excited to explore the world. Her thick brown curls, frizzy from Auckland's humidity, reinforced the puppy metaphor.

"Good morning, Ashley. How did the dinner meeting with the business leaders go?" Sheryl held a volunteer position, but her many years of experience and marriage to a senior Labor politician, plus her commonsense smoothed the edges of most emergencies.

"They listened to my speech detailing what we intend to do in the business arena, and I answered their questions without a hitch. My study paid off. I think it went well. Robert?"

He gave a brisk nod. "Your answers came across as thoughtful and honest. Even better, you didn't promise what we can't deliver. Capital gains tax will be a problem. It's a mistake to campaign on this issue. We're better to win the voters over with social policy."

Ashley sighed, tired of the subject and helpless to change her party's stance. "I hear you, but Geoffrey is the party leader. His say is final."

"He's making a mistake, and the polls confirm this. The voters want change. We'll remain the opposition party if we don't alter the way we're attacking this campaign."

"Geoffrey deserves our loyalty," Ashley said, her tone even and polite rather than the snappish chiding her instincts propelled her to unleash. "Is there much mail?"

The words, meant to distract him, pushed her heartbeat into a rapid *bang-bang-bang*. A chill raced down her spine while she waited for his reply.

"The normal stuff. I've dealt with what I can and written post-it notes for each piece."

Relief had her knees wobbling beneath her black trousers. "I'll deal with the mail before we head out to our breakfast meeting. Is there anything else requiring my attention?"

"A few letters from constituents. I've added them to the mail pile."

Ashley nodded. "If I don't emerge by seven-thirty, tap on my door. That's the latest we can leave for the union leaders' meeting."

She hustled to her office and stepped inside. It held a modest wooden desk, two comfortable chairs for visitors, and modular shelving full of books for research. A painting by her mother adorned the wall—a scene of Auckland Harbor and Rangitoto Island, the dormant volcano that dominated the city panorama. Although she often left her door open, today she required privacy to pull herself together.

After speaking to her parents and brother, she'd reported the threatening letters to the police.

Unfortunately, they couldn't do much, although they'd make their presence known whenever she attended outdoor events, which she appreciated. The truth—her brother had scared her silly with his security lecture and his list of rules. She was jumping at every strange noise, acting the ninny in public.

This had to stop.

Ashley's fight to retain her parliamentary seat required focus. Determination.

When she was five and wore her hair in pigtails, she'd told her parents she intended to be the queen of New Zealand. They'd pointed out the job was taken, so she'd decided the position of prime minister might be okay. Now, years later, her ambitions hadn't veered from her chosen course. She dreamed of following other strong New Zealand women who'd claimed the ultimate power and run the country. Women who'd effected change.

This...this stalker was derailing her plans. She checked her watch and gasped. He or she—whichever sex her stalker claimed—would also make her late. Her days were jam-packed as it was, and she couldn't afford to waste time jumping at shadows.

It was time for her big-girl panties.

Ashley dumped her folder and laptop on the desktop and got to work. Robert was excellent at his job, and each letter had suggestions for action. Some she agreed with while others, she let her opinion govern her final decision. Her rule about touching each piece of correspondence once helped her to plow through a pile of work. Next, she scanned the letters ready for her signature. Even though she trusted the staff, she always read each reply before adding her name.

The final one gave her pause, as did the original letter attached to the one Robert had drafted.

Dear Ashley, do you remember me from school? She scanned the request, her throat tight and a heavy weight pressing on her chest. Although a woman—someone called Felicity Barrowman—had signed the letter, the penmanship brought to mind her brother's masculine scrawl. Every instinct, jogged by the similarity in the writing, told her the writer was a man, and he was making his next move.

This man was her stalker.

"FROG, I GOT YOUR email. What's up?"

It was early evening in Eketahuna, and Josh Williams lay in a hammock in his parents' rear garden, having a beer and relaxing after a day of farm chores. Two weeks ago, he'd left his New Zealand Special Air Service military duties and the army for good, and now he was at a loose end with no clue of what came next. He was spending his days helping his older brother Dillon and taking care of his father's farm while his parents took the vacation his mother had dreamed about for years. They arrived home tomorrow, and it was time for him to find his adult boots and determine his next life chapter.

"I need a favor." Frog's face wavered on the screen from interference. Expected, given his friend was calling from

Afghanistan.

"No problem." Josh never hesitated. Matt Townsend was affectionately known as Frog because of his love of karaoke. He sang as often as possible but badly, hence the nickname. Frog was a fellow soldier and a member of the NZSAS team that both Josh and his brother Dillon had belonged to before taking retirement.

"My sister needs help." Frog's face etched into worry.

Josh sipped his beer and frowned, pulling one of Frog's family photos to mind. "Which one?"

"Ash, the youngest one."

"The politician?" He dug through his memories again and recalled a blurred photo of a woman wearing a cap and gown at a university graduation.

"Yeah. Ashley has acquired a stalker. She's reported the problem to the police, but they can't do much. It's bloody frustrating being stuck in Afghanistan and unavailable to help. This stalker has scared her, and Ash normally owns confidence."

"How can I help?" Josh asked.

"I need you to take charge of her security."

Josh blinked but agreed. "Sure, I can do that. Where is she? Christchurch? Mum and Dad arrive home tomorrow so I can catch a flight the day after."

"Wait. Damn," Frog muttered after a background shout. "I have to go. I need you to pretend to be her fiancé."

"Fiancé?" Josh spluttered.

"Yeah, but Josh, do not under any circumstances fuck with her. She's my baby sister, and you keep your hands off. Promise?"

"Wait, what?" His hearing was off. "You did say her fiancé?"

"Yeah, I'll email later with more details. It needs to be a convincing performance, otherwise you won't be able to stay close to Ash. Hands off my baby sister or I *will* take action. Got it? Will you do it? Watch over her?"

"Wait! You're certain you want me?"

"I don't trust anyone else. Hands off, remember?"

"Details," Josh prompted.

"As soon as we get back," Frog promised. "Maybe two hours."

"Frog!" someone roared in the background.

"Gotta go," Frog said. "Remember your promise, or I'll bloody your pretty face the first chance I get. I'll check in again soon."

"Yeah, man. Stay safe."

The call disconnected, and the screen turned black. Josh closed the app on his phone, appalled and terrified at his friend's request. Had Frog been playing him? Nah, his mate never joked about his family.

Well, he'd wanted something to do. He'd wait for details and go from there.

His phone rang. "Yeah?"

"Ella and I are coming into town for dinner. Meet us at the pub?" Dillon asked.

"What time?"

"Seven suit you?"

"I'll see you there."

Three hours later, Josh walked into the pub, and after getting a beer, claimed a table. His brother ambled inside with his arm curved around Ella's waist, their heads close together. Ella patted his cheek, and Dillon laughed at their private joke.

Josh took pleasure in his brother's happiness, and he genuinely liked his new sister-in-law. Ella had pink hair today, although the color changed from week-to-week. Yesterday, she'd had electric-blue. She wore what she'd informed Josh was a vintage dress and a swing coat. See? He was learning.

If he could learn about clothes and hair, politics shouldn't prove difficult.

"Hey." Josh rose to hug his brother and then Ella. "What can I get you to drink?"

"I'm driving," Dillon said. "Low-alcohol beer for me."

"A glass of Sauvignon blanc, please." Ella pulled out a chair and sat. She swept a lock of pink hair away from her eyes. "I'm exhausted. Your brother had me helping to shear the alpacas this afternoon."

"You should've called me," Josh said. "Dad has everything in hand, even though he's been away. All I had to do was shift the stock to a fresh paddock and check the water supply."

"I wanted to help," Ella spoke in a firm, no-nonsense manner. "It's fun to see the entire process of growing the wool to shearing and spinning."

By the time Josh returned with drinks, Ella and Dillon were perusing the menu and checking out the specials' board.

Dillon stood. "I'm having the roast beef. Ella wants salmon. What will you have, Josh?"

"Roast beef works for me," Josh said.

While Dillon stood to place their orders at the bar, Josh chatted with Ella about alpacas and the increasing number of native birds in the Eketahuna region.

"We're pleased the populations are recovering so well." Ella's head tilted slightly, her cheeks flushed with pleasure. "The poaching ring decimated some species, but they're bouncing back."

Dillon returned and claimed the seat beside Ella. "The kitchen orders are backed up. Our meals will be half an hour."

"That gives me time to tell you about my call with Frog," Josh said.

"How is he?" Dillon asked. "Problem?"

"He wants me to act as personal security and fake fiancé for his younger sister."

Dillon spat out a mouthful of beer, spraying the table.

"Did you say fake fiancé?" Ella dabbed at the beer with a napkin, her eyes rounded with astonishment.

"Not too loud. This is on the down-low, but I figure Frog won't mind you knowing. His sister has attracted a stalker, and the cops can't help much at this stage. The notes keep coming, but no one sees who delivers them."

"Have you met his sister?" Ella asked.

"No," Dillon said.

"No," Josh agreed. "I've seen photos. Until he told me, I had no idea Frog had such high connections."

Dillon leaned back in his chair. "Who is she?"

"Ashley Townsend." Josh's grin widened at his brother's blank expression.

Ella gasped. "The Labor MP? The one who gets a hard time from the press? They nicknamed her Legs."

"That's the one."

"She keeps her private life to herself." Ella sipped her wine. "How will you play the fake- fiancé angle? Won't everyone notice a fiancé popping out of the woodwork and ask nosey questions?"

"Frog has come up with a workable plan. He emailed me more details before I left home to come here. According to his story, I met Ashley through him, and because my job was sensitive, we kept our connection quiet. Now that I've retired from the army, we're able to make our engagement public. Frog briefed his parents and older sister. They'll confirm the story."

"Won't she get blowback for lying once the cops catch the stalker?" Dillon asked.

"I asked Frog the same thing." Josh rubbed the back of his neck. Although he understood, he didn't enjoy lying. "He thinks they can spin the situation to garner public sympathy, and meantime, the engagement will bring publicity for the Labor party. Hopefully, he's right."

Dillon's brows rose, curiosity glinting in his eyes as he considered the situation. "What does a fake-fiancé do?"

Josh shrugged. "According to Frog, I attend political functions with his sister and stand at her side while watching for threats and keeping her safe. In my spare time, I try to work out where the threat is coming from and shut it down. Old boyfriends. Upset constituents. Political rivals. That sort of thing."

"You'll need clothes," Ella said. "You can't wear your

scruffy jeans and a leather jacket while standing next to Ashley Townsend. She's a babe."

Josh scowled and smoothed his hand over his unruly beard.

"That will have to go. I trimmed Dillon's beard. I could—"

"No," Dillon said, straightening. "He can find his own girl to trim his beard."

Josh grinned and winked at Ella. "I'll have a fiancé to look after me."

Ella frowned at Dillon before turning back to Josh. "You will not play with her emotions and stop her from doing her job. This isn't a game, Josh. Fooling around might have consequences for Ashley and wreck her career."

Josh glowered at the accusation in his sister-in-law's words. Yes, he flirted with women. Yes, people might accuse him of hurting women, but never on purpose. He was always upfront regarding his expectations. No long-term commitment. Nothing more than friendship. Enjoy each other and move on with no hard feelings. His job as a soldier had made his stance on romance easier since he'd never been in one place for long. Now, it was different. He still didn't want to marry. He still wanted to have fun, but he required a new excuse.

"She's a public figure." Dillon paused with his glass mid-air. His brows drew together. "Why isn't she receiving DPS aid?"

"What's a DPS?" Ella asked.

"Diplomatic Protection Service. The Prime Minister and the Governor-General get a DPS, both in New

Zealand and when they're abroad. The ministers of the crown, members of parliament, the judiciary and the leader of the opposition only receive protection if the police think the risk warrants a DPS," Dillon explained.

"Huh." Ella sipped her wine. "I learn lots of new things these days."

Dillon picked up Ella's free hand and wove their fingers together. "You know what they say about curiosity."

"I've heard mention of major trouble and maybe cats." Ella grinned.

Dillon winked at her. "Exactly. Trouble. So, what's Frog's plan?"

Josh started with the easiest question first. "Frog indicated the cops considered the threat minimal. They've decided it's a crank. Frog told me the stalker has frightened Ashley, and she's not one who scares easily. He mentioned a milkshake assault?"

"Oh yeah!" Ella chortled with delight. "I remember that. A guy came at her with a milkshake, intending to tip it over the sexy red suit she was wearing. Ashley must've seen him coming. Witnesses swore she tripped, but the suit guy with the drink ended up with his milkshake over his clothes and face. The papers were full of it for an entire week. The cartoons were hysterical. That's when they started with the *Legs* nickname." She did air quotes to emphasize.

"I don't get why you can't just be security," Dillon said.

"Because Ashley travels often, and as her fiancé, I'll have full access to events while a security guard might raise questions. Ashley doesn't want this to derail her campaign. Frog came up with this plan. Said he trusts me with her safety while he didn't know dick about the men his parents wanted to hire." Josh paused to drink. "Frog wants me to stay with her until the election ends. I act as bodyguard, fiancé, and a second set of eyes to catch this guy."

"Could be a woman," Ella piped up.

"Yes, but Frog is leaning toward a man," Josh said.

"A stalker is often someone the victim knows. Has she any ideas?" Dillon asked.

"He told me there was trouble when she was younger. A passenger in a car Ashley was driving died. I'll check that out, but Frog seemed to think the accident wasn't a problem. That it had been squared away."

"What story will you tell your mother?" Ella asked, her eyes twinkling with suppressed merriment.

Josh gave a heartfelt groan. "I haven't thought that far ahead."

"I recommend the truth," Dillon suggested. "Less trouble that way. She won't blab. Not important stuff."

"When did you meet Ashley?" Ella asked, her hands fisted and held up like a reporter's microphone. "When did you know she was the one?"

Josh had memorized Frog's suggestions, sent via email with strict instructions for him to read, remember, and delete. "We met at Frog's birthday party and clicked. Ever since we've kept in contact and met when we could. Now that I've retired, we're taking our relationship to the next level."

"Not bad." Dillon lifted his glass in salute. "I believed

that."

"And other women?" Ella asked. "Not that I want details, but I'm putting it out there. From what Dillon has disclosed, you're not a monk."

"Hey! I haven't misbehaved in the last six months. Mainly, for lack of opportunity." Josh offered a rueful grin, his blue eyes crinkling at the corners. "Frog got to me before I mingled with the local ladies."

Dillon released a snort. "What about money?"

"According to Frog, most of the accommodation and flights, plus the food is included. Ashley will even pay for extra clothes. Frog offered a wage. I told him to pay me half of what he suggested. That he'd earned the friend discount. Besides, I have savings. At least this is space to consider my future. I loved army life, but it wasn't the same after you left. Two others who started the same time as me have retired too. I've been lucky and decided not to continue when my heart wasn't in the job."

"Do you have an engagement ring?" Ella asked. "Women notice that sort of thing."

"You can borrow Hana's ring," Dillon said.

"Are you sure?" Josh asked. Hana had been Dillon's first wife, and she'd died in a home invasion.

"Yeah. I wanted Ella to have her own ring. Hana's is sitting in the drawer. You might as well use it if you need it."

"Thanks," Josh said. "Have I missed anything?"

"Get Summer to help with research, et cetera. Barber, for instance," Ella suggested.

Josh nodded. He'd have to speak to his sister- and

brother-in-law anyway, and Summer was a wizard with research.

"Nikolai might offer back-up if you need help. Louie and Jake too," Dillon said. "If you're down this end of the country, I'll be available if you need me."

Ella's eyes brightened. "You can call on me too."

Josh laughed at his brother's growl of disapproval.

"*Pfff!*" Ella puffed up with indignation. "I am a kick-arse bitch. I can do anything."

"Steady, tiger. Remember our deal? I try not to act too over-protective, and you won't run into dangerous situations."

"You growled first." Ella sniffed, but mischief sparkled in her expression.

"You did," Josh agreed. "But you're off the hook, bro. Most of the functions will be in Auckland since Ashley's seat is in Manurewa."

"This election might prove interesting now," Ella said.

"One point." Dillon paused as if to collect his thoughts. "How will you keep your fiancée safe without a weapon? They won't give you a license to carry. Only the DPS are allowed to carry a gun."

"True," Josh said. "But given the tightening of gun laws in New Zealand, this works against the bad guys too. Frog told me he has taught his sister self-defense moves. I can make certain she practices in case she needs them and watch her back. That's the best I can do. Everything else we'll play by ear."

"Who are you voting for?" Dillon asked.

"National," Josh said promptly.

Ella giggled at Dillon's wink. "That won't go down well."

"No," Josh agreed, enjoying the gentle ribbing. "Which is why I will lie through my teeth and tell everyone I support my fiancée one hundred percent."

"When are you leaving?" Dillon asked.

"I've booked a flight to Auckland tomorrow. I need you to explain this to Mum and Dad when they get home, so they're not taken unawares. Tell them I'll call them. I'll speak with Nikolai and Summer when they pick me up at the airport. Once I've told them, I'll contact Ashley." He grinned. "I'm an engaged man. Wish me well."

2

THE STALKER MAKES A MOVE

ASHLEY SCANNED THE AUDIENCE in the church hall. She smiled and focused on projecting a friendly and approachable persona. Sincerity. *Heck.* Easier said than done when she kept jumping at shadows.

"In New Zealand, we face the same problems as other countries around the world. We have homeless people, families who live in poverty. The Labor party isn't promising an instant fix.

"No one can.

"But what we do promise is to lift the minimum wage. We promise to make more affordable housing available for those who need it. We promise cheaper doctor fees and twenty hours of cost-free education per week for your pre-school children. Free university education for the first year. A subsidized apprenticeship scheme for those teenagers who prefer to learn a trade. More funds pumped into mental health and suicide prevention. We want our children to prosper, their parents to have pride in their family and achievements. We want our children to have their health and become productive citizens.

"We aim to not just count dollars and cents and balance budgets but to look after the wellness of every New Zealander, no matter their age or ethnicity. Let's be happy, healthy, and mindful because that is the way forward for the future." Ashley paused. "I appreciate you coming out on this chilly night to listen to me discuss our policies. I hope you'll vote for me and give a tick to the Labor party for your party vote on election day. If you have questions, I'd be pleased to answer them."

Ashley scanned faces and smiled, encouraging the locals to engage with her. "I don't bite. I promise. Politicians, no matter which party we come from, serve you—the voters. To help us do a good job, we need your feedback."

An elderly gentleman wearing a navy beret raised his hand.

"Yes, sir?"

"What will you do for those of retirement age?"

"Well, we will raise the pension in line with inflation, and we understand how expensive heating can be during the winter months. We're proposing every resident eligible for the pension will receive an extra payment of twenty dollars per week during the coldest months of the year. We want you to stay warm," Ashley said.

The questions flew quick and fast after the initial one, and Ashley thought she did well. She'd prepared, and her extra diligence meant she didn't waffle or show a lack of confidence in providing answers.

"Ms. Townsend has time for one more question. Yes?" The local pastor nodded to a scruffy man in a long, black coat. He stood at the rear.

"Do you have secrets, Ashley?" The man's gap-toothed smile held mockery and challenge.

Ashley blinked. Her pulse raced, and she swallowed hard. She didn't recognize him. Conversation from her audience rose like the low buzz of bees, growing louder until she wanted to clap her hands over her ears. She forced a polite smile because smiles were her secret weapon. "I'm sorry. I don't understand your question."

"Do you have secrets?" the man repeated.

Ashley met his smirk with another courteous smile. "I believe I've been honest and open regarding our campaign and our policies."

The pastor shot Ashley a look, seeming as confused as she. He clapped, and the audience joined his applause.

Ashley turned to the pastor and offered her hand. After a firm and businesslike shake, she beamed enough to make her facial muscles ache. "Thank you for hosting me tonight."

"Did you know that man?"

"No." Ashley lifted her hand to rub her face and stayed the movement before her fingers settled. "I've never seen him before."

"Me neither. He isn't one of my parishioners." The pastor frowned, deepening the lines of experience on his forehead. "He... Never mind. The Labor party has my vote."

"Thank you," Ashley said. "We appreciate your support."

Ashley shrugged into her red coat, picked up her laptop bag, and her handbag, and made her way from the hall. Two steps into the floodlit car park, a woman stopped her. A junior reporter for the local newspaper. An ambitious one. Her business-smart attire of a blue jacket and matching skirt plus heels were the uniform of the woman this reporter aimed to be in the future. Ashley understood drive and goals, owned them herself, but on seeing the determined light in the reporter's blue eyes, tension slid through Ashley's torso to settle on her shoulders. No matter what, she refused to offer the woman a quote to boost her career at the Labor party's expense.

"*Ashley.*" The reporter's high voice grated Ashley. "Can you discuss the secrets the man mentioned?"

A flash of impatience struck Ashley, but her quick count to three had her instinctive retort dying and a more suitable soundbite emerging. "I'm sorry, but I'm as confused as you. If you want answers, you must ask him. Did you have any policy questions for me?"

"No, I have everything I need," the reporter replied, her manner calculating.

Inwardly, Ashley groaned. It wasn't difficult to imagine the angle of the woman's story. Unease engulfed her as she replayed the man's question and his odd behavior. Chill bumps rippled across her arms and legs. The man had acted smug as if he'd had the secret rather than her. Was he her stalker? Or was she jumping to conclusions because her stalker had her spooked?

"Thanks for coming to listen to me," Ashley murmured.

The reporter's cat-sharp eyes narrowed a fraction as she turned away. Ashley pinned on a smile and fought to keep it there as she searched the departing crowd. The crowd split off in twos and threes, laughing and chatting, piling into vans and cars. Others walking. Ashley scanned faces, studied vehicles. She searched the shadows cast by the hedge surrounding three-quarters of the parking lot.

She caught her breath and puffed it out in a slow exhalation. Her right hand trembled when she pulled her car keys from the side pocket of her handbag. Each new breath came in a wheezy pant.

Initially, she'd fought her brother's suggestion of a bodyguard. No, not just security, but a fake fiancé. Now, she couldn't wait for the chosen man to arrive from wherever her brother had found him. Matt had contacts, and if he trusted this man, that was good enough for her.

A man shouted from behind her, and she started. A quick glance told her it was a teenager hailing his friend. Heck, she had to get a grip. She'd been fine until the man in the black coat had mentioned secrets.

Her life was an open book.

All of it.

Mindful of her brother's advice, she forced herself to focus. *Be present and aware of your surroundings.*

Ashley strode to her car. Her keys were in her right hand, and she used the remote to unlock her vehicle once she grew closer. After a rapid perusal of the car interior, she slipped inside. A second later, she'd locked the doors. Her shaky laugh resounded as she clicked her seat belt into place.

She was all right.

Ashley ran her sweaty palms down the legs of her black trousers then started her vehicle. She had her fully charged phone. Matt had texted her the bodyguard—her fiancé's number. All she needed to do was drive home and meet the man who'd stay attached to her side for the next few weeks.

A secret.

Fudge, she did have one.

A fake fiancé.

He was so secret, she'd never recognize him in a line-up. Although she trusted her brother, she prayed this man he'd found had a brain. No one who knew her well would accept a man who couldn't hold a conversation. They'd become suspicious, but Matt had promised her this scheme was workable.

She pulled out of the parking lot, stopped for a truck, then merged with the evening traffic. Most of the people who'd listened to her speak had hurried home while she'd spoken to the reporter. The traffic was steady, but not as heavy as it had been when she'd visited the suburb and spoken at a marae two weeks ago.

She'd almost made it to the arterial road when her car started juddering. It jerked and spluttered, and she eased her foot off the accelerator before pressing down again. Her car didn't respond. Instead, it bunny-hopped for several feet before dying. The vehicle coasted a few feet farther as she steered it toward the curb. The driver behind her gave an impatient toot and overtook, speeding past her.

Ashley attempted to restart her car. "Come on," she muttered.

The car stalled. She tried again. This time nothing happened.

Her car was dead.

"Isn't she at home?" Summer asked.

"No, she attended a meeting tonight," Josh told his younger sister. "I suggested meeting her here. I can spend the time checking out her security." He turned to his brother-in-law Nikolai. "You and Summer should head home. You don't need to wait with me. Ashley told me she'd be home after ten."

Ashley's home was a 1920s wooden bungalow that occupied an extensive section on Mill Road. Mature trees grew at the rear of the house, casting deep shadows. Ashley had left a light on, and the illumination spilled across her front yard. Two garden beds full of spring bulbs flanked a path leading to the front entrance while a verandah wrapped around the house. Hanging baskets and several pots of flowers and herbs provided color and scent and hinted Ashley enjoyed gardening. A locked garage sat to the right. Frog had told him Ashley had inherited the house from their grandmother, and she took care of her inheritance.

Nikolai shot a wink at Summer. "We should meet your fiancée."

"We should." Summer leaned into her husband, her smile impish in the glow of the security light. "Mum will require a report."

Josh groaned. "Really, I appreciate you giving me a lift. Frog gave me permission to borrow his vehicle since Ashley is storing it for him."

"We'd never leave you alone here in the dark," Summer said. "Louie and Mac are looking after Sam. We're good waiting with you."

While her expression remained serious, his sister's blue eyes twinkled with mischief. Josh groaned again even as he admitted he deserved Summer's teasing. He and Dillon had interfered in her romantic life from the moment their parents had given Summer permission to date.

The riff from his phone—the first few bars of the *Jaws* theme song—stopped the conversation.

"Hello."

"It's Ashley," a tremulous voice said. "My car died."

"Where are you?" Josh demanded. "We'll come and get you."

Ashley rattled off the address, although it meant nothing to him.

"We'll be there soon. Are you off the road?"

"Yes."

"All right. Hang tight. Keep the doors locked. Ashley, I'm with my sister and her husband. We're in a black SUV."

"Okay," she whispered.

"Give me a sec to tell Nikolai where to find you, then we'll talk. You stay on the line."

"Yes." This time she sounded a fraction more confident.

"Where are we going?" Nikolai asked.

"I'm on Ruru Road. Do you know it?"

"No, but we'll find it with GPS," Josh said.

They piled in the SUV.

"Got it," Summer said after inputting their destination. "We'll be around ten minutes."

"Did you hear that, Ash? We'll be with you in ten minutes. Is there anyone nearby?"

"No. A few cars but no pedestrians. I was driving, and suddenly, the car stopped responding. It was fine during the drive to the meeting."

Josh listened with approval. Good, she was steadier now. He'd keep her talking, distract her. "How did your meeting go? Do you normally go by yourself?"

"The meeting went well. There was one guy who asked a strange question, but other than that, it was a regular gathering where I discussed our policies with a Q and A afterward."

"What was the strange question? Did you recognize the guy?"

"He asked about secrets. Everyone seemed confused, but no, he wasn't familiar. He acted as if I should know him or at least understand what he meant."

"Description?"

"A long black coat. A beanie covered his hair. I didn't see what color it was because of the hat. A black beard. Tall. Over six-feet, I'd say."

"Did you see him after the meeting?"

"No, he disappeared. I never saw him leave the hall."

"What is your schedule? I have a few clothes, but I'll

have to buy more while I'm up here. My sister tells me I mustn't embarrass you."

"Most of the meetings are in halls, so tidy jeans and a nice shirt and jacket are fine. Oh, I have a breakfast meeting with the local business owners. Next week, I have a meeting with the other Labor candidates in Wellington."

Josh pulled a face. "It sounds as if I'll be busy."

"What make of car does Ashley have?" Nikolai asked.

"A white Mitsubishi," Ashley replied before Josh could ask her.

Nikolai peered through the windshield. "I see it."

"We're here, but stay in the car until I come to the door."

"Matt didn't give me much of a description."

"Dark brown hair, blue eyes, six-three in height. I'm wearing jeans and a black leather jacket." Josh grinned. "Your brother didn't tell me much about you either."

Nikolai slowed and did a U-turn once traffic allowed the maneuver.

"We're parking behind you," Josh said. "I'm hanging up now."

"Summer, stay here in the warm. Josh and I will check out her car," Nikolai instructed.

"She might feel more at ease if I'm there," Summer suggested. "You're big men and tall. A bit overpowering for a woman who has suffered a fright."

Nikolai paused. "Excellent point, sweetheart. But monitor what's happening around us. Given the circumstances, we don't want any surprises."

As he climbed from Nikolai's vehicle, Josh probed the shadows, searching for anything out of place. His senses didn't indicate danger, so he strode around the car to stand in the light. Nikolai and Summer joined him, and the woman inside slumped before unlocking her car. She and climbed out, offering Josh his first glance of her.

Ashley Townsend was tall for a woman and slim. She had long, straight honey-blonde hair, and she wore it pulled back in a ponytail.

"You're prettier than your brother," he said.

She gave a tiny smile that exposed two dimples, one either side of her full lips. She wore makeup but still looked natural.

Summer snorted. "That's a cool thing to say to your fiancée."

Josh ignored his sister's input. "Ashley, I'm Josh. This is Summer, my sister, and Nikolai, my brother-in-law."

"Thank you so much for coming to get me. I wasn't sure what to do. I mean, I can change a tire and do basic car maintenance, but I've experienced nothing like this before."

"Pop the hood for us," Josh instructed, keeping his tone smooth, instinctively wanting to reduce the stress in her voice and muscles. "What happened?"

"The first thing I noticed was when I tried to speed up my car didn't respond. My car bunny-hopped, and I haven't done that since Matt taught me to drive when I was fifteen and shouted at me."

Summer snorted. "Dillon, my oldest brother, gave me my first driving lesson. He made me cry. I hear your brother is military too. Soldier types tend to own the bossy gene. We can compare notes some time. How many brothers do you have?"

"Only one. I have an older sister too."

Josh moved around the car to peer under the hood with Nikolai.

"Nothing obvious," Nikolai said.

"Could someone have added something to the fuel?" Josh prowled around the vehicle and spotted the damage straight away. He walked back to Nikolai. "Someone has tampered with the fuel. There are scratch marks on the flap where someone applied force. Might be best to leave the car parked here and get it towed tomorrow."

"Sounds like a plan." Nikolai shut the hood.

"The fuel cap was forced open," Josh said when he reached the women.

Summer's eyes widened. "I read a book club mystery where the baddie added water to the fuel. The fuel is lighter, and it floats to the top while the water drops to the bottom and creates problems with the fuel pump."

"That's our best guess." The snippets his librarian sister collected no longer surprised Josh. She'd always had a thirst for knowledge. "Nikolai and Summer will give us a ride home. We'll get the car towed tomorrow."

Ashley closed her eyes then opened them again. "Thank you. Let me grab my laptop and handbag." She opened the door and leaned inside to collect her belongings.

Josh's gaze zapped straight to Ashley's curvy arse and didn't leave until his sister dug him in the ribs with a pointy elbow.

"Ow!" he muttered.

Nikolai chuckled while Summer sniffed.

Ashley backed out of the car and locked the doors. "Did I miss something?"

"No." Josh winged a warning glare at Summer.

"Ashley, can you come to dinner one night? Since we'll be almost related for a while, it'd be lovely to get to know you better." Summer smiled sweetly, raising suspicion in Josh. "We live in Bottletop Bay, which isn't far from your place. You can bring Josh if you must."

Ashley smiled, and Josh stared, mesmerized by her dimples and soft, kissable lips. "Thank you. That sounds like fun. Most of my friends are involved in politics."

Josh walked beside Ashley and opened the door before stepping aside for her to enter. The back of his neck prickled.

"Nikolai," he murmured.

"Yeah," Nikolai agreed with his assessment. "Summer, move it. Please," he added when Summer sent him a look. He leaned closer. "Someone is watching us."

"Oh!" Summer lengthened her steps now that she understood the reasons behind Nikolai's demand.

Josh shut the door once Ashley was inside and rounded the car. He couldn't see anyone, but someone was there, watching them. He slipped into the SUV, his spidey senses still tingling.

"Anything?" he asked Nikolai while thinking it was good that whoever was watching was at a distance. They'd spot him or her if they were within listening range.

"No."

"What's happening?" Ashley asked.

Josh reached for Ashley's clenched hand and threaded

their fingers together. "We think someone was watching us."

"Me? My stalker?"

Josh tightened his grip until she glanced his way. "We're uncertain, but that's the obvious conclusion."

Ashley's fingers clenched around his. "I hate this."

"I know." Josh discerned the wobble in her voice. He drew her against his side and hugged her, offering comfort. She smelled of delicate flowers with a hint of lemon. He nuzzled her hair, and a fresh spring day popped into his mind. Frog had been right to warn him away from his sister. She was his type. "We will catch whoever is doing this. I promise. I won't let him hurt you."

"Is it possible my stalker did something to my car?"

Josh would take a bet on it, although he didn't verbalize his certainty. "We'll know once we get your car checked over by a mechanic."

She nodded, then her fingers tightened on his again. "Do you truly want to enter this craziness with me? Don't you have someone special in your life?"

"No," Josh said. Ashley interested him, though and brought out his protectiveness.

"You realize that as the children of farmers, both Josh and I are more likely to vote National." Summer raised her voice in an annoying sister-kind-of-way.

"Ignore her," Josh whispered.

"Is she telling the truth?"

Josh hesitated. "Yeah. I'm not a Labor supporter."

"That's terrible," Ashley said.

Josh had difficulty reading her, and the dim interior

of the SUV didn't help. He thought she was teasing but wasn't one hundred percent certain. "Would you prefer to forget your brother's crazy plan?"

Ashley was a soft weight against his side. She didn't speak, didn't breathe for a long five seconds.

"Ashley?"

"Can we talk when we get to my place?"

This time, Josh caught her wariness. "You can trust Summer and Nikolai."

"If this gets out—the lies. The fiancé fabrication. I'll lose my seat. The press will crucify me. I've wanted to go into politics ever since I was a kid at primary school. If people suspect, I'll lose everything I've worked for."

"Shush. Relax. We'll talk once we arrive at your place," Josh promised.

"Matt thinks it's easy for me to lie. I don't. Lie, I mean. I'm a terrible liar. I'm not good at it, so I don't do it."

"Look at it this way, sweetheart. We'll be friends. I'll be someone in your corner, someone you can trust. I won't speak to the press or do anything to hinder your chances of re-election. If anyone asks nosy questions, you tell them I'm your friend. Your best friend. That won't be a lie. If they ask when we're getting married, tell them the election is the most important thing at the moment. None of that is a lie. Don't worry. Frog's plan is perfect. It'll work."

"Frog? Is that my brother's nickname?"

Josh paused, tilted his head. "Have you heard your brother sing?"

She burst out laughing and something clenched in his chest. "He loves singing. It relaxes him."

Josh thought back, the comment bringing insight. Frog's terrible singing had made them laugh. His entire team had relaxed after the shared laughter on hearing Frog's singing. "It relaxed the team too because we couldn't stop laughing."

"I play the piano and Matt sings," Ashley said.

"Badly?" Josh wondered if lack of musical talent ran in the family.

"Josh!" Summer protested. "That was rude."

Josh huffed. "You haven't heard Frog's singing."

Ashley gave a light laugh, and the tinkling sound grabbed him. Suddenly, this favor to Frog was looking better and better. Ashley was a babe, and she had a brain. Acting as her fiancé... Well, it wouldn't stretch his performing abilities. Keeping his hands off and his word to Frog not to hit on his sister—that would take more effort.

·♥·♥·♥·♥·♥·

THE LETTERS HADN'T BEEN enough, so he'd upped the pressure. He wanted her scared. Terrified. He wanted her to suffer the same confusion and dread he'd experienced.

Because of her.

She'd got off lightly while he'd grieved and ached and endured years of nightmares.

By now, the man he'd hired had caused consternation at her meeting.

Her car would delay her arrival at home while he prepared to cause her more angst.

He knew what to do.

3

UNDIE-GATE

MATT'S FRIEND SEEMED NICE with his brown hair, twinkly blue eyes, and straightforward manner. Sexy, touch-enticing facial scruff. She had to remind herself his laugh lines disguised a tough military man. Not her type because she dated intellectuals, but Josh and his brother-in-law had blown away her stress with their no-nonsense investigation of her car problem. They hadn't waffled. They hadn't tried to placate her with half-truths, and she appreciated that. They reminded her of Matt, which helped her to relax even further.

Nikolai slowed and turned into her driveway.

Ashley scanned her yard and tensed, swallowed hard.

"What is it?" Josh demanded.

He'd noticed her reaction. Of course, he had. From her observation, not much escaped military-type men. "I have security lights in the front that flick on when I pull into the driveway. They were working when I left home to drive to the meeting. I never leave lights on inside my house."

Nikolai pulled up and turned off the vehicle ignition. "Are you positive? The light was on when we were here earlier."

"Yes!" Ashley snapped then regathered her manners. "Sorry. I don't mean to be rude. The interior lights were off when I left."

"All right." Josh removed his arm from around her shoulders. "Stay here with Summer while Nikolai and I check out your house. Do you have your keys?"

A shiver ran through Ashley. Contrarily, she wanted his physical touch again. That's what a fiancé did. They offered comfort—even fake ones. "I'm coming with you." He opened his mouth, but she spoke again before he could. "Please. I hate this mind-numbing fear. I have to act."

The two men shared a quick glance before Josh said, "Promise to stay behind me."

"I promise," Ashley said. "If my stalker runs past you, I'll make sure to land a few punches so he doesn't escape."

Summer snickered. "I like you, but I'm still not voting Labor."

"No worries." Ashley slid from the vehicle when Josh opened the door for her. An old-fashioned gentleman. She couldn't remember the last time a date had offered her this small courtesy.

"Remember, stay behind me."

"I will," Ashley promised. She was not the stupid blonde who ventured into a basement. Nope. Not her.

"We'll check inside first," Josh said.

Nikolai gave a quick nod.

Josh tried the door. Locked.

Ashley handed him the key for the front door.

"Do you have an alarm?" Josh asked.

"I've never needed one."

Josh unlocked the door. The laundry light was on, and Ashley reached past Josh to switch on the hall lights.

"Tell me if anything is out of place."

Ashley's breath eased out as she followed Josh deeper into her house. Chill bumps pebbled her skin, but as she flicked on more lights, her tension released at the normalcy of her surroundings. Everything seemed in its place. Nikolai prowled into the kitchen while she trailed Josh and drifted along the passage.

Josh slowed. "Is this your bedroom?"

"Yes." She rounded him and gaped at the tidy piles of underwear sitting on top of her bed. "I-I-someone else did this." A sick feeling settled in a lump in her stomach, much like she felt after eating a portion of her sister's meat stew. Someone had come into her house and gone through her possessions. They'd invaded her privacy, touched her things. *Intimate things.* She gulped and clenched her hands to stop them from trembling. "I don't understand. I locked the door."

An arm came around her shoulders, offering silent comfort. Josh tugged her against his muscled body. "We need to call the police, Ashley. Get this on record."

"But I locked my door." She felt stupid repeating the point even if it was true.

JOSH'S FAKE FIANCEE

"It's an old lock and easy enough to pick," Josh said. "Do you leave any of your windows open?"

"I used to. Matt lectured me on security, and I lock everything. Since I told Matt about the letters I'd received." Her brother had warned her the stalker might escalate. "Is this..." She swallowed the lump that had formed in her throat. "Is this the same person who's sending the letters to me?"

"It might be unconnected, but I don't think so," Josh said. "Frog told me the police weren't helpful when you reported the letters."

Ashley shrugged. "To be honest, I understood their point of view. It was a few letters. They're busy." Her gaze slid to the piles of her lingerie. "They'll laugh at this, talk behind my back. If this story gets out, I'll look stupid. Too girlie for responsibility." Tears stung her eyes, and she blinked hard.

"Call the police anyway," Josh said. "Even if they can't do anything, this breach of your security must go on record. What would your brother tell you to do?"

"That's low," Ashley whispered.

"I promised Frog I'd keep you safe." Josh tipped her chin up with a forefinger, and their gazes connected. His was full of concern and what she called he-man determination. "Tell me, what would he say?"

"He'd tell me to report the crime."

"Exactly. I'll be there with you, and tomorrow, we'll install a new security system. Okay?"

Ashley sighed. He was right. She knew it, but already, she could imagine the cops' reaction. Big girl panties, she reminded herself. Besides, she was in politics. People always made snide comments about politicians. No matter what she or her colleagues did, someone disliked their actions. It was the nature of the game.

"Is there anything else out of place?"

"Just my underwear." A shudder ran through her. She'd have to squeeze in shopping time. The idea of wearing clothes a weird stranger had touched sickened her. That meat-stew sensation again.

The police came, took her statement, and left. The two police constables who'd attended had regarded her as if she was crazy. Not that she blamed them, but she'd followed Josh's advice and done what Matt would expect. The police had a report to file with her name attached to it.

"Discuss an alarm system with Louie," Nikolai suggested.

"Great idea," Josh said.

"Summer, we should head out." Nikolai turned to Josh. "You'll let us know if we can help with anything."

"Yeah. Thanks."

"Thank you for your help tonight." Ashley attempted a friendly smile when she'd rather cry angry tears. Maybe mutter one or two of her brother's descriptive curses. Instead, she forced her smile wider. "I appreciate it."

"No problem." Summer winked at her brother. "You're family now. I'll call you about dinner."

Nikolai and Summer left, leaving tension of a different kind. Ashley trusted her brother, so she believed in Josh, but it was still weird. This fake fiancé thing. And the boundaries. Did they hold hands in public? Kiss?

JOSH'S FAKE FIANCEE

What did a fake fiancé do?

Her gaze slid to Josh's mouth, and a whoosh of heat ran through her, leaving her knees weak and her heart strangely wanting. Josh Williams was a capable man. Strong. Masculine. Sexy. She jerked her gaze away and mentally listed Labor's policies.

"Should I clear your bed for you? I got the impression you intend to toss your lingerie after tonight."

Ashley shuddered. "Yes, please. I can't sleep in there tonight. I'll take a spare room."

"Which room is mine?"

"The room next to the master," Ashley said. "It has an en suite."

"Why don't you take that one?" Josh's understanding had her blinking away another bout of potential tears. "I'll take your room."

She bit her lip. Withheld her tears. She'd worked hard to contain her emotions. Yes, she smiled, but she never showed sadness because that made her appear weak. The last thing she ever wanted was to seem over sensitive or out of control. An emotional candidate repelled the voters.

"Are you sure?"

"I get to have a king bed rather than the single. Win-win."

"I'll grab clean sheets for you."

"I can change the sheets. Take a bath or something. Chill out. Summer swears by a bubble bath."

Ashley stared at Josh, nonplussed by his understanding. His charm. His niceness.

"Ashley." Josh moved closer. His hands landed on her

shoulders and their gazes connected. "Don't worry. We'll get you through this. I promise."

Ashley nodded, although she didn't think this pretense would be as easy as he thought.

Josh woke to a scream. He bolted upright in the bed, confused for an instant until the cry repeated, rippling down the passage.

Ashley.

He jumped off the bed and slinked through the darkness. He cast out every sense, searching for danger. The clock on the kitchen wall ticked the seconds. The wooden floors creaked beneath his feet. A whimper had him hurrying into the spare room and to the bed.

"Ashley," he murmured, cautiously shaking her. "Ashley, wake up. You're dreaming."

She groaned, whimpered again.

Josh sat on the edge of the bed. "Ashley." He hesitated to touch her, not wanting to upset her more than she was already. "Ash, sweetheart."

She jolted, her gasp of fear striking him like a blow.

"It's me. Josh. You're safe. Should I turn on the light?"

"Please."

Big brown eyes fixed on him. Without makeup, the shadows beneath her eyes were noticeable. Her blonde hair covered her shoulders in a shiny mass, and she had a beauty spot to the right of her mouth. He hadn't noticed earlier, but now that he had, his mind dwelled on kissing the sexy mark. She wore an old T-shirt, and it molded to her curves.

He shook himself, forced his gaze back to her face. Frog

would kill him if he ever discerned Josh's inappropriate thoughts.

"Bad dream?" he asked.

She nodded.

"Do you want a drink? Tea or something stronger?"

"I don't drink alcohol, but a cup of green tea sounds good."

"I'll make one for you." Josh stood, glad for a task. Looking at her, sitting on her bed gave a man ideas.

Ashley ran a trembling hand through her hair. "We should discuss how this relationship will work."

Josh's mind took a turn onto Sexy Drive again. He forced himself to move, to walk to the door. "I won't be long."

When he returned, Ashley had a planner open and was tapping a pen on the page, a frown twisting her soft lips.

"Something wrong?" He wrenched his focus to the teacup and saucer in his hands.

She sighed. "There's so much to do before election day. The Labor party..." She blew out another sigh. "I shouldn't say this, but given our current progress, we'll crash and burn."

Aware normal conversation would settle her, he set the cup of tea on a nightstand and sat on the bed. Close enough to be sociable but not slide into intimacy.

Yeah. Now, what were they discussing? Huh, okay. "Do you have a plan? What would you do if you had your way? Frog said you're high in the party rankings."

She replied without hesitating, impressing Josh. "We should stop talk of a capital gains tax and focus on our strengths. Our social policies."

"Can you tell your party that?"

She nibbled her bottom lip, and Josh glanced away from her cute beauty mark. *Get control of yourself.*

She tapped her pen again, narrowed her eyes. "Well, I can, but Geoffrey is determined. He says it will make a more balanced playing field."

"In theory. Normally, the wealthy who have the assets to attract the tax can afford to pay a smart accountant to minimize their payments. It's the people in the middle who get hit hardest. They're the ones who work hard, save, and pay most of the tax, which will go toward your social programs."

Ashley made a humming sound. "Yes, I know that. We'd be better to raise taxes in other areas. More tax on petrol, for example. Road user charges. We'll need to do that to add more infrastructure and ease the road congestion."

"Is that the topic for your Wellington meeting?"

"Yes, we'll look at the poll results, discuss, and focus on areas where our policies resonate better with the voters," Ashley said. "As a party, we'll have a better sense for how we're doing once the poll results are in, and we can report back from our different electorates."

Josh nodded. "How will your engagement figure in this? Will it cause problems?"

"Maybe. I don't know." Ashley did her pen tap thing. "When we discussed this, I told Matt a security company might work better. I thought they could keep to the background, and that would be enough. He refused to trust anyone I might hire and told me I needed someone twenty-four hours. I joked and said that sounded like a husband, and that's when he came up with the fake fiancé idea. At first, I thought it was overkill. The letters made me uneasy, but the idea of someone coming into my house..." She trailed off. Blinked. "I'm scared. I don't even know what I've done to deserve this level of attention. That terrifies me too."

"You've probably done nothing more than smile or offer kind words," Josh soothed. "Are you tired?"

"Yes, but every time I close my eyes, I imagine someone inside my house, invading my privacy. I start shaking."

"Put your planner away, and we'll go through your background. Frog filled me in on as much as he knows, but if you're like my sister, I figure you don't share everything with your big brother. Tell me about your boyfriends. Who have you dated in the last couple of years? Any nasty breakups?"

Ashley scowled and set aside her planner. She sipped her tea. "Is this necessary?"

"We have to start somewhere."

"I haven't dated much. I spent time with Cole Mackinson. He's a lawyer for a firm in the central city. We had dinner together a few times, but there was no spark. Murray Anderson. We went bowling and for dinner, but we're both busy. It was difficult to find nights we were both free, so we gave up trying. I heard he's dating a school teacher now."

Josh took notes, clenching his pen. He loathed hearing Ashley's history with other men. "Anyone else?" He forced out the words, both wanting and not wanting to learn the answer.

"I've gone out for casual dinners with guys I've met via party functions. I haven't had anyone serious in my life. No bad breakups." She laughed, and it held an edge of distress. "Sort of sad, right? But the thing is, I work hard and put most of my energy into my job. I intimidate a lot of guys."

Their loss. She didn't scare him. Intrigued him. Challenged him. And where the hell was his mind wandering? Ashley was Frog's younger sister. He'd made a promise to his friend, which meant he'd keep his hands off and do his job.

If only she wasn't so pretty. So enticingly sexy.

"What about when you're in Wellington for the parliamentary sessions? Do you see anyone there?"

"I went to the movies with a guy I bumped into in a restaurant. Frank Paulson. I still see him, and we might go out for a drink if I have time. We're friends rather than anything romantic."

Josh jotted a note. "Any problems related to your electoral seat? Maybe a constituent who disagrees with the party direction."

Ashley frowned. "There was a woman who volunteered for us, and her husband arrived to drag her home to cook him dinner. We helped her get into a women's refuge. That was hairy. We served him with a restraining order because he kept hassling me and the staff. That was last January. I heard he moved to Australia."

"Name?"

"Justin Watkins."

"Anything else?"

Ashley shook her head. "Nothing I can think of. My life is busy and drama-free. No, nothing else because I never have time to get into trouble. That's what I told Matt. What if our engagement"—she did air quotes—"makes things worse?"

"As your fiancé, I can hang around more than a security man. It means you can focus on your work and holding your seat. Frog suggested we say we met through him and kept the relationship low-key because I was overseas on active duty. You didn't want to draw attention."

"Yeah, but what Matt hasn't considered is the possible flak I might receive when we call off the engagement. That's the part that makes me unhappy. I'd hate to come across as flighty."

"Blame me. I've got broad shoulders."

Her gaze flickered to his shoulders and chest, and a flash of raw need struck him along with confusion. Why did the first woman who'd interested him in months have to be Ashley Townsend?

He hustled into speech, ripping his gaze off her to focus on his list. "Well, you could mention you had a stalker and required protection. Or, if you want to keep the issue private, you can tell them I had trouble settling and fitting into civilian life again. That's not a lie. I have no idea what to do with my future. I'm tired of war, and it wasn't the same after my brother Dillon retired. Helping you gives me time to make a plan."

"We don't even have a ring," Ashley muttered. "I'll get questions."

"Actually, I have a ring for you," Josh said, and for once the mention of an engagement ring didn't make him nervous.

"Oh." Her gaze met his, her brown eyes full of wonder and feminine mystery. "I hope you didn't waste money—"

"It's a nice ring, one Dillon let me borrow. It belonged to his wife."

Ashley's brows rose.

"Dillon has been married twice. Hana, his first wife, was killed during a home invasion. He wanted to get Ella, his second wife, a ring that was hers."

"Oh."

"Hana was lovely. You would've liked her. Everyone did. She was a practical woman, and she'd be pleased someone is using her ring."

"If your brother is certain."

"He suggested I borrow the ring. I'll give it to you tomorrow before you go to work. What time do you start?"

"I arrive at the office by eight at the latest. Sometimes much earlier. I'll go through the mail and correspondence before heading out on the campaign trail. The poll results hit tomorrow. What will you do?"

"I'll be trailing you. Don't worry. I'll keep to the background and won't get in your way, but I'll be close enough if you require help."

"But what will I tell everyone? About why you're there, I mean."

"Tell them I'm your fiancé, and I'm helping you with the campaign. You have volunteers, right?"

"Yes."

"That will be my position, except I won't be leaving your side. Do you have a crazy file? You know, a bunch of letters or correspondence that's strange or unusual?"

"My assistant Robert might."

"We'll check with Robert tomorrow. I'll organize upgraded security here at the house, and I'll double-check the security at your office. I'll check on the names of the men you've given me. Do a background on them as much as I can. Don't worry. Everything will be fine. Can you sleep now?"

"This pillow isn't the same as mine."

Josh grinned because she sounded young and cranky instead of the mature politician image she usually projected. "You can swap pillows with me, or you can sleep in your own bed. It's big. I promise to keep to my side."

She stared before giving a decisive nod. "All right. I sleep better in my bed."

Josh stood and waited for her to get out of bed. The T-shirt fell to mid-thigh but not before he got a great view of the legs the reporters had nicknamed her for.

"Want the rest of your tea?"

"No, it's cold now. I'll get the cup in the morning." She led the way to the master bedroom and climbed into the king-size bed. After plumping a pillow, she lay back with a contented sigh and closed her eyes. "Can you get the light please?"

Josh gave a quiet huff as he obeyed her. The darkness in the bedroom held a different ambiance when Ashley was here, and he fancied he could smell flowers that hadn't been there earlier. Already, her breathing sounded soft and even as if she'd dropped off to sleep. Not the scenario that usually occurred when he shared a bed with a woman.

He climbed under the covers and lay in the dark, assessing everything she'd told him and making mental notes on what to do first. Email Frog and ask if he'd thought of anyone else who might mean his sister harm. Maybe he could shed light on this because stalkers rarely fixated on someone without reason.

Josh must've drifted off to sleep. When he woke, it was with warmth at his back and a feminine arm curved around his waist. He moved a fraction, and Ashley grumbled. Desire shot through him along with her floral scent. His cock lengthened since this was the closest he'd been to an unrelated female in months.

It wouldn't take much to turn in her arms and kiss her in the way he'd wanted to from the first moment he'd seen her pale, terrified face. He shoved away the temptation. Not the time nor the place. He couldn't take action or grab the kiss he craved, not when she trusted him to protect her.

· ♥ · ♥ · ♥ · ♥ · ♥ ·

THE COPS HAD COME and gone while he'd watched from a safe distance. He had practice at hiding in plain sight, and the police never looked twice at him.

One problem, though.

The guy.

He had no idea who he was, but the man acted chummy with Awful Ashley.

Bet she'd lied to him, kept her dirty little secrets.

She thought she was safe. *Wrong*. No one was secure in their little square homes, and he'd prove that soon.

He started his vehicle and departed.

"She thinks she's protected," he said to the dummy he'd arranged in the passenger seat. "*She's fuckin' not.*"

His lips stretched into a grin that felt as if it didn't fit his mouth. Not surprising, given he'd had little to smile about since he was a kid.

But now—now that was changing, so he'd keep smiling at Awful Ashley's expense.

4

SWEET TEMPTATION AND VISIBLE PANTY LINES

Ashley woke wrapped around Josh. She blinked, not moving for long seconds. Because of her brother's confidence in the ex-soldier, she'd trusted Josh not to make a move on her. She'd trusted him to keep her safe and had slept better than she had in weeks.

Instead of Josh misbehaving, she'd accosted him, treating him like a cuddly toy. She sucked in another quiet breath. He was still asleep, so she made a stealthy retreat. She peeled her arm away from his trim waist and separated her chest from his muscled back.

Thank the stars, he'd worn his boxer-briefs to bed. The man was way too tempting to her peace of mind. Not her typical type but that didn't stop the fantasizing. He'd popped into her dreams like a magical genie, and they'd…they'd…

Heat collected in her cheeks. Luckily, he was a heavy sleeper. Unlike her older brother. Once she'd created space between their bodies, she started shaking, and it wasn't with fear.

She liked him.

Ashley bit back a groan. Only she could make a relationship difficult. Josh was doing her brother a favor. The ex-soldier was marking time until he decided his future.

The truth—with the campaign at full-tilt plus her constituent duties, a man was the last thing Ashley needed. Men were demanding. Men were possessive. Men were plain hard work. At least, that was her latest experience. Oh! She'd missed telling Josh about her relationship with Charles. The man bore a grudge and was still sore at her for winning the nomination for the Manurewa seat when he'd been confident it was his. Perhaps she'd better mention him to Josh. Although, she doubted Charles would stoop to breaking into her home.

A quick glance at her watch told her to hustle. She had a lot to do today, and dreaming of the impossible was a waste of her day.

She wasn't Josh's type. Too serious, one of her previous boyfriends had told her. Too busy, another had declared. Too organized. Lacked spontaneity. She sighed and rolled out of bed to hit the shower. Time to roll on with the political campaign—the part of her life she *could* control.

After a quick shower, she realized two things. One, she'd forgotten to organize her clothes the previous night.

And two, she refused to wear the lingerie her intruder had pawed through. Ashley wrapped a towel around her body—thankfully a large one—and scuttled to her bedroom. She poked her head around the door.

Josh was awake and speaking on his phone. *Of course.* His gaze tracked to her as she hovered in the doorway.

"Just a sec, Louie." Josh quirked his lips, his humor reflected in his ocean-blue gaze. "Would it help if I closed my eyes?"

"Yes, please." So polite when her stomach churned with excitement. That sensual gleam in his expression made her feel special.

"I'll keep them closed until you tell me." His cheeky grin pushed heat through her body.

She swallowed, saw his eyes were closed and rushed toward her wardrobe. What could she wear? If she'd been thinking clearly the previous night, she could've washed the underwear she'd had on that day. Somehow, she'd have to find time to purchase lingerie today. Meantime, she'd go commando and wear trousers. She shuddered, thinking of the infamous legs episode. Definitely trousers.

She remembered a camisole top and a bra. She'd put them on a drying rack in the laundry. Panties too. Triumphant, she grabbed a rose-colored merino jumper and black trousers before retreating to the laundry.

Her drying rack was empty, her lingerie gone. She stared at the white plastic frame. Her intruder had stolen her laundry too? Muttering under her breath, she stomped back to her clothes where she'd left them in the spare room. She pulled on the trousers and maneuvered the jumper over her head before surveying the result in the half-mirror. The slacks fit well, but any fool could see she was braless.

Ashley checked her watch and muttered again. She needed a scarf or something to hide her chest.

"I've made tea," Josh called. "Should I pour it to go?"

"Yes, please."

Josh appeared and stared at her, blue eyes so full of heat she froze.

"What?" A defensive note filled her question.

"You look gorgeous."

"The intruder took my underwear from the laundry. I don't have any," she wailed. "I need a scarf to divert gazes from my boobs."

"Where are the keys for Frog's car?"

It took Ashley a beat to make sense of the question. Oh! Matt's car. "They're in the pantry on a hook. Won't be long. I need to fix my hair and put on makeup. And find a scarf," she muttered.

"Leave your hair loose," Josh suggested, his grin slow, hot, and very male. "It's beautiful. You look sexy."

No! She wailed inwardly. That wasn't the right image to project. Ever since the legs incident, she'd attempted to downplay her appearance. Yes, she'd been lucky in the gene department, but that wasn't beneficial for politics. Her skin was excellent, and her smile worked for her. But she wanted people to appreciate her brain, not her outer shell. Politicians required smarts. People-skills. They had to think on their feet, communicate concisely. That was what she wished people to remember. Her hard work. Her dedication.

Not her stupid legs or face.

She stomped into her bedroom and brushed on mineral powder and a layer of mascara. A plum lipstick finished her look for the day. Yes. Perfect for her visit to the local school this morning.

Ashley found a cream scarf covered with polka dots in various shades of pink and twisted it into position around her neck. Better. With a black jacket and her black leather ankle boots, she was ready for anything.

Josh was waiting for her in the kitchen with her go-cup, her handbag, and laptop bag ready for her to scoop up. He gave a whistle. "No one would guess you're not wearing underwear."

Ashley gasped and tugged at her jersey hem. "You are not a gentleman."

"Nope," he said cheerfully. "I'm your beloved fiancé. Give me your hand. No, your left one."

While she hesitated, he produced a ring from his pocket.

Ashley bit her bottom lip, realized she was chewing off her lipstick and held out her hand. He took it between his calloused ones and slid the diamond solitaire onto her ring finger.

"Thank you. It's beautiful. I'll take good care of it," she said.

"You're trembling. Don't worry. I'll be with you every step of the day. No one will hurt you while I'm watching over you."

"Thanks." She let him think he'd guessed the reason for her shakes when it was him, his touch that toppled her off balance and the idiotic part of her that wished this was a real engagement. "Have you ever been engaged?"

"No. You?"

"My first time," Ashley said. "I'd better get moving. If I miss putting an hour in at the office, it throws off my day. My first meeting today is at a school. I'm reading a story to the kids and meeting the parents and teachers for morning tea."

"I rang a garage to tow your car. Nikolai suggested the guy who does his vehicle repairs. Is that okay?"

"Thank you. I hadn't got that far yet."

"Frog's car started without a problem. Louie will drop around this morning, so I'll drive you to work and come back to let him inside. His quote won't take long since I have a good idea of what you need. I'll be back at your office before you head off for your school meeting."

"Thanks."

"You're very welcome, sweetheart."

During the ten-minute drive to the office, Ashley pondered over what she'd tell her assistant and the volunteers who worked with her consistently. She wriggled, and her mind slid to underwear and her lack of. "With my luck, the local ladies' magazine will investigate VPLS today."

Josh took one hand off the steering wheel and squeezed her knee. "Don't worry, no one will notice you left your lingerie behind this morning. Besides, I thought visible panty lines were undesirable."

Ashley couldn't prevent her small start of surprise at the tingles that ran from his hand and spread up her thigh.

"How do you know about VPLS?"

"I have a sister, remember? I learn random factoids from Summer. She's a librarian and a research whiz."

Ashley nodded. "Our engagement announcement is worrying me. People's possible reactions."

"It'll be fine. Stick to the story and divert anyone who questions you with policy. You gave me details of past boyfriends. Tell me about your workmates."

"They're friends. I trust them." She'd mention Charles later when they had more time.

"Yet telling them you're engaged makes you nervous."

"They'll wonder why I haven't mentioned you."

"Tell them it was a security issue. That's not a lie." Josh indicated a right turn and pulled up in front of her office. "What time will you leave to go to the primary school?"

"Quarter past nine?"

Josh nodded. "I'll be here." He leaned closer and kissed her. A quick press of lips before he returned to his seat.

She blinked, raising her hand to finger her tingling lips. "Why did you kiss me?"

Josh chuckled. "I'm your fiancé. People will expect us to show affection. Come on. I'll walk you inside before I meet with Louie."

"You don't have to escort me."

"I want to make sure no one is loitering where they shouldn't be."

"It's three steps to the entrance."

In lieu of an answer, Josh opened his door and rounded the vehicle until he reached the passenger side. "Come on, sweetheart. You have work to do."

Ashley unfastened her seatbelt and exited the vehicle into the circle of Josh's arms. His lips twitched as if he tried to stifle his reaction. Epic fail. His grin burst out at her swift intake of breath. Heat crawled through her cheeks as her breasts flattened against his hard chest.

Josh kissed the tip of her nose. "You look gorgeous." He urged her to the entrance. Josh shouldered open the door, the *ting-a-ling* of a bell signaling their arrival.

"Good morning, Ashley," Carrie trilled. Today she'd tamed her thick, frizzy hair with straightening irons. Curiosity shone in her brown eyes as her gaze zapped from her to Josh and back. "Who is this?"

"You must be one of Ashley's volunteers," Josh said, extending his right hand in greeting. "I'm Josh Williams, Ashley's fiancé."

Carrie's mouth dropped open, and her eyes bulged until she resembled a bullfrog.

"Congratulations!" Sheryl spoke from behind them. "Is this recent?" Curiosity and speculation filled her gaze.

"Why didn't you tell us you're engaged?" Robert snapped. "You don't wear a ring. We didn't even know you had a boyfriend."

"Ashley and I met through her brother. I'm ex-army. New Zealand Special Air Service. Since my job is sensitive, we decided it was better to keep our engagement private until I retired," Josh said.

Ashley smiled, thankful to Josh for answering their questions.

"Oh, you're wearing an engagement ring," Carrie cried.

"I'd better go to meet Louie." Josh kissed her on the lips

and brushed his fingers on her cheek. "See you soon."

Josh strode from her office, and the tinkle of the bell filled the silence that had fallen.

"He's a babe," Carrie blurted. "Why don't you look happier?"

"I had car trouble last night. Luckily Josh had arrived at my place and was able to pick me up. It's a problem having my car out of commission." The excuse emerged without a blink. *Whoa!* She pressed her lips together in case she blurted an intruder had rifled through her lingerie.

"Oh! Let me see your ring." Carrie reached for her hand and squeaked. She bounced in excitement. "It's gorgeous. I adore diamonds. You're so lucky. Congratulations!"

"Thank you." Ashley smiled at Carrie's excitement. "I'd better get to work."

Robert followed Ashley into her office. "The polls are in."

His voice held disapproval, and that irked her, caused suspicion. Did he have something to do with—*no!*

She gave her head a hard shake, forced a smile, and sat behind her desk. They'd worked together since the last campaign. He was hardworking and trustworthy.

To ease the discomfort that had fallen between them, she followed Josh's suggestion and sought refuge in her job. "What do the polls indicate?"

"Not promising for us. The campaign manager is calling the entire caucus to the meeting tomorrow morning at nine."

"Bother. Can you change my flights? I'd prefer to fly tonight rather than take an early morning flight. I'll need a seat for Josh too."

"Of course," Robert said. "Will you need me to travel with you?"

Again, Ashley's mind slid to the letters she'd received, and guilt surfaced. But Robert had an opportunity...

"No, I'd prefer you to cover here. Is that okay?"

"Perfect." A quick grin wiped away his professionalism. "I have a hot date tonight."

"Someone I know?"

"No, I met him during my morning run. It progressed to coffee, and now we're going on a date." Robert's blue eyes shone with excitement and anticipation.

"That's great! I'm so pleased for you, and I hope to meet him soon. Anything important in the correspondence today?" Good for him on sticking his toes back into the dating pool.

"No." His smile faded to a frown, his brow creasing as he glanced at her. "There was something odd, though. Someone delivered a bouquet."

Ashley's brows rose.

"The flowers were dead."

She blinked, unsure she'd heard right. "Dead?"

"Yes."

Her pulse jumped, started to race. She coughed to clear her throat. "Was there a card?"

"I put it with the correspondence."

"Thanks."

Robert withdrew and shut the door, leaving Ashley alone with her correspondence and her fears.

5

CHOCOLATE BISCUITS AND GOOD NEWS

Josh returned to pick up Ashley, his mind in turmoil. Frog was right. Someone wanted to scare her, and whoever it was, they didn't intend to backpedal.

They'd sent her notes.

They'd put water in her petrol tank.

They'd entered her home.

He made a mental note to ask to see the correspondence.

Louie was busy installing a security alarm in Ashley's home, and the mechanic was fixing her car.

Time to dig into her background, past boyfriends, her work colleagues to see what shook loose. He'd speak with Frog, ask for any further info he had that might suggest the identity of whoever was trying to scare Ashley.

After parking, Josh entered the electoral office.

Sheryl glanced up from her desk where she was folding leaflets.

"Hi, is Ashley ready to leave?"

Sheryl smiled, her eyes crinkling behind her blue-rimmed glasses. "Tap on her door and let her know you're here. She won't mind. And congratulations on your engagement. You've got yourself a winner."

"I think so," Josh said.

Robert exited an office, a sheaf of papers in his hands. On spotting Josh, he stiffened a fraction before stretching his mouth into a welcoming smile. The type a crocodile wore before it snapped its dagger-sharp teeth together.

Josh inclined his head. "Is Ashley ready to go to her meeting?"

"I can drive her while her car is at the mechanics," Robert said. "You must have other things to do."

"Nope." Josh took pleasure in disagreeing because it was no hardship to spend time with Ashley. "We haven't seen each other for ages. We're catching up."

"She can't afford a distraction." Robert scowled. "I question your timing during her campaign."

Pompous twit. "I understand Ashley's ambitions. We've discussed it, and I support her wholeheartedly." He turned his back on the man, rapped his knuckles on the door and stuck his head through the doorway. "Hey, sweetheart. Just wanted to let you know I'm here."

"Come in," she said. "Shut the door."

Josh took one look at her face and slid into her office. "What's wrong?"

"I received flowers today. Robert threw them away

because they were dead, but he kept the attached card." She opened her handbag and handed him a green card.

I know what you did.

Josh lifted his head to study Ashley's pale face. "Any ideas who might've sent the flowers?"

She shook her head. "No. According to Robert, they were on the doorstep when he arrived."

"We should install security here too," Josh said.

"I want people to feel welcome. Security cameras everywhere do not signal hospitality to the people who live in my electorate."

"Whatever you think. Louie might have something to blend into the background. A less obvious camera, its position unknown to staff and visitors. Think about it. Ready to go?"

"Yes." Ashley stood and grabbed her handbag. "I'm looking forward to this. By the way, I'm flying to Wellington tonight. I asked Robert to book you a ticket."

"I'd better pack then. What will we be doing in Wellington?"

"I'll be in a strategy meeting. You'll have to amuse yourself for two hours."

"Where is your meeting?"

"At the Condor Hotel. It's near the Beehive."

Josh had gone on a school trip to the Beehive, the colloquial name for New Zealand's parliament buildings, and knew the area well. "Do you have everything you need?"

"Do you mind going to Wellington?"

Josh winked at Carrie who was unashamedly

JOSH'S FAKE FIANCEE

eavesdropping on their conversation. "We can hold hands on the plane and catch up."

"Ashley needs to study the notes sent to her, ready for the Labor caucus meeting," Robert said, his voice stuffy.

Josh rolled his eyes. He'd be checking on Robert. He had an entire list of names to review and with Summer's help, he'd ferret out anything suspicious. This latest note suggested something from her past. He hated to upset Ashley with his prodding, so he'd contact Frog again and hope his friend wasn't away from base.

The press ambushed them as they arrived at Wellington airport later that night.

"Ashley, the Labor party is behind in the latest poll out this morning. What do you think is going wrong with your campaign?" a reporter demanded.

"Well." Ashley dredged up a smile for the young reporter in his ill-fitting black jacket and crooked red tie. "It's still early days. Of course, we'll take the results on board and discuss our action plan, but we're not worried. Other polls have reported different results."

Josh stood behind her, carrying their overnight bags.

"Ashley! Ashley!" The short brunette struggled to push past the taller reporters blocking her way. "Ashley, I understand you're engaged. Who is your fiancé, and why have you kept your engagement so hush-hush?"

Ashley turned to him, a smile plastered on her face. "This is Josh Williams. My fiancé."

"A secret engagement? Why?"

Josh set their bags at his feet and slipped his arm around

her waist. Ashley leaned into him a fraction, relieved by his presence.

"Should I answer?" he whispered.

She nodded.

"Because I've been overseas and haven't been home for long. Just long enough to pop the question." He grinned and leaned in to kiss her cheek. Her skin prickled. Every one of his touches had her pulse racing, her nerve endings at high alert. Her nipples pulled tight, and she was fiercely glad of her polka-dot scarf. With her day compressed because of this flight to Wellington, she still hadn't purchased new lingerie.

"When are you getting married?" The young brunette shouted, bouncing on her toes so Ashley could see her. "Have you set a date?"

"Not yet. Ashley is busy with the upcoming election," Josh said. "Now, if you'll excuse us. I've organized a special dinner for my lady, and we're going to be late if we chat much longer."

Josh picked up their bags and ushered her from the airport.

They'd already discussed getting a cab into the city, and with Josh at her side, procuring a taxi was straightforward. Josh urged her inside. After placing the luggage in the trunk, he slid in beside her.

"We're having dinner?" she asked when the cab pulled away from the curb.

"We are, but that's all I'm telling you. I meant it to be a surprise."

Ashley sighed. "I hate to sound ungrateful, but I was

looking forward to an early night. I thought I'd have a shower, jump in bed, and catch up on reading before tomorrow's meeting."

"That shouldn't be a problem."

"I'd hoped to have time to go shopping today."

"Give me a list of what you want, and I'll go shopping while you're at your meeting."

"I... No."

Josh clasped her hand, squeezing in a silent demand for her to glance in his direction. "My job is to help you. You're busy. We'll have a receipt and can exchange pieces that don't work for you."

"I'll consider it."

"I have excellent taste."

"And a big head," she said sweetly.

Josh laughed.

"We could've stayed at the flat."

"No, a hotel is better this time. It's best if we shake up your routine. We don't want to be predictable. It makes your stalker's job easy. Have you received any correspondence while you've been in Wellington?"

"No, everything has arrived at the electoral office."

"So we can presume your stalker lives in Auckland. If that changes, we'll have another string to follow."

Ashley hated the idea of someone watching her, and she must've made a sound because Josh's hand tightened on hers again.

"Don't worry, sweetheart. We *will* catch this guy."

The cab dropped them off in the hotel foyer, and Josh took control. It was nice having someone to take charge when she normally had to do everything herself. And for once, she wasn't continually glancing over her shoulder.

"Come on." Josh let the staff commandeer their luggage and clasped her hand. He led her to reception and took care of that too.

"The honeymoon suite," she whispered, her cheeks flushed after intercepting the receptionist's speculation. A professional, the hotel employee hadn't commented or asked questions but she'd sure communicated with her eyes.

"It was all they had left. The hotel security is excellent here. I've spoken to the manager and they'll make sure no unauthorized visitors get anywhere near our room."

Their special dinner turned out to be room service. Ashley arrived at the table wearing a robe, after taking a shower and hand-washing two pieces of underwear she'd fished from her dirty laundry pile. She refused to go commando again.

She sat at the table opposite Josh and waited while the room service attendant served their dinner.

"Just call if you require anything else," the woman instructed and departed.

"There is only one bed," Ashley said.

"Yes."

"Aren't you worried I'll accost you while you're sleeping?"

Josh chuckled. "I hope you will."

Ashley reached for her glass of sparkling water. "You think I'm joking. Do you realize I haven't had sex for months? I might appreciate the masculine attention."

"I enjoy kissing you, although I refuse to do it too often. Your brother wouldn't approve."

"What's Matt got to do with this?"

"He instructed me to help you, to protect you, but he promised he'd break my nose if I put a foot out of line." Josh grinned at her indignant gasp.

"Matt has no right to tell me who I can and cannot kiss." Ashley cut a piece of salmon and popped it into her mouth.

"Your brother is protective. I get it. Dillon and I used to watch out for our sister in the same way."

Ashley cut more of the delicious salmon. "Matt is in Afghanistan. You're working for me, keeping me safe. Not Matt. The next time I speak to him, I'll tell him so."

"It won't stop him worrying."

"Probably not, so you should tell him what he wants to hear and keep the rest to yourself."

"Lie?" Josh asked.

"Yes." Ashley scowled. "I guess that wouldn't work either."

"No."

"All right, but you tell him I disapprove of his tactics and will have words with him the minute he sets foot on New Zealand soil."

"That should make him shake in his shoes," Josh said.

Ashley sniffed. "Now you're laughing at me. I'm not useless, you know."

"I'll make sure Frog is aware of your position when I speak to him again," Josh promised. "Are you going to let me shop for you?"

"You'll promise to buy *exactly* what I ask for?"

"Of course," Josh said. "I'm your fiancé. I should have intimate knowledge of your underwear."

"Huh."

"I'll let you see mine."

"I've already seen yours," she blurted.

"Yes."

A suspicion occurred. "Were you awake this morning?"

"Sweetheart. I'm ex-NZSAS. We're trained to sleep light."

Ashley relaxed more than she had in weeks. Josh's teasing charmed her and eased her fear. Against her better judgment, she agreed to let him do her lingerie shopping.

"What will happen at your meeting tomorrow?" Josh asked.

"Hopefully, Geoffrey will review the party stance on capital gains tax. That's one thing killing us in the polls. Other than that, I'm sure we'll continue in the same vein."

Josh walked with her to the hotel and insisted on escorting her to the meeting room. She introduced him to several of the other Labor party members, and on hearing their explanations, they didn't ask awkward questions. They merely nodded and extended congratulations.

"How long will the meeting take?" Josh asked.

"They run around two hours."

He led her off to the side, out of visibility from most of her coworkers, leaned closer to her and whispered. "I added my contact details to your address book. Text me when you're almost done. I think you're safe here, but I won't take chances. If I get back earlier, I'll grab a coffee and wait for your text."

"Thanks."

Josh's grin was all the warning she received. She blinked, heat roared through her and the next second, he was kissing her. It wasn't one of those quick brushes of his mouth against hers or a peck on the cheek. This was an open-mouthed, tongue-tangling kiss of seduction. Ashley tightened her hands on his shoulders and held on because she feared her knees might buckle. This kiss, his touch, his scent... Everything knotted together to befuddle her senses. When he parted their mouths, she was breathing hard and craved a repeat.

Josh Williams knew a thing or two about kissing.

He leaned closer again, his eyes a darker blue than usual, and stole another slow, decadent kiss. "See you later, sweetheart. Don't forget. Text me."

With her power of speech AWOL, she nodded instead. He winked and left, his long strides carrying him to the lift. When it arrived, he held the door for an elderly secretary to exit, then the doors closed behind him, and he was lost from sight.

Ashley sighed and reclaimed her political persona.

The first person she saw was Charles, and the man sure held resentment close and wielded it like a club—usually on her head. *Suck it up, princess.* She brought out her secret weapon and beamed at him.

"Hi, Charles. I hear your campaign for the inner-city seat is going well. Congratulations."

"I work hard," Charles snapped.

"Of course you do. I don't doubt that for a moment. You're an excellent politician."

He blinked at the praise, but Ashley had had enough of the prima donna. "Oh, there's Christine. I need a word with her. Please excuse me."

Ashley walked away before Charles could reply. The man was an idiot. "Hey, Christine. How are things with you?"

Christine was standing for a seat in Christchurch, but they had met as students at Auckland University.

"Someone has been keeping secrets." Christine, a petite blonde who preferred bright and bold colors, waggled a finger at Ashley.

Ashley stilled. "What secrets?"

"That hunk of a man who kissed you a few minutes ago. Heck, my toes curled from the heat. Ah! That's why your brain is sluggish. His kiss muddied your mind."

Ashley giggled. "Josh is a great kisser."

"How did you meet him? Wait? Are the weird rumors true? I heard on the news this morning you were engaged. I thought it was the press inventing stuff again." Her gaze darted to Ashley's finger and widened on spotting the ring. "It's true?"

"I met Josh through my brother."

"Ah! That explains the sexy physique. Josh is a soldier."

"Yes. Or at least he was. He left the army a few weeks ago." Ashley noticed her colleagues drifting into the meeting room. "We'd better hurry or we'll miss out on the chocolate biscuits."

Christine tapped her handbag. "I brought my own. You can share."

In the conference room, they sat next to each other.

Geoffrey strode into the room with two senior members. They took their seats while Geoffrey remained standing.

"Earlier this morning, our senior members held a meeting. The polls have us trailing by a huge margin. This election needs a shakeup to improve our hopes of winning. With that in mind, we've decided to rejig our party line-up and present something new to the voting public. I will resign and step into a senior role."

A buzz of conversation sprang up, and Ashley shared a glance with Christine.

"Who will they appoint?" Ashley whispered.

Christine shrugged. "Who knows?"

Geoffrey raised his hand for quiet, and silence fell. "Last night and this morning, we discussed my replacement. We looked at achievements, popularity, and a host of other circumstances." Geoffrey scanned faces, his search halting when he met Ashley's gaze. "The new Labor party leader—if she will accept the post—and we hope, our next prime minister, will be Ashley Townsend."

Ashley blinked, uncertain if she'd heard correctly.

"Yay!" Christine leaped to her feet and wildly applauded. "Go, Ashley!"

The party members joined in the applause, and several of the younger ones hooted and hollered with approval while Ashley continued to stare at Geoffrey.

"Speech!" Christine shouted. "Speech!"

Geoffrey signaled Ashley to stand and join him. Her legs trembled, but she managed the short journey.

"Thank you, Geoffrey. I know this can't have been easy for you," Ashley murmured.

"You'll accept?"

"I am honored," Ashley said in a total understatement. It was something she'd dreamed of since she was five-years-old and learned she'd lost out on the queen position. Although she hadn't been elected yet, she could be the prime minister if the Labor caucus swayed the voting public.

"Ashley has good news," Christine shouted above the chatter. "She got engaged this weekend."

"Congratulations!" several of her colleagues called.

Ashley listened to the congratulations for a few more minutes before raising her hand for silence.

"Thank you. I am honored to accept the leadership of the party. I know we have had problems, and I have my own ideas and suggestions of what to change. Shall we pull up our shirt sleeves and get to work again? We have a lot to do before Election day."

6

SEXY LINGERIE

Josh hadn't realized lingerie shopping would provide entertainment. He'd gone to the shop Ashley had suggested, and the instant he'd stepped foot inside, an assistant had made a bee-line to him. After he'd pulled out his list, the middle-aged woman had helped him meet Ashley's requirements.

He'd added a few requests of his own since he believed Ashley should embrace her sexy. She could turn heads and still do an efficient job for her electorate.

They'd sorted out bras, getting the sizes and makes Ashley had specified since she knew they fitted well.

"My fiancé is often in the public eye. She wants to make sure her lingerie doesn't show beneath her clothes," Josh said.

"We have this new line. The boy-shorts are perfect to wear beneath trousers, yet they're still very feminine." The assistant held up plain black panties in a silky fabric.

Josh imagined Ashley wearing them and nodded. "One set of black and one set of beige."

"They come in three-packs."

"Even better," Josh said.

"I think that's everything on the list."

"I'd like to add two more sets. These are for my viewing pleasure." Josh winked at the assistant, and she wagged her finger at him, but her eyes twinkled.

"Your fiancée is a fortunate lady. What did you have in mind?"

"I'll take a set of the pale pink you showed me earlier and something in that ruby-red color. Perfect."

Ashley had warned him of the expense, but the total had him blinking twice. Still, he handed over the money Ashley had given him plus his credit card to cover the rest. He couldn't wait to see her in this lingerie, and after their earlier kiss, he thought they might both desire the same outcome.

"Thank you," he said to the sales assistant. "You helped to make this visit stress-free for me." He glanced at his watch. "I promised to meet my fiancée in two hours, so I'd better hustle."

Josh stopped by their hotel to drop his shopping with the luggage they'd left for later collection and continued to the hotel where the Labor caucus was meeting. The session was still in progress when he arrived, and he retreated to the coffee shop to wait for a text from Ashley.

His phone rang as the waitress delivered his coffee.

"Hey, Louie," he said. "What's up?"

"I left Ashley's place to meet Mac for lunch, and when I got back, I found a dressmaker's dummy on the front lawn, by the mailbox. It's dressed in lingerie. A red G-string and a bra that's more thought than substance."

"Crap. Is there any note attached or in the mailbox?" Josh asked.

"Just a sec."

Josh heard a series of taps.

"There's a plain envelope."

"Open it," Josh ordered.

"A single sheet of paper. The note says *home wrecker*. That's all."

"Crap. This person who is hassling Ashley is escalating. Can you snap a photo of the dummy and the note and send them to me?"

"Should I call the cops?"

"So far, they're telling us they can't do much. We need cameras. Physical proof of mischief. I've emailed Frog. I'll question Ashley and ask if she knows what the note means. She's not a woman who'd flirt or have an affair. She's genuine. Sincere. She works hard and doesn't have time to play."

"There has to be something to drive the notes," Louie said.

"Yeah."

"I'll send the photos through now. Let me know if I can help with anything else."

"Thanks, Louie. Appreciate it."

Josh busied himself with research and poking into Ashley's background. Then Summer emailed him a copy of an article showing a picture of an eighteen-year-old Ashley. Josh fired off another email to Frog, asking for further details, other than what he'd already mentioned. Could this be the source of the danger after all? He'd ask Ashley, but he hated tears, and this might be a touchy subject. Was the public aware of this and how deep was the story buried? He sent Summer another email asking his sister's opinion.

It was another two hours before Ashley sent him a text. Josh packed up and strode to meet his fiancée, his heart heavy at the discussion they needed to have soon.

When he arrived at the conference room, Ashley stood chatting to a group of older men and women. Each shook her hand, and there was an electric vibe, an air of excitement filling the air.

"We scheduled the press announcement for one." An officious lady tapped her pen on her clipboard. "Do not be late."

"I won't," Ashley promised with her trademark smile. She lifted her head and spotted him, her smile widening. "Josh."

"What's going on?" Josh asked.

"Geoffrey resigned," Ashley said. "I'm his replacement."

Josh stared, seeing her excitement, yet taking a beat to reconcile the words with what they meant. "You're in charge?"

She nodded. "As of two hours ago. I'm so glad we booked late afternoon flights because I have a press conference at one."

"Congratulations." Josh grinned because her dream

stood that much closer, although worry slid through him. As the leader of the opposition, she'd have a higher profile. She'd present a bigger target, and with the increased public appearances, his job to watch her had become more difficult.

Ashley threw her arms around Josh. "I'm so excited. This is such a big deal. I hope I can turn around the poll numbers."

Josh hugged her back, still concerned, but not willing to share his disquiet where others might note her reaction. "You'll be great. I know it. What does this mean for your workload?"

"It means I'll be traveling more and campaigning countrywide instead of around Auckland. I have a proposed schedule, and I'll get Robert to book the travel, hire a car, and organize accommodation where necessary."

Josh nodded. "Are you ready to go now? Where is your press conference?"

"In front of the parliament buildings. The Beehive." Ashley speed-talked and grabbed his forearm. "I'm starving. Can we have a sandwich and coffee?"

Josh slung his arm around her shoulders. "We can't have your stomach grumbling loud enough for the reporters to hear."

She grinned. "No, we can't."

The press conference took place with quick efficiency. Josh stood away to the side, close enough to get to Ashley, but most of those present were Labor Party supporters, curious tourists, and several bored reporters.

It didn't take long before the reporters perked up. Geoffrey Turbott, the former party leader, announced his intention to step aside for the younger guard and announced Ashley Townsend was the new party leader.

"Did he say Legs?" a man standing near to Josh asked.

"Yeah."

"That should make this campaign more exciting. It's not a hardship to look at Ashley Townsend."

Josh's hands curled into tight fists even though he agreed with the man's assessment. While her rise in the ranks thrilled Ashley, Josh saw problems keeping her safe. He needed to make a request for the Diplomatic Protection Squad to protect her now, given the threatening notes arriving so regularly. The members of the Protection Squad carried weapons while he couldn't because of New Zealand's current laws.

"Is it true you're engaged?" a reporter asked.

"It is." Ashley flashed her engagement ring.

"When will we meet your fiancé?" a female reporter asked.

"Just this once, since this is a day of new beginnings. Josh." She turned to where he stood off to her right. "Josh, the reporters want to meet you."

Josh snorted under his breath. For a woman who stressed minimizing lies to the press, she didn't have a problem drawing attention to their engagement.

"How did you meet?" the female reporter asked.

"We met through my brother," Ashley said.

"Have you set a date for the wedding?"

"Not yet." Ashley gave a throaty chortle. "I'm busy for

the next few weeks."

Most people surrounding Ashley laughed, apart from one man in a gray suit. Josh scrutinized him, taking in the man's tension. Although he'd fastened an impassive expression to his features, his sharp brown eyes gave away his turmoil. He was pissed.

Josh snapped a photo of Ashley with his phone before taking a clandestine one of the grim man.

Ashley continued answering the questions the press fired at her. The woman was in her element and offered smart, concise replies while sending a few zingers that made the reporters and cameramen laugh.

Finally, she wrapped up the session, and the crowd dispersed.

"You're really doing this," Josh murmured. "Frog will be so proud of you. Who is the guy in the gray suit? Do you know him?"

Ashley followed Josh's line of sight and grimaced. "That's Charles."

"He wasn't on your list."

"Charles is a colleague. I meant to tell you about him."

"He doesn't like you."

"He resents me," Ashley corrected. "The man covets what I have—my seat and now my position as leader."

"I'll check into his background. Anyone else you missed from your list? Pissed off colleagues?"

Ashley released a snort. "Right now, several of the Labor politicians have their noses out of joint. What they don't realize is that if I don't perform well, I'll be out on my butt too."

7

RECALLING THE PAST

THE NEWS BEGAN AS he was driving past Awful Ashley's house. His hands tightened on the steering wheel when the lead story mentioned *her*.

Huh.

She'd be in the public arena more. Harder to get at without one of her adoring fans seeing him, perhaps witnessing something they shouldn't.

He replayed his plan, glanced at Awful Ashley's driveway. She had a visitor. *Bugger.* No spray-painting this afternoon.

He considered his plan for Robert, his schedule, and his frown cleared.

Even better.

Given her position as the new opposition party leader, this brainwave would injure her chances of election, cast doubt on her suitability to run the country.

All he needed was to cause a diversion, get people talking, wondering.

The old story to surface to injure her reputation.

The truth.

And if that failed, he'd resort to Plan B.

Didn't matter what happened to him afterward.

He'd died a long time ago.

· ♥ · ♥ · ♥ · ♥ · ♥ ·

THE FLIGHT BACK TO Auckland was half-full, which gave Josh the opportunity to speak with Ashley and question her regarding his discoveries.

This morning she'd slicked her hair into another ponytail. He cast his mind back to Summer's instruction on hairstyles. Yeah, she'd called it a high ponytail. It gave Ashley the cute factor, but he preferred her hair loose. The tousled and just out-of-bed look did it for him.

"Tell me more of this envy thing with Charles."

"My best guess is Charles Jamieson is pissed because the party chose me to be their new leader. He hasn't forgiven me for winning the nomination to stand for the Manurewa electorate. He hated that. Charles coveted the seat. What you're seeing is plain jealousy."

"Enough to spiral into stalking you?"

"No, I..." She shook her head. "He might dislike me, but that doesn't mean he's the person sending me weird notes."

"Did you date him?"

"Once. He didn't ask me out again after I won the right

to stand for the Manurewa seat."

"Nothing surfaced on my research dives. I'll see if Summer can learn anything new."

"But I earned my position. I've worked hard," Ashley said. "Charles wouldn't be that petty."

"Look at this photo. He's puffed up with his righteous fury. If a man is pushed hard enough, he'll revert to caveman behavior."

"But he's standing for a seat now. He's polling well, and I'm confident he'll win his seat for Labor."

"But he's not the leader of the opposition," Josh pointed out then hesitated. He should question her about the accident details Summer had unearthed, yet he hated to pierce her excitement with his nosy questions. No, better a pissed alive fiancée than one attacked by a stalker. "Summer found something else. The accident where the girl died."

Every bit of color fled her cheeks, and she wrapped her arms around her torso before slumping. She sucked in a hoarse breath and struggled for composure, leaving Josh feeling like a bastard for putting her through this pain.

"Ashley?"

"No, you're right to ask. Matt suggested I should tell you, make sure you had the facts, but it was a dark time in my life. Occasionally, I still have nightmares of that night, wondering if I'd done something differently, it might have changed the outcome."

A flight attendant approached, offering them a hot drink and a cookie. They both declined and waited for the attendant to move out of hearing.

"W-when I was eighteen, I attended a party with my friend. It was when we lived in Onewhero on the farm. Jess Harrison, my friend, was older and had a full driving license. I could drive but held a restricted license, which meant I couldn't drive after ten at night without a licensed driver in the car with me. My friend had broken up with her boyfriend, and he was there with his new girl. Jess drank and drank and created a drunken scene. She punched Allen's new girlfriend in the face. With the help of two other friends, I got Jess into the car. I'd had two glasses of wine, but my friends told me I was fine to drive safely."

Josh nodded in encouragement. He recalled the rules for holding a restricted license because they'd chafed him and his friends. Zero alcohol and no driving after ten at a time when they were testing the freedom of being eighteen and legally allowed to drink under New Zealand law.

"The friends who helped me with Jess told me we were in the country, and they doubted cops would pull me over on the short drive home to Jess's house." She paused and swiped at her eyes before scrambling for her handbag. She pulled out a travel-size pack of tissues and used one to blot away her tears. "I knew the roads well and wasn't speeding. I drove at the legal speed because it was a clear night with a full moon.

"Jess started ripping off her seatbelt and insisting on returning to the party. She wanted to confront Allen again, demand he gave her another chance. I took my eyes off the road for a few seconds. When I looked back at the road, there was an animal on the road. A d-dog. I swerved. I know you're not meant to. It was instinct. I hit the dog and ran off the road into a tree. Jess ended up tossed from the car. I was okay because of the seatbelt and the airbag. Jess died."

Josh wrapped his hand around Ashley's, and she burrowed against his chest.

"Is everything okay, sir?" the flight attendant asked.

"Thanks, we're fine." Josh waited until they were alone again. "What happened after the accident?"

"They charged me with manslaughter and I lost my license for two years. Because of the circumstances, I received community service. I was lucky. I know that. Jess died because of me. She was pregnant. I didn't know. She never told me."

Josh didn't agree with Ashley taking the full blame, but he let the murky circumstances and what-ifs slide. "What about Jess's family? How did they cope with her death? Did they blame you?"

"They knew she'd been drinking. Allen told the cops Jess had attacked his girlfriend, and the friends who helped me confirmed she'd been wearing a seatbelt when we left. One of them had clicked it into place. Her parents acted cool toward me, but they never blamed me outright. At least, they never spread rumors or chided me to my face."

"Did she have brothers or sisters?"

"Two younger siblings. One brother and one sister. After Jess died, things fell apart for the family. Jess's parents separated. I haven't seen any of the family for years. I doubt I'd recognize them if I saw them."

"Does the father still own the same farm?"

"I'm not sure. I moved in with my grandmother because I was at university in Auckland, and it was easier living with her since it was closer and I could catch the train. My sister married and moved up North while Matt joined the army. None of us were interested in the farm, so my parents sold up and moved to Tuakau. They love their new place. They have a few acres, yet they're closer to the city if they want to go to a show or a special event."

"Okay," Josh said. "I'll check out this Charles and look into Jess's family."

"Jess's death upset them. I know that, but I don't think they'd do this all these years later. That makes no sense."

"Don't worry. Concentrate on your campaign."

A shudder ran through Ashley. "I hope this doesn't get dredged up in the press again. I mourn Jess's loss every single day. If I had my time over, I'd do things differently. I haven't touched alcohol since that night, and I'm a conscientious driver. When I first started in politics, I told my advisor about this part of my life, and he suggested—if the press ever asked questions—I should tell the truth. The subject hasn't come up once."

"It might now that you're the opposition leader," Josh said.

"Yes, I guess I should prepare my answer if anyone asks."

"Sweetheart, tell them what you've told me. That you regret the accident and it caused you to change your life. Say you took the punishment the courts set, and ever since, you've tried to live a good life. Most of us have mistakes in our background. It's how we deal with consequences that help us to grow as an adult."

"The captain has turned on the seatbelt sign," a voice came over the speakers. "Please return to your seat and prepare for landing. Place your seats in the upright position and secure your trays."

Josh fastened his seatbelt and saw that Ashley's had remained in place from the onset of their journey. When he considered it, he could see how she followed rules. His heart ached for her. While she'd come through the accident and lived, she still suffered from the fallout. Hopefully, the person terrorizing Ashley had nothing to do with her past, but he'd check to make sure. His list of suspects was getting longer, and it made him feel as if he was doing something productive to keep Ashley safe.

He huffed out a burst of air when another thought occurred. Wait until he informed Dillon and Summer he was now engaged to the leader of the opposition. They'd bust a gut laughing.

They'd left Frog's car at the airport, and after collecting their luggage, exited the terminal.

"Do you think it's someone I know? Someone close to me?" she asked once they were inside the car.

"I'm not sure, but we'll find out," he promised. "Louie gave me the code for the alarm. We can change it to something easier for you to remember."

"No, whatever he's done is fine. My district has always been safe. I hate being forced to install an alarm."

"What do you have in store for tomorrow?"

"The party have given me details of the meetings they'd organized for Geoffrey. I'll fulfill the promises we made for this week while they're revamping the plan. I'll be in

Auckland tomorrow and in Waikato the next day. The one after that it's Northland."

Josh nodded. "Are you driving or flying?"

"Both. I can fly up to Whangarei, but I thought I'd drive to Matamata to meet local farmers. I'm not looking forward to that one. There's bound to be questions regarding climate change and our current farming methods. It will be a difficult line to straddle."

"I bet you've done your research," Josh said. "You know your party's position on climate change, so tell it like it is. No matter what you say or do, you'll never please everyone."

"Tonight, before I go to bed, I'll shuffle responsibilities for the senior spokesmen roles. That will be fun." Her grimace told him she hated to ruffle politician feathers.

"Frog told me you decided to be the prime minister when you were five-years-old. You're not going to let a few politicians scare you, are you?"

"You haven't seen their teeth," she retorted.

Josh grinned and guided their vehicle to the on-ramp and onto the southern motorway. The more he came to know this woman, the more he enjoyed her company. The constant kissing was getting to him too. He had to keep reminding himself this wasn't a real engagement. Ashley didn't belong to him or think of him as anything but a protector sent by her brother.

Josh forced his mind to more practical matters. "Anything else I should know about the upcoming days?"

"We'll be busy. Luckily, I won't need to do the scheduling. Robert will do that."

"He adores you." Josh might as well use the time to prod. It sure beat pining after something he couldn't have. His thoughts slid to his siblings. Yep, they'd bust a gut for sure.

"I like him too."

"No, he is in love with you. Every time he looks my way, he bristles. Reminds me of a dog defending its territory."

"You're misreading the signs. We're good friends. Nothing more. Robert is gay."

Josh frowned. How had he missed that? "How long has he worked for you? What do you know about his home situation?"

In the dim light of the car interior, Josh caught Ashley's scowl. She didn't see what he saw in Robert. The man *was* in love with her.

"He's in his early thirties and has worked with me for the last five years. We met at a Labor party meeting when we were both in our teens and got on well. We're very similar. Robert was married briefly, then divorced. He told me last time I saw him, he's met someone. I'd say he's more concerned my sudden engagement might derail my political career."

"Why did the marriage fail?"

"That's kind of personal. We don't have those kinds of conversations. We work together. I... We're colleagues. Nothing more."

"Did you meet his wife?"

"She was...*is* a nice lady. I didn't know her well, but whenever we spoke, she was pleasant. Intelligent and stylish. The kind of woman who was perfect for Robert."

"They're not together anymore."

"Stop. No more. You'll make our working relationship uncomfortable if you continue in this vein. Robert and I are colleagues, and that is all we'll ever be." She cast him a quick glance, her gaze bouncing away when it connected to his. "Blame it on my brother and his rugby-playing mates, but I favor more intellectual men. I dated men of my brother's ilk, but they grunted, and that does not a conversation make."

"Interesting," Josh teased. "Who knows of your preference for intellectuals?"

"My family. My close friends."

"Why haven't I met your friends or heard you discuss them? I need names so I can check them out."

"Josh! No, I won't have you investigating my friends."

"Ashley." Josh strove for patience. He got it. He did, but couldn't she see that the nuisance notes had increased in frequency? Someone had broken into her home. Hell, he hadn't informed her of the dummy wearing her underwear yet.

Maybe he should. He hesitated, not wanting to spoil her day more than he had already when she was on such a high. Then, he remembered Frog—his demand to watch his sister. He had to keep Ashley apprised of what was happening. This was her life.

"When Louie installed the alarm, he had to leave for an hour. When he returned, someone had left a dummy by your mailbox. They'd dressed it in your missing lingerie, and the person who'd left it had cut off the dummy's head. The severed head lay a few feet from the dummy."

"That's sick." Ashley swallowed hard. "Why would someone do that to me? What could I have done to attract this attack?"

Josh reached over to grasp her hand. He squeezed it before returning his grip to the steering wheel. "Don't worry. We'll find whoever is doing this to you. Each time they do something, they're leaving clues. All we need to do is put them together and see where they point."

"You make it sound easy."

"Don't worry. You're safe with me here." He'd make sure of it, and tomorrow, he intended to demand she received protection from the cops. If he told them everything, they'd change from their previous stance, especially now that she'd be more prominent as the leader of the opposition.

Once Josh turned off the motorway, the streets were quieter with less traffic. Ten minutes later, he pulled into Ashley's driveway. The extra security light he'd asked Louie to install along with the alarm bathed the side of Ashley's house with brightness.

"Oh! That's brilliant. I've meant to get a security light in that spot for ages. Matt told me I should have one there."

"Now you do," Josh said. "Wait here while I check out the house."

"Don't treat me like a child," Ashley snapped. "I'll stay behind you and keep my wits alert, but I will not quiver in a corner. I refuse to give this person power over me."

Josh had seen her fear, and he mentally cheered her bravery. "Come on then. Let's get our bags so we don't need to make more than one trip. Then you can get on with your work while I cook something for dinner."

"I can cook."

"I'm sure you can, but why don't I do it, so you don't have to work late into the night? You have a heap of meetings and public speaking gigs scheduled. You need your rest, so take my offer and hit the ground running."

"Thank you, Josh." With that, she exited the car and grabbed her handbag, laptop bag, and one piece of luggage.

He followed her. "I'm only behaving like a fiancé."

"Huh!" Ashley snorted. "Most of my past boyfriends expected me to wait on them. Another bad quality of brawny, grunting men."

"Hey." Josh prodded his broad chest and bulky biceps and narrowed his eyes at her. "I don't grunt. I've known lazy intellects too."

"You don't grunt." Ashley's chin dipped, but not before he'd glimpsed her far-away, almost wistful expression. "Your admirable qualities far outweigh your cons. It's a pity this engagement is fake because I'm starting to enjoy your company very much."

Stupid. Stupid. *Stupid*. Ashley castigated herself as she followed Josh to the rear of her house. A second security light lit the yard, and no one lurked where they shouldn't.

Josh unlocked the door and reached around to get the passage light.

Ashley held her breath until she saw everything was as she'd left it. Her breath eased out with relief. She hated the teetering-on-eggshells sensation that stalked her. That was the reason for her proposing to Josh earlier. Plus the euphoric remnants of joy from learning she was the one the party deemed suitable to lead them to victory at the election.

Yes, the two moods combined and had her mouth motoring out of control.

Matt had warned her Josh was a player who never settled with one lady. Matt had also told her he'd trust Josh with his life, and he presented the best solution to keeping her safe and on track to obtain her goals.

Her brother's warning had slipped away in the wake of the kisses and sleeping in the same bed. Heck, a woman just had to look at Josh before she was aching to test those hard muscles beneath her fingertips. Being the recipient of his charming smiles and cheeky winks turned her to mush. She defied any red-blooded woman not to experience the same reaction. On top of that, he could hold an intelligent conversation, he was supportive of her work even if he didn't agree with her party's policies, and the man was plain nice. He was respectful, charming, and insightful.

And she was a drowning woman.

Her heart refused to listen to her practical head.

Snubbed. Rebuffed.

Rejected each and every warning.

Yep, no doubt about it. She was toast where Josh Williams was concerned. The man would break her heart when he left her. No need to cry pity tears when genuine ones awaited.

Work.

That was something she could count on to maintain her

sanity, so that's what she'd do.

"Josh, I'll be in the dining room if you need me. The table is big enough for me to spread out."

"Would you like a cup of tea?"

Charming and nice combined well with sexy. Ashley blinked at his genuine smile and held back her sigh. "I have a packet of ginger and quince green tea in the pantry. Could you make a pot for me?"

"Sure. Any requests for dinner?"

"Surprise me." She shrugged from her jacket.

"I'll put the bags in our rooms," Josh said.

"Thanks," she murmured as she pulled out her notebook and her laptop. Already, her practical mind had decided she should bury herself in work. Work was her safe zone, and a way to realize her aspiration to be prime minister.

Ashley scanned the list she'd made while waiting for their flight and started to complete her tasks.

In the distance, the phone rang, but since it wasn't hers, Ashley ignored the summons. The ringing ceased, and soon her work consumed her. She let instinct guide her, taking what she knew of her colleagues and their strengths and remade her team. When she'd finished, she scrutinized her new chart. She gave a decisive nod.

Radical but refreshing. *Perfect*.

This might rock her team but in a good way.

Ashley continued with her next task.

"Ashley!"

She started and dropped her pen.

Josh retrieved it from the floor. "Sorry I frightened you.

Dinner is ready. I've set everything up at the breakfast bar since I thought you'd prefer not to tidy away your books and papers. Did you get much done?"

"Yes."

"Your tea has gone cold."

"I didn't even hear you bring it."

"I spoke to you. You went *hmm*, so I figured you knew it was there. I'll make another pot for you after dinner. Come on. The pasta will get cold."

The scents wafting from the kitchen made her stomach rumble. "That smells delicious. Who taught you to cook?"

"My mother taught us the basic skills. She loves to cook and believes everyone, male or female, should learn. Once I joined the army, I found cooking relaxed me." He grinned. "My girlfriends have always appreciated my skills in the kitchen."

Ashley pushed out a laugh, although his casual remark and the implications burned her. A reminder to stay away from Josh. If she wished to progress, she couldn't have a philandering boyfriend or fiancé.

But you're not going to listen. Her heart sang with joy at the decision.

Josh seated her at the breakfast bar, his strong fingers flexing around her waist as he lifted her onto the bar stool. Although she was tall, he tossed her into place without a single grunt.

He grinned at his easy accomplishment and swiped a finger over her cheek. "You have ink on your face."

She started to get up to clean it off, but he stayed her with a hand on her arm.

"Leave it. It makes you look cute and studious. Eat your dinner."

"Yes, Dad," she quipped.

"Ashley." The strange note in his voice drew her attention from the pile of glistening spaghetti to him.

His blue eyes glowed, and a soft smile curved his lips. "The last emotion on my mind is fatherly. Frog warned me not to do my normal flirt and leave. With you, it's hard."

"Why, because I'm a nerd?"

"No, sweetheart. It's because you're sweet and sexy and intelligent. Every time I glimpse you, I get an urge to strip off your clothes and feast on you. I'm eager to see you in your new lingerie."

Her eyes narrowed. "I hope you followed my list."

"I did, but I added a couple of items for my viewing pleasure. Cheeky, I know, but a man needs hope."

"You want me too?"

"Very much. You're an unexpected package, Ashley Townsend. Any man is lucky to have you in their life."

Ashley speared her spaghetti with a fork and twirled the pasta onto the tines. "I'm hearing a *but* in your words."

"I promised Frog I'd keep my hands to myself. I'm a man of my word."

"Hmm." Ashley forked pasta into her mouth. She moaned at the hint of truffle oil, the spinach and corn and herbs, and the al dente spaghetti. It was sex in a mouthful. Ashley swallowed and twirled more pasta around her fork. "This is delicious. Thanks so much for cooking dinner, Josh."

His phone rang again. "Sorry, I'd better get this. It's my

sister. Keep eating." Josh stood and retreated, but Ashley could still hear his side of the conversation. "Fuck," he said. "Send it through. They're trending on social media? Yeah. All right. Thanks for letting me know."

Josh hung up and returned to his seat.

Ashley took in his expression, and her stomach did a slow churn. Tension bled into her, and she clenched her fork until her knuckles whitened. "What is it? What's happened?"

"Your *friend* has started a social media campaign. They've flooded the different channels with posts saying you're unfit to lead the country and that voters are stupid if they vote for you or your party."

Ashley scooped up her phone, and almost instantly, it rang. She frowned at the unknown number. Every instinct told her that whoever wished to talk to her meant her harm.

"Hello."

"Ashley." A husky voice. Masculine, but one she didn't recognize.

"Who is this?"

"Put the call on speakerphone," Josh whispered.

"Who's there?" the man asked.

"My fiancé. We were eating dinner. How can I help you?"

"You ruined my life. Because of you, I lost everything."

"Who is this?"

"Have you seen my social media posts? I will destroy you," the man snarled. "Once I'm finished, you will lose everything." Seconds later, he disconnected the call.

Ashley let Josh take possession of her phone. "I don't give out my phone number to people. Not this one at any rate. How did he get it?"

He tapped several keys and studied the screen. "If he's the one who broke into your house, he might have noticed a phone account or paperwork."

"But I had my laptop with me. I receive electronic statements." This man... She...

Numbly, she lifted her gaze to Josh. He wore what she privately labeled his warrior's face. Her brother possessed a similar one which always meant it was butt-kicking time.

A pain in her hands had her releasing her grip. She'd gouged crescent marks into her palms. The sense of violation, the spreading tingle of fear had tears burning her eyes. This was meant to be a day of celebration. A day of personal triumph. She'd taken a giant step toward obtaining her driving goal, and this man had spoiled the sweet taste of success for her.

She bunched her hands to fists. This time, she embraced the pain and let it center her mind, to beat back the terror. Did she want to be a sniveling coward? Give up and go away to cry in a corner?

She. Did. Not.

Maybe she should go public about her stalker. At the very least, it might swing the tide of votes her way. Her party deserved a turn in government, and she was determined to do good and help the New Zealanders who required their support. The children. Low-income families. Those who currently struggled to get ahead under the incumbent National Party.

"Ashley."

Something in Josh's tone slashed at her burst of confidence. He radiated pity, concern.

"What is it?"

"The guy has flooded social media with obnoxious posts concerning you. He's attempting to smear your reputation."

Ashley swallowed hard and steeled herself. "Let me see." She retrieved her phone. Seconds later, she was scrolling through a social media feed. Dozens of posts, tagged with her name, filled the page. They called her a criminal. They accused her of wrecking homes. They stated she was unfit to run for parliament.

Each post insulted her integrity.

Anger was a fiery ball in the pit of her stomach. It pulsed and expanded with each lie she read. The comments... Well, some were plain disgusting. Ashley moved on to the next social media app. In this one, she was trending as #AshleyCriminal.

Ashley heaved out a harsh breath, fury pumping through her veins. "What happened to the business card the cop gave me?"

Josh rose and retrieved it from the stack of opened mail and flyers she'd tossed in a basket on the counter. "What will you do?"

She dialed the number and held up a hand for silence. "Detective Alexander? It's Ashley Townsend here, the leader of the Labor party. Can I talk to the contact person for the Diplomatic Protection Service? Yes, I'll wait." Her gaze met Josh's, and his bright blue eyes glittered with approval. "Yes, I'm here." She reached for a pen and pad and noted the phone number he'd given her. "I received an anonymous phone call a few minutes ago. The man threatened to destroy me and told me to check the social media. He has flooded the internet with slanderous posts and graphics. No, I've no idea of his identity. Yes, I'll speak to the DPS. No, my fiancé is here with me. Okay. Thank you." She hung up and set her cell phone on the countertop with a firm click. *There! Take that.*

"Good girl," Josh said with approval.

"I refuse to let this cowardly arsehole ruin everything I've worked for. I'll fight to the end." Her pulse raced, and in truth, dizziness had her clutching the counter for stability. But she also felt empowered and damn glad she had Josh at her side.

"What do you intend to do?"

"Well, I won't post on social media. That would be fruitless and a waste of my time. I believe I'll use my first public meeting tomorrow, which is a talk to university students, to speak out against bullying. It's a huge issue worldwide, and kids growing up in New Zealand suffer as much as others. And I think it's best to ask for help from the DPS. The leader of the opposition party is sometimes offered security under certain circumstances. Let's see if this situation warrants their help."

Ashley picked up her fork. "Might as well do it on a full stomach."

Her phone rang again. Charles. *Of course.* She'd return his call later after she'd put her plan into motion.

8

Extra Protection

Two DPS officers arrived at Ashley's house at seven the next morning, which pleased Josh because he worried at the way this situation was heading. Ashley's stalker had sounded angry yet controlled. The man had a plan and possessed the patience to follow it. Josh got the impression her stalker was toying with her at present.

The DPS officers, both men, were older than him but bore fit physiques and sharp gazes that never settled but constantly assessed for risk.

"Thank you for coming," Ashley said. "Your boss told me you'd require nearby accommodation and one of you would drive my car since it's big enough for all of us."

"Yes, ma'am." The man stood at around Josh's height of six-four and held himself with a military bearing. His tan skin suggested Maori ancestry as did his close-cut black hair and brown eyes.

"Call me, Ashley," Ashley said. "*Ma'am* always makes me feel like my old school teacher. The one who used to rap us across the knuckles with a ruler if we misbehaved." She paused to peer at them, her lips twitching. "You don't come bearing rulers, do you?"

The other officer chuckled. "They're not standard issue. I'm Gerry. That's Nelson."

Gerry was a fraction shorter, which made his shoulders appear even broader. He reminded Josh of a rugby player—one of the powerful and bulky forwards—because his gray suit struggled to contain his shoulders. He had a shaved head, blue eyes, and groomed, two-day stubble on his powerful jaw.

Josh held out his hand to Nelson. "Hi, I'm Josh Williams." He shook Nelson's hand and turned to Gerry to repeat the action.

"You're ex-NZSAS," Nelson said.

"I am. Only recently retired, and I'm helping Ashley with behind-the-scenes stuff while I decide on my next steps."

"You're not carrying." Nelson's expression indicated trouble if Josh supplied the wrong answer.

"No, that would be against the law. I do have a firearm license, and my rifle is locked up at my father's farm in Eketahuna." Josh didn't doubt they'd checked him out because he'd have done the same.

Ashley glanced at her watch. "It's time to hit my office and my first meeting at the university. Who wants to drive?"

"I will." Gerry held out his hand for the car keys.

"I have two spare bedrooms. You want to stow your gear now?"

"It's fine in the car," Nelson said. "We'll sort it out when we get back."

Ashley collected her handbag, laptop, and briefcase and exited the house. Josh grabbed his phone and the notebook where he'd been scribbling his investigation details. He shoved them both into his inside pocket before setting the alarm and locking the door.

"You have a decent alarm system." Nelson's deep bass held approval.

"A mate put it in yesterday after Ashley's stalker broke into the house. Hopefully, that will put a stop to him breaking in again."

"Is it monitored?"

"Yes," Josh said. "The alarm company will contact the police should anything go awry." He joined Ashley, and Nelson took the passenger seat.

Ashley was hard at work, returning phone calls from her fellow members of parliament. Her voice was crisp and decisive and kind of hot. Josh grinned. She hadn't realized that he'd need to share her room now that the DPS were underfoot.

"Charles, this is none of your business," she said.

Josh started to pay attention to the conversation. He hadn't liked what he'd seen of the man while they'd been in Wellington.

"I have this situation under control. You know that none of those posts are true. I am not a criminal or any of the other things they accuse me of. I have been upfront

JOSH'S FAKE FIANCEE

with the party regarding my history. No, I do not intend to resign." She listened, frowned, her brow puckering. "Stop. Enough. You go to the party manager and complain. Do what you have to do. You'll just look like a dick. Oh, wait. You are a dick." She hung up and groaned. "I shouldn't have spoken that way. Charles was probably taping the call."

"Who was that, Ashley?" Nelson asked.

"That was Charles Jamieson. He's standing for the Auckland Central seat and thinks he can do a better job than me. We dated once. Once was enough. He tried to tell me women belong in the kitchen where they can cook meals for their man. He believes a woman like me, one who might have a family in the future, has no right to stand for a parliamentary seat. The man is an ass. He certainly brays like one." She slapped her hand over her mouth. "I apologize. You did not just hear me slag off a fellow MP. I won't do that again."

"I didn't hear a thing," Josh said.

"We're covered by confidentiality. As long as you don't break the law, you're good." Nelson spoke in a deadpan voice, but his eyes flashed with humor before he turned back to Gerry.

Gerry pulled into a parking space outside the electoral office. "How long will you be here?"

"Half an hour." Ashley opened the door to exit her vehicle, and Josh stayed her.

"Let the guys check things out first. Let them do their job."

Josh watched in approval. The two men scanned for

danger then Gerry opened the door for Ashley while Nelson waited to flank her as she walked to the office entrance. Josh followed at the rear and took a seat in the waiting room while the DPS officers did their thing.

Charles Jamieson.

He'd poke deeper into the man's background and see what he discovered.

Josh fired off an email to Summer. She'd promised to dig into Ashley's accident further to see if anything raised alarm bells. When his sister didn't reply, he figured she was busy with the baby or at work. Instead, he started his search for online material relating to Charles Jamieson. Social media pages. Full of inspirational sayings—one for each day. He also posted photos relating to his campaign. Nothing contentious here. The guy had a gift for social media and kept things real but never stepped over the boundaries.

Next, Josh did a general search and checked each link as far back as ten pages of the search results. Nothing jumped out here either. Solid education. Trained as a lawyer, but he'd never practiced. Politics seemed to be his passion, and like Ashley, the man was a career politician. He lived and breathed politics. Hadn't jumped into any scandals. Worked hard. If he played hard as well, he did it in private.

"Josh, we're on the move," Gerry interrupted his research.

"Thanks." Josh put away his phone and notebook, waved goodbye to Sheryl and Carrie, and followed Ashley and the DPS officers from the electoral office.

Ashley worked and fielded phone calls during the drive

into the central city. Josh knew she hadn't slept much the previous evening because her bedroom light had remained on into the small hours of the morning. When most women might've cried themselves to sleep, Ashley had straightened her shoulders and marched into battle. He couldn't have been prouder.

The hall where Ashley was to speak to students was standing room only. As Ashley entered with Gerry and Nelson, the chatter died before bursting into life again—a flurry of whispers. Since Josh was satisfied with Gerry's and Nelson's efficiency, he remained at the rear where he could scan the crowd and keep watch from the back.

Ashley strode the aisle to the podium at the front with her head up, her shoulders straight and a smile on her face. She wore a forest-green suit that clung to her curves and made the most of her figure, yet it never strayed into tacky. Her blonde hair shone under the lights, and the loose strands bounced as she walked.

Pride burst in Josh again. She was class, and although her stalker had rattled her, she hid her fear well.

When she reached the front, two men and a young woman greeted her and shook hands. Then, the young woman bounded up to the podium and raised her hands for silence.

"Thank you for coming today. The day before yesterday, we were excited to have a young and upcoming Member of Parliament coming to speak to us. Today, we're thrilled to introduce you to the leader of the opposition." She paused to laugh. "I told my friends this woman was going places, but the dizzying rise of her star surprised me too.

I knew she was ambitious and talented and popular with her constituents, but her fellow Labor party politicians value her too since yesterday, they chose her to lead them into this upcoming election. I am proud to welcome today, Ashley Townsend."

Applause broke out in pockets around the hall, but Josh could see Ashley needed to work hard. She'd intimated she had a plan, but she hadn't given him details. It was obvious most of these students had seen the social media posts. Neither he nor Ashley had bothered to listen to the news or check the online newspapers for public reaction, but he imagined the press and the response of other members of parliament. Give them a taste of blood, and they became ravenous sharks. Ashley swam in dangerous waters.

Ashley stood and approached the microphone. Once she reached the spot, she glanced around the hall and took in faces. She smiled—a genuine smile of happiness, and one Josh hadn't seen since the posts had hit social media.

"Good morning. I'm thrilled to have the opportunity to speak to young New Zealanders. I'm going to take a safe wager. I bet you and your friends, your parents and university tutors too, are wondering what's up with the nasty posts that appeared online last night. They're calling me a criminal and accusing me of gross misconduct and other crimes. To be truthful, I stopped looking at my social media apps after reading the first couple.

"Firstly, none of what you might have read, or the press speculated about is true. I follow the law. The Labor party, and I presume the other political parties vying for seats, have a process in place to vet our candidates. No one gave me my position. I earned it because I am a decent human being who tries to do the right thing.

"During the last few months, I've received threatening letters. None of them bore a signature. Someone sent me a bouquet of dead flowers, also with an alarming note. My car refused to work after a mystery person forced open the fuel tank and added water. My home was broken into..." She paused and pulled a face. "The person who entered my home without my permission removed my lingerie from the drawers I keep it stored in and stacked it on top of my bed. They helped themselves to items of laundry and used these to dress a shop dummy. Yes," she said. "For several hours last week, anyone who drove past my house would've seen a dummy dressed in my favorite pair of red undies and a matching lacy camisole.

"Then we come to the flurry of posts on every social media channel. The police have checked for the source of these posts, but unfortunately, most of the profiles where these posts originated are dummy accounts, opened for the purpose of harassing me."

Ashley paused again to scan the faces. Admiration grew in Josh. This was a ballsy step and one that might backfire. On the plus side, these students were paying attention. They hadn't expected her to come out with the truth. They'd expected spin.

"Yes, the truth is an insidious one. I've attracted a bully. These days, kids are taught about bullying. Our parents tell us what to do if we're bullied. Report it to an adult, right? But not all those bullied are young children. Adults are just as likely to suffer from bullying. It might be in the workplace or in our social lives. Perhaps a family member.

"People of any age can attract bullies, and we must stamp it out and fight back if necessary.

"So how do we do that? We speak out. We tell people in authority or instigate a complaint. In my case, I've informed the police, and as the bullying has escalated, I now have two muscular men following me around during my workday." She indicated her DPS officers, both of whom remained stony-faced and watchful.

"That is my bullying story. I'm not going to answer further questions regarding this situation but know this. I dislike bullies, and I refuse to let him or her run my life. Just know I won't cower. I will fight back. I will not take this bullying or let it affect my reputation. Speaking out takes away the bully's power. If you have any questions on how to deal with bullies, my team have collected several fantastic resources. If you or someone in your circle is facing the same problems as me, grab a handout on the way out of the hall.

"Now, I know you're busy, and I've been speaking for a while now, but before I open the floor to questions, I thought I'd give you a quick down and dirty bullet-point speech of how the Labor party intends to help students. Which of our policies apply to you?"

The vibration of Josh's phone distracted him, and he pulled it out of his pocket to glance at the screen. It was Frog. Josh briskly exited the hall before answering.

"Frog," he said, while automatically making a time calculation. It was past midnight in Afghanistan.

"What's going on over there, Josh?" Frog's low voice

JOSH'S FAKE FIANCEE

held demand and frustration.

"Didn't you get my email?"

"I did. Your verbal report?"

Josh described what was happening and mentioned Ashley's bullying speech.

"Does Ash realize she's rattling his cage?" Frog demanded.

"She knows what she's doing." Pride and admiration filled Josh. Like a military boss, she'd employed a strategy. "She's counting on her situation swinging the vote to the Labor party."

Frog barked out a laugh, but Josh could tell he was worried and irritated because he was so far away. "She has always had good instincts. I hope she's right and this doesn't push her stalker into taking radical action. Hell, I can't even believe my baby sister is the Labor party leader."

"Frog, the accident Ashley was in where her friend died. Are you positive there was no blowback at the time? The social media posts accuse her of murder and wrecking homes. Your sister assures me she's never had an affair, and my investigations make me believe her."

"Ash doesn't lie," Frog barked.

"Put yourself in my shoes. If it was Summer, and you were looking after her, you'd check and recheck every angle."

A sigh echoed on the line. "Sorry. It's driving me crazy I can't be there for Ash."

"She has two DPS officers with her right now plus me. They'll be with her every moment until the threat passes. The cops aren't brushing her off any longer. They're taking this seriously."

"Okay. Ash's friend who died was the oldest in the family. She was a wild child, and my parents worried about her influence on Ashley. She had younger siblings, and Jess's parents did split after her death. I don't know if Jess's death was the wedge that drove them apart or not."

"Anything else? I've tried to trace them, but not even Summer has located them."

"Bloody dog. I told Ashley to never swerve to miss an animal."

"Since we lived in a rural area, it was one of the first things my father told us when he taught us to drive. It's instinct though, Frog. You can't blame Ashley for that."

Frog sighed again. "I know. *I know.* I've been racking my brain. I can't think of any reason for someone to stalk Ash. She's dedicated and focused on reaching her goals and never dated much." He barked out a laugh. "Most of her dates when she was younger were dumb Neanderthals, according to Ash. She felt her time was better spent socializing with her political friends and mentors. Honestly, Josh. Ashley is a straight arrow. She doesn't lie. If she'd had an affair, she'd tell you, but she's not the cheating type. I've never met anyone with more integrity than my sister."

"That's my reading too," Josh said. "Do you know Charles Jamieson?"

"Yeah. I met him once. Man's a dick."

Josh grinned. "Those were Ashley's exact words."

"I doubt it's him," Frog said. "At school, he was the kid who dobbed in his mates and ran tattling to the teachers. I mean, check him out, but I doubt I'm wrong in thinking he's innocent of the stalking."

Josh snorted. "The guy has already tattled to the campaign manager, but he and the senior party members are standing by Ashley. This situation is frustrating as hell. Ashley has offended her stalker, and he wants everyone to know. Her schedule is available to everyone. It's easy for this guy to learn where she'll be. Hell, if he's smart, he'll case each place she's due to make an appearance beforehand. It's too damn easy for him to pull out a weapon and attack. If he doesn't care if he gets caught and merely wants to shoot Ashley, there might not be much I or the DPS officers can do."

"Ashley needs to be smart with her appearances."

"The campaign manager has organized them," Josh said. "Everything was arranged before the flood of social media posts. I doubt they can change things now or that Ashley will want to lose any opportunity to bolster the Labor party's chances to win over the voting public. You haven't seen her since her promotion. She's scared, but she has this determined glint in her eyes that wasn't present before. She wants to win."

"I got that impression when Ash emailed me last night," Frog agreed. "Keep me posted."

"Will do."

"Oh, and Josh. Don't play with my sister's emotions. She has wanted this since she was a kid, and she's worked hard. If you put her off her stride in any way, I will break your pretty face."

"Hey, it's not me distracting her. It's her stalker. You

focus on him. I'm the innocent party—the one who's doing you a favor." Josh's stomach clenched at the white lie. He liked Ashley. A lot. Their kisses had become personal and more than a token show of an affectionate couple.

Frog snorted, apparently unimpressed by Josh's protestations. "Don't forget. I've seen you in action. I've seen the way the women clamor for you. Don't mess with my sister. Keep her safe and leave it at that."

"You're lucky you're not saying that to my face," Josh snapped, guilt still prodding his conscience even as he denied the charges. His remorse turned his voice sharper than usual.

"We'll settle any problems the next time we meet." Distinct relish shaded the promise from Frog.

"You and what army?" Josh snorted. "You'd better keep up your fitness levels. Even then, you'll be pushing it." He checked his watch. "Gotta go. Ashley should be finished soon if she hasn't already."

"Keep her safe."

"Will do," Josh promised.

As he returned to the hall, his phone vibrated again. Summer. He tapped out a quick message, promising to contact her soon. When he entered the room, Ashley was fielding questions.

"When are you getting married, Ashley?" a young man with a long black beard and his black hair styled in dreads asked.

"We haven't set a date yet. Right now, I'm focusing on the campaign."

"Do you intend to have children?"

"I love children," Ashley said without hesitation. "Children are our future, which is why Labor is keen to implement changes to the education, early childhood, and community sectors."

"If you're prime minister, how do you expect to do your job while you're pregnant or have children to look after?" the young man fired out.

Josh watched the guy closely, but the grins from the men and women sitting nearby suggested they knew him. He was a student rather than a physical danger to Ashley.

"I will do what any modern parent does—share parenting duties with my husband and hire help where necessary. You know, nobody asks these questions of our current prime minister because he's a man. He has children, yet they never come into the conversation. The queen had children and continued with her duties. Why should I be called out as different? Know this. If or when I have children, I will give them the best care and as much love as I can. I will nurture and shape them into productive citizens, just as my parents did with me. I can, and I will carry on with my political duties. Whatever my job or my situation, I will give New Zealand and its people one hundred percent of my effort." She removed her gaze from the young man and smiled, warmth and sincerity pouring from her in invisible waves. "That's all the questions I have time for today. Thank you for listening to my vision for our wonderful country. Don't forget to grab a handout as you exit. I trust you'll exercise your right to vote on election day and hope it is one for the Labor party."

The students broke into chatter then. Most stood and filed outside, many stopping to collect one of Ashley's handouts. Josh remained where he was, scanning faces as the attendees left.

Once the room had cleared, Josh joined Ashley. Nelson and Gerry stood close, alert for danger or students who came too close.

When Ashley was ready to depart for her next speaking engagement, Nelson led the way, Josh walked at Ashley's side, and Gerry followed.

"I'm surrounded by brick walls," Ashley joked.

"It's our job to maintain your safety," Josh murmured. He frowned, experiencing a faint prickling at his nape. He surveyed their surroundings, attempting to discover the source of his unease. Nothing jumped out at him, but he noticed Gerry's scowl as he too scrutinized faces.

"Ashley. Ashley! Can we have a quick chat?" A female reporter waved her hand, and Ashley's steps slowed.

"I can give you five minutes." Ashley softened her words with a smile. "After that, I must leave to reach my next engagement."

"Social media has been flooded with posts. Is it true you killed one of your friends?"

Ashley's cheeks paled, but her smile remained intact. "When I was eighteen, the passenger in the car I was driving died when we crashed into a tree. That part is accurate, and there isn't a moment when I don't wish my friend was here with me today. The part that isn't true is your implication I'm a murderer. I was young, and I made a mistake. I paid for that mistake by losing my best friend.

"Along with that, I paid fines, lost my driving license, and did community service. I suggest you do your research instead of relying on fake news from social media."

Ashley stalked off, leaving the female reporter gaping like a fish struggling to breathe out of water. The reporter spoke to her cameraman, and they trotted after Ashley. Gerry and Nelson pushed them back when the reporter attempted to ask further questions.

Josh slid in beside Ashley, his senses still jumping in preternatural awareness. Ashley's stalker was here in the crowd, watching. He was smart about it, though, and Josh couldn't spot him. He waited until Nelson and Gerry sat inside the vehicle.

"Did you see anyone?" Josh asked.

"No," Gerry barked, frustration tightening his stubble-covered jaw.

"He's here." Nelson scanned their vicinity. "I can sense him, but damn if I can spot him."

·♥·♥·♥·♥·♥·

HE TREMBLED, HIS ANGER a tangible thing. Her minders might give her the illusion of safety, but Ashley Townsend should think again.

He refused to give up.

His plan was working. He'd rattled Awful Ashley with his notes. Invading her home had upset her too. While the new security alarm might stop him rifling through her underwear, it wouldn't stop him from achieving his goal.

She was frightened.

The online posts had caused talk, provoked curiosity.

He'd caught part of her talk about bullies. *Bah!* If she thought this was bullying, she'd whimper at what was to come.

An old scar on the top of his hand reminded him of the past, of punishments, the withholding of treats and privileges. No, the bitch didn't understand what it was to be persecuted and punished for something someone else done.

She believed she'd paid for the crime.

She hadn't even started.

9

POLITICS AND DANGER

It was two hours later when Josh returned Summer's call.

"What's up?" he asked when she answered the phone.

"I've gone through everything published in the papers at the time of Ashley's accident, and I've started to research Jessica Webster's family. She had a younger sister and brother. From what I can work out, the parents split up about nine months after the accident. The father worked on a cattle station near Queenstown. He retained custody of the son while the daughter remained with the mother. I've found the daughter and mother on social media. The mother lived in Auckland with her parents after the divorce. Irene, the daughter, is currently working in England, and judging by the mother's social media page, she is visiting her daughter and taking the opportunity to see the European sights with her current husband of six years."

"And the father and brother?"

"The father died in a quad bike accident on the station where he worked. I found a death notice in the local paper plus a write-up. He was a popular guy and coached the local rugby team. I found photos of Joseph—the brother—at school, but nothing after that. He doesn't appear to have a social media presence. I've tried everything I can think of to learn what happened to him. Nada."

"Is it possible this Joseph is our stalker?"

"I don't know." Summer pursed her lips. "Nothing stands out as odd. The divorce went through quickly, and there were no associated legal battles. Oh, that Charles character. He has alibis for days and nights when things have happened. He might've hired someone, but from what I sense of him, I'd place him low on the list of suspects."

"All right. Keep digging, just in case. I'll ask Ashley tonight if she knows anything about Joseph," Josh said.

"The online posts are awful." Summer muttered under her breath. "Trolls! Some have been taken down, but people are still commenting and sharing them. How is Ashley holding up?"

"She's taking this in her stride. The posts upset her, but she decided to use them to her advantage to sway public opinion. She has likened it to bullying."

"You like her," Summer said, sounding surprised.

"Why is that so strange? She's attractive and smart. Contrary to popular belief, I don't hit on every woman I meet. I enjoy a decent conversation."

"Even if it is about the Labor party and their policies?"

"We discuss things other than politics," Josh said tartly.

Summer paused for a beat. "Are you sleeping with her? Josh! You cannot play around with her. She has an important job and doesn't need you playing mind games."

Josh gripped his phone more tightly. Indignation rose, and he ended the call before he uttered something he'd regret. "Thanks for the info. Later, Summer." Why did everyone assume he intended to walk away, leaving Ashley in a helpless puddle of femininity? For one, the assumption was an insult to a classy lady. And two, he'd never, ever made promises to women about a future. He'd always made his stance clear before he started anything. With Ashley, it was different. She intrigued him, and he found himself wanting more, wanting to deepen their connection, not that he'd confess this to Summer. A scowl dug deep into his features, Summer's assumptions irking him.

He strolled over to Nelson and told the cop he was going for coffee. With Nelson's and Gerry's coffee order in mind, he stomped away to regain his equilibrium.

One meeting and talk flowed into another. Josh wasn't sure how Ashley kept her smile fixed in place since the media and the public asked her the same questions over and over again. Ashley remained patient while giving her answers a spin to impart information covering Labor's policies and their promises to voters.

"You're doing great, sweetheart," Josh whispered as he slipped into the car beside her. "What's next?"

"We have an hour at home to change for a business meeting and cocktails, then we're going to the red-carpet showing of a new fantasy movie set in the South Island."

"Fantasy?" Josh suppressed a groan. "Not with Hobbits?"

"This time it's dragons. We'll get to meet the director and stars, including the dragon, from what I hear."

Oh, joy. Josh buttoned his lips, deciding to follow his mother's oft-heard advice of it you can't say something nice don't say anything at all.

Ashley hid her amusement. Matt hated what he called airy-fairy crap, and obviously, Josh stood in the same camp. Her brother enjoyed car crashes and high-octane thrillers. You'd think he got enough of that type of action during his workday.

When they arrived back at her house, Ashley showed Gerry and Nelson to her spare bedrooms, and since Matt had ordered her—for reasons he failed to expound on—to continue the pretense that Josh was her fiancé, that meant she and Josh had to share.

Josh had dumped his things in her bedroom before Gerry's and Nelson's arrival. Now, she pulled clean linen out of the cupboard.

"Gerry and I will make our beds." Nelson wrestled the sheets from her hands, determination stamped into his features. "You take a break and get ready for your evening."

Ashley brushed a lock of hair from her face, glad to have one less task. "Thanks."

Josh appeared, carrying a tray. "I've made you a cup of tea. Should I run the bath for you?"

"That sounds heavenly," Ashley said.

"I'll leave the tray in the bedroom."

In her room, Ashley kicked off her shoes and wriggled her toes. As much as she hated heels, they were a part of her political uniform. They turned her height into an asset and stopped any male patting-of-the-head ideas.

She poured a cup of tea and closed her eyes to savor the scent. She had a thing for the ginger and quince tea and loved the surprising aroma that reminded her of a bazaar with its Turkish delight fragrance. While she waited for the tea to cool a fraction, she removed her jacket and unbuttoned her blouse to reveal the red bra Josh had purchased.

Apart from thanking him for doing the shopping, they hadn't discussed the contents.

Although red wasn't a color she'd have purchased herself, she'd adored the vibrant ruby color of the lingerie set at first sight.

Josh pushed the door open. "The bath is almost—" He turned away to close the door with a loud click and leaned against the wood to study her with greater intensity.

Ashley swore she felt his touch as his gaze roved her curves.

"You are more beautiful than I imagined." His gaze slid to half-mast. "Are you wearing the matching panties?"

"Of course."

"Can I see? Please."

"What do I get in return?" she asked.

"I'll strip for your viewing pleasure any time you want, sweetheart."

"Matt wouldn't approve. I had him lecture me this morning."

"Fuck, Frog." Josh grimaced. "He harangued me too. My sister also warned me not to play fast and loose with your heart."

"We're not five-year-olds," Ashley said. "Have they forgotten we're adults?"

"You don't look like any five-year-old of my acquaintance." Josh pushed away from the door to stalk closer.

Her heart gave one hard thump before jumping into a frenzied race. She held her ground. *Just.* "W-what are you going to do?"

"I *really* want to see the full effect of your sexy red lingerie."

"It's ruby, not red."

Josh shrugged. "Please."

Her mouth grew dry, and she licked her lips. Once. Twice. With his gaze caressing her all over, she decided to do as he requested. But she had to remember. Josh was no tamed cat to put outside whenever it suited her. If she opened this door...

Aware of the passing time and the fact she'd need to strip anyway, Ashley unfastened her skirt zipper. With the zipper spread, she did her regular careful shimmy to peel the fabric over her hips. This time, she had the added challenge of leaving her panties in place and not taking them off with her gyrations to remove the skirt.

"Do that shimmy thing again." His voice was low, gritty while his electric blue gaze held her captive.

A blast of exhilaration stole her breath, tightened her chest. Her mouth grew dry as she stared at Josh. She stood with her skirt still caught on her backside, her bravery abandoning her. What was she doing?

"I. Dare. You."

Her gaze flew to his, and she rocked her hips, gave a tiny twist, and her skirt pooled at her feet. She stepped out of the green fabric.

"You're gorgeous, sweetheart. All that creamy skin. Your curves. You hide them."

"I don't want the voters distracted from business."

He grinned. "Concealed weapon."

A snort escaped her. "Don't give the press any ideas. I'd better jump in the bath."

Josh rose from the bed and intercepted her before she'd taken two steps. "One kiss."

She stared, sensed the tension riding him, and knew, *just knew*, letting him kiss her was a bad idea. But she craved his touch, wanted to feel a proper kiss rather than one of his quick pecks meant to solidify their pretense. Instead of replying, she continued to stare at him, fighting an inner struggle.

His callused hands curved over her shoulders, the rough spots on his palms and fingers eliciting a shiver. His gaze dropped to her lips, and he slowly lowered his head. At any time, she could've stopped him, should've stopped him. She didn't. His mouth brushed hers, firm and competent. Hot and decadent. The intimate caress teased a moan from her, and he drew her closer, his hands slipping to her hips and pressing her nearer until she felt the solid ridge of his erection. Heat whooshed through her, and her mind hazed, her thoughts narrowing to the man who held her.

Big. Strong. He focused on her mouth and detonated her barriers. Instead of clear-sighted thought, a picture of them moving to the bed formed in her mind. Her hands roved his back, but she gained the merest impression of his musculature.

Too many clothes.

Skin. She needed to run her fingers over his torso, to experience the give of his muscles, and that wasn't happening. Ashley struggled to move, to get her hands on that real estate.

Josh nipped her lip, and when she opened her mouth to protest, he slid his tongue against hers.

Oh. *Oh!*

That was better.

She stopped fighting and relaxed to enjoy herself. He pulled away, and with a moan of protest, she followed him, mashing their lips together with far less expertise than him. Not that Josh laughed. He gave a groan of his own and sank into a kiss again. His fingers kneaded the cheeks of her arse and not an inch of space separated their lower bodies.

Yes! Oh, this was so, so good.

Much better than the lukewarm, fumbling sex she'd experienced at university.

A foreign sound intruded.

Josh tensed then parted their mouths and pressed his forehead against hers. "Damn." He pushed away from her. "Yeah, what is it?"

"There's a woman and a kid here. She says she's your

sister," Nelson called through the door.

"Summer? Thanks. I'll be there in a sec," Josh replied.

Ashley wanted to cry, but perhaps the timely interruption was a wake-up call. He was a soldier—ex-soldier—and she was a prime minister in waiting. At least, she hoped this office lay in her future.

"You'd better bathe and get ready for your next gig. Do I break out the suit?"

She nodded, not trusting herself to speak. Bother. She'd already liked Josh, and now she'd discovered the man had lots of sensual skills in his arsenal. Perhaps she should listen to Matt and buckle down to concentrate on the campaign. Men weren't to be trusted—not in the romantic sense when she had so much to lose.

Without a word, she turned away to gather clean underwear and prepare for her evening.

Josh straightened his button-down shirt and left the bedroom, closing the door after him. In the kitchen, he nodded to Nelson. "Where is she?"

"I made her wait outside in her vehicle."

Josh grinned. "I bet that went well."

"Do you have a sister?"

"Yes, younger than me. She's married to a military man, and they have one boy. Can Summer come inside once I verify she is my sister?"

"She can," Nelson said.

Josh strode to the rear door and peeked through a crack. He spotted Summer leaning against the car, impatience etched into her frown.

When she saw him, she straightened and placed her hands on her hips. "You kept me waiting long enough."

Josh grinned and saluted her. "Nelson says you can come inside now that I've vouched for you. Did you find anything?"

"Yeah. Let me grab my laptop to show you. Can you get Sam for me?"

"Sure." Josh jogged to the SUV. "Hi, Sam." His one-year-old nephew held out his arms and beamed at him with a gummy smile. "I'll have you out of your car seat in a trice." True to his word, seconds later, he carried Sam toward the house.

Inside, he gestured to Nelson and then Gerry. "This is my sister Summer and her son Sam. Summer, Nelson, and Gerry. They're Ashley's DPS squad until we work out this stalker stuff."

"Did you ask Ashley about Joseph? I found an article written by a local journalist at the time of the inquest. Joseph was noticeably upset and blamed Ashley for killing his sister."

"Do you have a copy of that article?" Nelson asked, stepping forward.

"I do. Let me fire up my laptop, and I'll show you." Summer pulled her laptop from its protective bag. "I haven't been able to locate Joseph, not since he left high school. There is nothing online for him that I can find, and that's unusual these days."

A door opened and shut down the passage, and Josh had to force himself not to react. A naked Ashley slipping into the bubble bath or getting out, bubbles running down her breasts. His imagination—hell, he didn't require sounds or sight to get a hard-on. The more he learned of Ashley, the more he admired Frog's little sister.

He forced himself to concentrate on Summer. "Do you think he's the one?"

Summer wrinkled her nose. "I honestly don't know."

Nelson and Gerry spoke in undertones after reading the article Summer had discovered.

Gerry turned to Summer. "Anything else? Other family members?"

"You should go to the source." Ashley padded into the kitchen, her body swathed in a robe and her feet bare. "I'd hate to think you were gossiping behind my back."

"Of course we weren't," Summer retorted. "I came here to speak to you and Josh. I didn't realize you'd have a goon squad in residence." A mischievous smile crept into evidence. "Well, I knew you had one living here, but I hadn't expected them to multiply."

Josh groaned. "Not helping, Summer."

"What info do you want?" Ashley persisted.

"We wondered if Joseph Harrison might be the one behind the trouble you're having."

"No." Ashley shook her head. "Not Joseph. I doubt it's any of the Harrison family. Jess was a wild child. She was acting out, and I suspect she was dabbling with drugs. I feel terrible for saying this, but if she hadn't died in the accident, chances were she'd have hurt herself in other ways. Her parents were strict with their children. Stricter than most of our friends. Jess was a rebel. Not one family member blamed me for Jess's death. Not one, despite the stories in the papers."

"What about the article that says Joseph was upset and blamed you?" Summer asked.

"My older sister was standing nearby when the journalist approached Joseph outside the courthouse. He was a kid, and they confused him with their questions. My sister told me they twisted his words, and I believed her. The local reporter tried to interrogate me too, but Dad had my back."

Josh watched her closely. "What aren't you telling us, Ashley? You're careful with what you're saying."

"Miss Townsend, if you know anything to clear Joseph Harrison please tell us," Gerry said in a firm voice.

Ashley fought a visible inner battle before her shoulders slumped. "All right, but this can't be made public. It's not as if I'm certain, anyway. The reason Joseph has fallen off the face of the Earth is that I think he followed through and became Josephine. Jess wasn't the only one with problems in the family."

Summer's hands flew over the keyboard. "Ah, Ashley is right. There is a profile for Jo Harrison here."

"Let me see," Ashley demanded.

She pushed past Josh, and he got a whiff of lavender. Summer murmured something, and when Josh's gaze jerked to her, he found his little sister smirking at him. *Busted.*

"That's Joseph," Ashley confirmed. "Or Jo. The face is the same. Joseph always had a girlish appearance."

"Not a suspect then," Summer said.

"We'll check," Nelson stated in a no-nonsense voice.

Efficient and protective. "We'll have a chat with this Jo. No one needs to know."

"Thanks." Ashley turned to him, her brown eyes serious. Her features in what he was beginning to recognize as her work-mode. "Josh, you'd better hurry if you want to shower before we leave again."

"That's my cue to leave." Summer stood and packed away her laptop. "Nikolai will be wondering where Sam and I have got to."

"Thanks, Summer," Josh said. "I'll carry Sam out to the car for you."

Outside, he opened the vehicle's rear door and fastened his wriggling nephew into his car seat.

"You're falling for her," Summer accused.

"Butt out."

"Do you want to live in a fishbowl with the press watching every little thing you do? That's what will happen."

Josh glanced around him and lowered his voice, even though they were alone. "We're friends."

"Kissing friends," Summer retorted. "Ashley has the appearance of a well-kissed woman."

"Butt out."

Summer laughed. "So if someone from the press corners me, I should tell them *no comment*."

"Summer," he growled.

His sister laughed again as she settled behind the wheel. "Emotions are tricky things, brother, mine. They sneak up and pounce when you're not looking, not ready, not prepared. And they pack a punch. Don't say I never warned you."

Josh scowled as Summer drove away. As he turned for the door, he caught a glint of something in the trees. Curious, he took two steps closer before every well-trained instinct screamed a warning. Josh dived to the right as the gun fired. Hot, agonizing pain seared his left arm.

The door burst open behind him, and Nelson and Gerry appeared, both with weapons raised.

"Rifle, eight o'clock," Josh snapped. "Flesh wound. I'll live."

With a nod, the two cops cautiously ran from bush to bush, seeking cover where possible. Josh yanked on his shirt and held the fabric to the wound on his arm.

"Josh? What's happening?"

"Get back inside. Close the door and don't come back out until one of us says it's all right. Move!" Josh barked when Ashley hesitated.

In the distance, a car started and roared as it accelerated away. The bastard was making a run for it.

Josh pushed to his feet and lifted his makeshift pad to check his wound. The bullet had furrowed across his upper arm. It throbbed and bled, but he'd been lucky. If he hadn't moved when he did, the bullet would've struck him mid-body.

Nelson appeared from the shrubbery. "You'll need medical attention. I'll ring for an ambulance."

"No, I'll go to the emergency medical center on Great South Road."

Gerry sprinted up the driveway. "He got away. I know the color and make of the car. Guy is smart. He covered the plates with mud."

"This is going to cause complications," Nelson said.

A siren blasted in the distance, the din indicating an approaching vehicle.

"A neighbor must've rung it in." Gerry eyed the blood staining Josh's T-shirt. "Come inside and let me check your arm. Nelson, get the cops to wait. They can drive Josh to the clinic. I think we should stay with Ashley. For all we know, the guy might decide to double back and try again."

"Give me a sec." Josh pulled his phone out of his pocket. He'd cracked the screen when he'd struck the ground. He pushed a button and the screen lit. With relief, he dialed Nikolai.

"Josh," Nikolai said.

"Ashley's stalker shot me. A flesh wound. Nicked my upper arm. I'm bleeding like a stuck pig. Thing is Summer and Sam had just left."

"Fuck." Nikolai's curse trembled with fear for his wife and son.

"Yeah, you're probably okay, but watch security around your place. Maybe now is a good time to visit the folks in Eketahuna. I'd never forgive myself if this guy hurt any of you."

"Aw, I've grown on you."

"Like a rash," Josh fired back, not bothering to hide his grin. He and Dillon had disapproved of Nikolai's relationship with their sister. They'd tried their best to talk around Summer and break up the pair. They'd changed their minds about Nikolai, although neither of them admitted it aloud.

A police car pulled up, and Nelson strode over to liaise with the driver.

"Summer will refuse to go," Nikolai said.

"I'll talk to her. She can do her research from Eketahuna. Are you at home? Is she home yet?"

"That sounds like her now. I'll go and meet her. Hang tight."

While he waited, Josh tried to remember details. The guy had worn dark clothes that allowed him to blend. A beanie had covered his head. He couldn't even say for sure how tall the guy had been although he'd given off an air of competence. He hadn't hesitated to shoot at Josh.

"What's going on? How bad are you hurt?" Summer demanded.

"Just after you left, I spotted a glint in the trees. The guy was there. He had a rifle, and he shot me. It's a flesh wound. I'm fine, but I'd be happier if you and Sam were in Eketahuna."

"I didn't see anything. There was a car parked down the road. I noticed it because the rear was filthy. You couldn't see the numbers and letters on the plate for the mud. The car was empty."

"Which means the guy was staking out Ashley's house while you were there. He saw me with you and Sam. Knows you might be a weak spot. Please go to stay with Mum and Dad. At least for a week or two."

"All right," Summer said.

"What?" Josh asked, shocked at her easy acquiescence.

"We have Sam to consider. I didn't go through hours of pain for him to die at the hands of a madman. I'll see if we can get flights for tomorrow morning. Dillon or Ella won't mind picking us up from the airport in Palmerston North."

Josh closed his eyes briefly, relieved that maturity and responsibility had softened his sister's impetuous tendencies. "Thanks."

"I'll send you links to Jo's social media page, so you can message her. If you're polite and explain the circumstances, I'm sure she'll cooperate."

"Josh," Ashley called from inside the house. "I don't want to be late for my meeting. What's happening?"

Josh glanced toward the doorway. Gerry was standing guard and making certain Ashley didn't come outside.

"Summer, the police will contact him. I'd better go. I have two functions tonight and need to get changed." And have something done with his arm. It throbbed like a kick from a feisty cow. He lifted the pad to study the wound. The bleeding had halted. It wouldn't stop him from protecting Ashley.

"I thought you were shot. Won't Ashley cancel?"

"I'm fine. We can't let this guy dick us around. Keep in touch and let me know when you're heading to Eketahuna." Josh ended the call and scowled at his wound. Close call.

"How is it?" Nelson asked.

"I think it's okay, but I should get it looked at. How about I meet you at this cocktail thing? You'll watch Ashley closely?"

Nelson nodded. "We'll look after your girl."

"Tell the cops I'll be five minutes. Better grab my

wallet." Josh entered the house and found Ashley dressed in a long, form-fitting red dress. She'd done her hair in an up-do thing, baring her shoulders and neck. "You look gorgeous."

"Thanks." She spotted the pad on his arm, the blood on his shirt, and her eyes grew wide. Her hand pressed against her chest. "What happened? Gerry told me everything was okay. He told me to go and get ready. He did *not* tell me you're hurt."

"I'm fine, but because it's a gunshot wound, I need it checked."

"Josh." His name held panic and concern dug into her features. "Oh, Josh! Are you sure you're okay? You should go to hospital. Let me ring an ambulance."

"No, it's okay, sweetheart. Truly. I'm going to the emergency medical center. I'll get my arm looked at, and I'll meet you at the cocktail party."

"I should cancel," Ashley said. "Go with you to the medical center."

"No, please. You'll lose all the impetus you've gained this morning. You have an important job to do, and even though I wish you could, you can't hide away and let this guy win. Gerry and Nelson will watch over you," Josh said, praying like hell they did keep her from harm. "Every cop is searching for this guy. As long as you pay attention to your surroundings and follow their instructions, you should be safe enough tonight. I'll join you as soon as I can."

Still Ashley hesitated, her face pale and worried. Her gaze kept darting to his arm.

Josh nodded, understanding her shock and hesitation

because she wasn't used to this sort of thing. "I promise I'm fine and well enough to watch dragon movies with you."

Ashley straightened, obviously coming to a decision. She reached up to kiss Josh's cheek. "He wants to scare me. He's succeeded. I'm terrified, but you're right. People are counting on me. I have a responsibility to my party and my colleagues. I'm willing to follow any instructions the DPS give me. You too. This bully mustn't win."

"Go you, sweetheart." Unable to resist, Josh stole another quick kiss. He pulled back and smiled, wishing he could drag her off to bed or spend a quiet night with her. "I'll meet you at the party."

"You should stay at home."

"No. Nelson and Gerry are skilled policemen. They're efficient, but I gave Frog my word I'd look after you. I keep my word."

"This is selfish of me, but I feel safe when you're around."

"Josh!" Nelson shouted.

"See you soon, sweetheart." Josh grabbed his wallet and stuffed it in his pocket. At the last minute, he jogged along the passage to get a clean T-shirt. "Give 'em hell with your speech."

10

SEDUCTION AND SIN

"Will Josh be okay?" Ashley asked after he left in the cop car.

"He will," Nelson assured her. "He's a tough soldier. Don't worry. Right, this is what we're going to do. Gerry will back up the vehicle. Once we're positive it's safe for you to leave the house, I will come to collect you. Under no circumstances are you to leave our sight when we're at the cocktail party. Tell us if you exit the room, even if it's a trip to the restroom. One of us will be with you at every moment."

"I understand," Ashley said.

"The other thing. If anyone asks about the shots fired here, tell them you know nothing. We have officers checking into the incident, but we want to keep your stalker in the dark. Going forward, we'll maintain silence about him."

"Why?"

"Because he shot at Josh and intended to kill him," Nelson said bluntly. "He's made a statement, which tells us he won't stop. We can't be sure if it's publicity he wants or if he doesn't care who he hurts to get to you. We want to keep him off balance. We'll also take a look at your schedule. You need to shake it up, so your stalker isn't positive where you'll be."

"That's going to irritate the press."

"It's not our job to placate the reporters." Nelson quietly observed her, his stance wide and open. Alert. "We're here for your safety."

Ashley nodded. "Can I tell the senior party members what's going on? I'll need some of them to cover for me if I can't go to the meetings and functions they've organized."

"Give me a list of who you're telling and make sure everyone understands they can't discuss your daily location with anyone who rings for details."

"That will prove difficult. We share our itinerary with our support staff."

Nelson fell silent. "How about this? Choose one politician and combine your schedules. Each day discuss between yourselves who will cover which function."

Ashley scowled. "No, you know what? This is stupid. I can't let a stalker derail my planned program during the run-up to election day. I have a full schedule, as do other party members. It will cause chaos trying to shuffle everything. I'll continue with my scheduled functions. And on that note, I'm going to be late if we don't leave soon."

"Wait here." Nelson disappeared.

Ashley blew out a shuddery breath. She picked up her clutch bag and pulled on her evening jacket. Josh had to be okay. In that moment, she realized she cared for him. Along with relying on his presence, Ashley enjoyed his company and eagerly anticipated each day with him at her side. She inhaled and exhaled again. Despite Matt's warnings about Josh, she'd come to appreciate her fake fiancé. The idea of growing their relationship appealed to her. Enticed her. Made her inner woman whisper a plea for her to take action. If Josh was on the same page as her, she'd happily offer her body and enjoy the heck out of the interaction.

Half an hour later, Ashley entered the Edwardian Hotel. Only delayed by five minutes.

"Ashley." A gray-haired woman hurried forward.

"I'm so sorry I'm late." Ashley held out a hand and offered an apologetic smile. "I hope I haven't kept everyone waiting."

"The attendees are busy inhaling drinks and cocktail snacks." The woman gestured with a chuckle. "I doubt they've noticed the time, but if you don't mind, we'll get you to speak straight away."

"No problem." Ashley followed the woman into the lift.

Her DPS officers stepped inside with them, and the woman gave Ashley a startled look.

"They're my escorts," Ashley explained.

"Is it true you have a stalker?"

"I'm sorry, but I can't discuss details. I'm looking forward to sharing our vision of the future with your attendees."

"We're glad you could come tonight." The woman continued to give Nelson and Gerry a side-eye.

The lift doors opened on the twentieth floor.

"This way, please."

Even if the woman hadn't met them in reception, Ashley doubted they'd have trouble finding the function room. Loud chatter poured from the open double doors. The woman led them through the groups of men and women. Some sat at tables while others stood chatting. Soft music poured from concealed speakers and waiters wandered from table to table with drinks and snacks.

"We've reserved this table for you. Can I get you a drink before you start?"

"I'd love a glass of water. Sparkling if you have it." Ashley placed her clutch bag on a seat and removed her jacket. "Where should I stand?"

The woman gestured at a microphone stand on a raised dais. "I'll introduce you right now. You can come forward once my intro ends. Will that work?"

"Perfect," Ashley said.

The woman spoke to a waiter and disappeared out a side door.

Ashley accepted a glass and the bottle of sparkling water a waiter delivered. She took a sip and placed it on the table.

"Nelson, where will you and Gerry be?" she asked.

"Gerry will stand over to the right, slightly behind you, and not visible to most of the attendees. I'll be on your left. We'll be watching everyone as you speak."

The woman who'd greeted them returned and someone

switched off the background music. "Good evening, ladies and gentlemen."

The chatter faded, and the woman plunged into her welcoming spiel. Ashley retrieved her notecards from her bag and listened with less concentration than usual. Her stalker had shot Josh. Josh's sister and nephew had been there minutes earlier. What would've happened if he'd shot one of them?

"Put your hands together to welcome Ashley Townsend, the Labor party leader."

Ashley strolled to the dais. While she normally dressed conservatively and didn't flaunt her body, this evening she'd gone with more daring. A side split on the right of her long red gown gave glimpses of her thigh, and she overheard a couple of whispers mentioning legs before she reached the microphone stand.

Ashley turned and offered the attendees a bright smile before she began her pitch about opportunities for business owners and their proposed policies for the economy.

One of her gifts was a great memory, and as usual, she picked several faces in the audience and spoke directly to them. She finished, not needing her notes.

"I have time to take a few questions," Ashley said.

A woman's hand shot up.

"Yes?"

"Where did you get your dress? It's stunning."

"A new, young designer made it for me. Bronwyn is a local girl, and I love her work."

"Where is your fiancé?" another woman asked.

Ashley's smile faltered before she shored it up enough to project confidence. "He had another engagement, so he's running late, but he should be here soon."

"Have you decided on a wedding date?"

"We're not discussing that until the election is over. One thing at a time. Are there any questions concerning our policies? That's what I'm here for—to answer questions."

A skinny male reporter jumped to his feet. "I understand shots were fired on your property late this afternoon, and the police were called. Was this a domestic dispute between you and your fiancé? Is that why he isn't here?"

"I'm here," Josh called from the back of the room. "We heard shots too, but I've no idea what they were or where they came from." He flashed a grin, looking suave in his black suit while the sexy scruff on his cheeks gave him an edge of danger. "It wasn't us arguing, that's for sure."

Several people tittered, and the women closest to Ashley whispered amongst each other.

"As you can see—my fiancé is here. We're not arguing or having domestic disputes. Josh and I are very happy together," Ashley said. "Now, political type questions. Does anyone have one?" Ashley scanned the room, praying for a sensible question. The male candidates didn't receive this kind of crap, and it irked her something fierce.

"Will you be conducting a roundtable and discussing your proposals further or does your party intend to take immediate action with the apprenticeship scheme for young people?"

"Some of our youngsters want to attend university and

study for degrees while others are more practical and prefer to work in a trade. We intend to fund a year of free education at university, so it only seems fair to do the same for apprenticeships. Both policies will start at the beginning of the new year to coincide with the school term."

Ashley fielded a few more questions, before thanking the crowd for attending. "Thank you for giving me the opportunity to speak about our policies. Have a wonderful evening."

She retreated to her table and sipped her water.

"Great speech." Josh took possession of her hand and squeezed it. "I heard part of it from outside."

"Are you okay?" A whisper so no one overheard or jumped to conclusions. No one looking at him in his black suit would guess a man had shot at him earlier. "How did you get here?"

"Nikolai drove me. Summer insisted he check on me. My arm is dressed, and although I'll end up with a scar, there isn't any other damage."

"I'm in a scary movie. This man is out of control."

"We're doing our best to keep you safe. The police are checking on leads. At least they're taking the threat seriously now."

"Yes, but you almost died today." She scanned his black suit and the pale blue shirt that brought out the blue of his eyes. "You look wonderful." She reached up to straighten his black-and-blue tie and gave into the temptation to run her fingers over his jawline. His facial hair tickled her fingertips. "Very sexy. It makes a woman imagine what you might look like out of your suit."

He grinned. "You're the only woman who has a chance of finding out."

"Promises, promises," she murmured.

"Excuse me," a masculine voice interrupted.

Ashley turned, and as she did, she noticed Nelson and Gerry stood close at hand. "Can I help you?" she asked, recognizing the reporter who had asked about the shooting earlier.

"New posts have popped up online this evening."

Ashley froze. "What sort of posts?"

"Accusing you of holding back information the public has a right to learn. What secrets are you covering up?"

"I honestly have no idea what you mean," Ashley said. "Excuse me. I have another engagement."

"So you're denying everything the poster is accusing you of?"

"Someone is attempting to derail my campaign. I have nothing in my background to concern me and have the full confidence of my fellow colleagues. Otherwise, they wouldn't have chosen me to lead the party into this election. Now, please excuse me. I'll say my goodbyes and leave or I'll be late."

Ashley plucked her jacket off the back of the chair and shrugged into it. "Ah, there is Jenny, our host for the evening. I'll say goodbye to her. Did you have something to eat? I'll have to grab something before we get to our next engagement otherwise my stomach will grumble all the way through the movie."

Josh ignored the faint throb of his arm as he checked and rechecked those standing around Ashley. Now that her stalker had used a gun, it made protecting her more difficult. He didn't relax until they were inside the vehicle, and he noticed the DPS officers were on edge too.

"Do you have any outdoor meet and greets this week?" Josh asked.

"Yes. I'm visiting a farm in Northland and several in the Waikato. I'm scheduled to visit a new farmers' market in Pukekohe. I have several engagements in the rural sector."

"We'll have to increase security measures at each venue," Nelson said.

"Maybe we should come clean about Josh getting shot," Gerry suggested. "That way, the public might help us keep an eye out for anyone carrying a gun."

"What if it keeps voters away? It's important to meet as many of the voting public as possible. That's the purpose of a campaign." Ashley blew out a breath. "What type of gun did he use?"

"A rifle," Josh said. "He'll look out of place toting one of those around the city."

"He knows where Ashley will be each day. That's the problem." Gerry said.

"He didn't shoot at me, though. He shot at Josh. What if I'm not the target but Josh is?"

"I haven't been home long enough to piss off anyone," Josh said. "Besides, you were receiving odd notes and dead flowers before I arrived in Auckland."

"That's true," Nelson said. "It might simply be that your stalker wants Josh out of the way or wishes to hurt you as much as he can. Removing your fiancé would do that. A public figure such as yourself is under scrutiny from the press twenty-four/seven. You'd need to mourn in public while doing your job."

"That theory makes more sense," Josh agreed.

Ashley shuddered. "I don't understand. What have I done to cause someone so much pain they're willing to go to these lengths to hurt me?"

Josh took her hand, which was icy cold, despite the warm vehicle interior. He wove their fingers together and squeezed lightly in silent commiseration.

"We're looking at every angle," Nelson soothed. "But the truth is sometimes people are strange. They take offense at the smallest thing and an *insult* snowballs inside their head until it becomes a life and death matter. You might have smiled at the wrong time or ignored a question. You might've done a dozen different things to upset your stalker."

"He's accusing me of murder," Ashley said with quiet dignity. "Which simply isn't true. Murder is not a little thing. That last reporter intimated there were new posts."

"More posts?" Gerry pulled out his phone and scrolled. "Yep, more posts. We've spoken to the social media company. They say this person has opened new accounts. When they check the name and address details of the users, they're fake, yet their systems don't catch them until later when they scratch below the surface. None of their bots or machine learning is picking up these false accounts."

"What do I do?" Ashley asked.

"Carry on as you have been," Josh encouraged. "You've

publicly labeled him a bully, which is basically the truth."

"I agree." Nelson nodded in approval. "Until he makes his next move, we can't do a thing. We have to catch him breaking the law."

"What if he kills someone before you catch him?" Ashley asked. "I don't want anyone to die. It was bad enough that Josh—" She swallowed hard. "Josh came close to being seriously hurt this afternoon."

"Ashley, try not to worry. Continue doing your job, and we'll do ours," Nelson said.

By the time they arrived back home, Ashley was exhausted. Her stalker was interrupting her sleep and that, plus her long days, was catching up on her.

Used to the routine now, Ashley waited in the vehicle with Nelson while Gerry and Josh checked the house. The new security lights had come on when Nelson nosed the car into its normal parking space at the rear of her home.

Ashley scanned the areas of her garden still in shadows, anxiety doing a number on her stomach. It churned while her pulse raced. She hated this. This was New Zealand. People didn't, as a rule, go around shooting each other with guns.

A light came on inside the house, and Josh returned to the entrance. He nodded, and Ashley waited for Gerry to come around and open the door for her.

"Anyone want a hot chocolate before they go to bed?" Ashley asked.

"I'll make it," Josh said.

"But I make it a special way—"

"Frog told me one night when we were on watch together. I know how to do it. Go. Get ready for bed, and I'll make the hot chocolate."

Ashley didn't argue any further. If the hot chocolate wasn't up to her standards, she didn't need to drink it.

"She's scared," Nelson said.

"Wouldn't you be?" Josh asked as he opened the pantry to grab hot chocolate ingredients. "We're no closer to discovering the person responsible. We've probed her background, and apart from the accident where her passenger died, nothing jumps out at us."

"We've looked into that too," Gerry admitted. "She took responsibility and did her community service. We've tracked the family, and they say they bear her no malice. It was an accident. The only one we haven't spoken to is the young boy."

"We have someone checking on him," Nelson said. "I mean her."

Josh heated the milk, added the chocolate mix, and whisked everything together. Next, he poured the frothy liquid into mugs and dropped in marshmallows. "There you go. I'll see you nice and bright in the morning. I'll text you the details of what my sister discovered in a few minutes. That will give you something to work on before your official details come through."

"Thanks for the hot chocolate," Gerry said.

"Goodnight," Nelson said.

When Josh entered the room, Ashley sat on the bed, still fully dressed. Her eyes were damp when she turned in his direction.

"I'm scared, Josh. You got hurt today because of me. What if the man had shot at your sister or your nephew? What if this stalker hurts someone else? Should I step away from the campaign?"

"Sweetheart." Josh strode over, set down the hot chocolate, and hauled Ashley into his arms. "I'm fine."

"This time," she retorted. "I couldn't concentrate on the movie. All I could think of was the consequences of having a stalker. Maybe if I back from the public spotlight, he'll stop."

"That's silly talk. Use that beautiful brain of yours. This man, whoever he is, won't stop until he gets what he wants."

She stiffened in his arms. "Me."

"Yes."

"Ashley, you've always wanted to be a politician. You can't let this man derail your life. Your dreams."

"Well, what do I do? I'd hate for someone else to get injured."

"Nelson, Gerry, and I are working to keep you and everyone else safe. Is there anything in your past? Another incident where someone blamed you for the outcome?"

"No. I've racked my brain. The truth is the accident scared me. It changed me for the better. Because my friend died, I don't drink alcohol and haven't touched a drop since that party. I changed my behavior and concentrated on learning the skills I required to go into politics. Jess's death turned me into a goody-two-shoes."

Josh's heart ached for her. Her regret was transparent,

her sorrow at losing her friend. Nelson had shown him the accident reports, and although Ashley had alcohol in her system, she'd been nowhere near the limit. The judge had slammed her for having a blood alcohol reading while driving on a restricted license, but she hadn't intended to drive that night.

"I'm tired of being good, Josh. Tonight, I crave sin." She yanked at his loosened tie, leaving him in no doubt of what she had in mind.

Every muscle in Josh tensed. *Sin*. Yeah, he was up for that. He ached for her. "What about your brother?"

"Don't ask. Don't tell," she spoke in a solemn voice. "I'm an adult, and I have a stalker chasing me. If something happens to me tomorrow, I won't have regrets involving my career path, but I will mourn not getting my hands on your splendid body."

Josh grinned. "Splendid body, huh?"

"From what I've seen so far. I might've missed two skinny, spindly legs."

He should keep his word to Frog. His word—it meant something to him. "According to my friends and family, I have an atrocious record with women. The second thing—I promised your brother I wouldn't put my hands on you in an inappropriate manner."

Ashley released a snort. "Fine, let me do the work." She dragged off his tie and started on the buttons of his shirt. "I'll be the bad guy."

Josh's pulse jumped at her cool fingers on his flesh. Hell, he wanted her so much. He'd never spent so much time with a woman and not had sex. The thought brought a frown. "No, Ashley. Wait."

"What happens if my stalker kills me tomorrow? Or you. I need this. *I want you.* I know what I'm doing. I'm clear of mind, and I'm a mature adult. My party thinks I'm capable of running the country, so I'm certainly competent to make this informed decision. Think of it this way. We're two adults who want each other. Neither of us is making promises nor have expectations for the future. This is a slice of time we're carving out for relaxation. Something private for us."

He didn't want to be her man of the moment.

The thought whacked him over the head. Even though they hadn't known each other for long, he admired her. Liked her a lot. Hell, was this how his last serious girlfriend had felt when he'd walked away? He'd warned her, given her the truth, but she'd wanted more. Tried to force his hand, which led to him making his famous one-date rule.

"Hey!" Ashley knocked her knuckles against the side of his head, hard enough to gain his attention but not hurt him.

"Sorry. Thinking about the past."

"Been there." Ashley scrambled off his knee. She slid down the side zipper of her red gown and shrugged from her dress. Josh started to get a clue.

"Are you trying to tease me into jumping you?" Not that he required any sort of show. The moment Ashley had mentioned sex, his body had reacted.

"I'm not proficient at seduction."

Josh came to a decision and stood. "You're a sexy, gorgeous woman, Ashley Townsend. I surrender. I can't fight this any longer." His voice was low and gritty, his cock turning hard and heavy when he saw her in another of the sets of lingerie he'd chosen for her. Black lace. Sexy black stockings that hugged her stunning legs and ended in a lace band on her upper thighs. If she thought he didn't want her, she wasn't the smart woman he'd thought she was. "When Frog comes home, I'll confess. He can punch me in person."

"Not if I get to him first," Ashley promised. "He can't tell me who I can or cannot see. I mean, if I tried that with him, he'd tell me where to go."

"Let me undress you," Josh whispered in a verbal surrender. He reached for her, noticed his right hand tremble as it settled on her shoulder. "I thought the black lace would suit you." He ran his hand over her arm, savoring the silky skin. Her swift intake of air brought a smile.

It seemed they were both in new territory here.

Although he wanted to take things slowly, this time he embraced the idea of failure. He brushed a kiss on her shoulder and inhaled lavender. An old-fashioned scent and a contrast to the sexy underwear and dress, but the fragrance suited Ashley.

"Did I tell you how beautiful you looked tonight?"

"Ever since the legs episode, I've dressed more conservatively. After this afternoon, I realized I needed to live for myself. Since Jess—the accident—I've tried so hard to do the right thing, but I'm human. I'm not perfect. All of that hit me like a bombshell when I worried my stalker had killed you. I intend to *live* my remaining days. Existing is fine, but living each day as an adventure is better. I do this for Jess. For my job. *For myself.* I have to trust the police will catch this guy, and meanwhile, I'll show every Kiwi voter the best part of myself, which I think is a mix of who I was and who I've become."

Josh laughed, so impressed with this courageous woman. "The voting public won't know what or who has hit them. They'll start calling you Hurricane Ashley."

"Excellent. I'd prefer that nickname more than Legs. Now, shut up and kiss me. It's way past time to get down and dirty."

"Yes," he whispered. He claimed her mouth, intending to start slow. The first press of their lips blasted his plan away as Ashley worked her seductive wiles.

Yessss. Ashley sank into Josh's kiss, every feminine part of her saluting his masterful actions. She didn't want friendly sex. Gentle sex. She needed hot and passionate, and she communicated that by dragging him close and wrestling off his clothes.

"Hey, easy with my arm."

"Sorry. I forgot. Should we stop?"

"Hell, no." He nibbled her neck, eliciting a delicious shiver from her.

Her bra loosened, freeing her sensitive breasts. Josh lifted her and positioned her on the bed. His mouth settled over a nipple, and he sucked hard even as his fingers teased her other one. Pleasure roared through Ashley. It had been so long. She bit her lip as she recalled her houseguests. Nope. Not gonna worry about them. As far as the world was concerned, she and Josh were a couple.

He lifted his head and moved away from her. "Condoms?"

"Bedside drawer," she said immediately.

Josh nodded and removed his shirt. A dressing covered his arm, pristine white against his tanned skin.

"Is it sore?"

He winked at her. "My cock is hurting more than my arm."

His words reassured her, and while he stripped off his clothes, she wriggled from her panties.

"Let me do the stockings." Josh returned to the bed, naked. "So, Ms. Townsend. What is your opinion of my legs?"

Ashley giggled. "The spindly comment hurt, huh?"

"Yes."

"I understand," she murmured. "I'm kind of sensitive about my legs too." Her lips twitched as she tried not to laugh.

His eyes narrowed a fraction—all the warning she had. The next second she found herself stretched over his knee.

"Josh." Her voice held shock.

"I thought you were ready to step into the wild," he whispered. His big hand cupped her bottom, his fingers callused as he smoothed across the sensitive skin of her buttocks. "You have a mighty fine backside, Ms. Townsend."

"Thankfully, the reporters and cameramen didn't get a shot of that. Just my legs."

"My eyes only," he growled.

"Caveman much," she taunted.

"No more than any red-blooded male."

As he spoke, his hands squeezed. His fingers wandered, drifted. A sharp crack then a sting on her backside had her rearing upward.

"Shhh," he whispered, rubbing the smarting spot until Ashley relaxed.

He'd smacked her, and she couldn't decide what to think, how to react because the sting had turned to warmth, and it traveled to an achy spot between her thighs. As she pondered, the silence between them lengthened and astonishingly, sensual excitement licked her limbs.

Another sharp tap had her starting a second time. This time, the pain of it roared through her, an instant later morphing to heat and decadence and dare she say it, pleasure. Who knew? His hand smoothed again. His fingers made teasing forays between her legs. A tiny moan slipped free without permission.

Josh moved then, lifting and dropping her back on the mattress. He levered over her, giving Ashley a brief glimpse of hard muscles before they pressed her down. His mouth claimed hers, hard and desperate. The instant she parted her lips for him, his tongue tangled with hers. Heat. Delicious and inspiring. Ashley gripped his shoulders, intent on making certain he continued this drugging pleasure. She needed it. Craved it. His hands wandered her shoulders, her breasts while she did some exploring of her own.

"Let me taste you," Josh whispered, his voice ragged, which made her feel better because her pulse was racing like a car without brakes.

He made his way down her body, kissing and nipping, giving her more blissful pleasure along with the sting of sharp teeth. The small nips switched or confused her pain receptors. Each tiny jolt had delight frisking her senses. Feminine moisture readied her body for his possession, and she craved the feel of him sliding between her thighs.

"Now," she demanded.

"Not yet. When I say it's time. I've waited for you, and I plan to enjoy every moment."

"Yes," she whispered, her fingers ruffling his black hair as he licked her inner thigh. *Ooh!* The moves in his sensual arsenal were exquisite. Who knew? She certainly hadn't.

"Tell me if you enjoy this," he ordered and proceeded to lick her slit. He dallied at her entrance, lapping at the moisture her body created.

"Yes," she said on a hoarse gasp. "I enjoy everything you do to me."

His head lifted, and she met the glitter of his blue gaze. "Everything?"

"Yes," she admitted.

"Perfect." His eyes glittered with blue fire and promises as he licked his lips. He lowered his head again, this time lapping exactly where she needed his touch most.

It didn't take much. Two slides of his tongue, the slight suction of his mouth, and she was flying, hurled into an intense orgasm that stormed her body, her mind, her soul. Her torso arched, and she released a loud moan.

Josh laughed, and when the spasms tapered off, he peeled her stockings down her legs, kissing patches of revealed skin and launching another sneaky attack on her virtue.

"Josh."

"I'm here, sweetheart."

"Are you sure your arm isn't sore?"

"No, it's forgotten. You distract me." He reached for a condom, his gaze full of warmth and sensual promises. "Let's see if I can distract you too."

Yes. It wouldn't be difficult. All that prime male real estate. Her tongue darted out to moisten her lips. She couldn't wait to get started. Ashley reached for him, but he caught her wrists and guided them above her head and held them there.

"No touching," he ordered. "Not this time. I want you too much."

She offered what she suspected was a cheeky grin. "My hands have a mind of their own when it comes to you."

"Naughty girls get spanked."

"Some girls misbehave to get spanked," she countered.

He gave a bark of laughter. "Thought you enjoyed that. Has anyone spanked you before?"

"You're my first," she said solemnly then spoiled the moment with a girlish giggle. She clapped a hand over her mouth. She was not a giggling girl.

"It's good to see you happy and relaxed." Josh ripped open the foil package and donned the condom. "Smiling more. Your smile is stunning. It lights up your entire face." He rose over her, kissed her gently.

Too lightly.

"Harder. More," she ordered. "I won't break."

JOSH'S FAKE FIANCEE

Josh eyed her for a long moment, gave a slight nod and fitted his shaft to her. He surged inside her with one powerful, seamless stroke that had her breath hitching, her toes curling. For an instant, he hesitated, remaining embedded in her, his gaze questioning.

Without breaking their visual connection, Ashley raised her hands until she gripped the headboard. She winked. "Bring it. Make me scream."

Josh shook his head. "Not too loud, baby. We don't want your protection squad bursting in here, thinking your stalker has attacked. This sexy body. Your beautiful curves. My eyes only."

He retreated, leaving her empty, but thankfully, not for long. He eased back into her with an unhurried glide.

"No, not slow."

"I'd hate to hurt you," he said.

"You won't. I need—yes," she hissed, her body bowing as passion claimed her again. "Perfect."

Josh hastened his thrusts, cursed, and slid his hand between their bodies. His soft tap against her nub forced a groan past her lips. Ashley's eyelids lowered as she sank into a perfect storm of pleasure.

"Open those pretty eyes of yours," Josh demanded. "Watching you come is part of the fun."

"I won't climax again. I never do."

"Huh. One thing you should learn about me. I'm an over-achiever. You say I can't, just pisses me off. Makes me try even harder." He slid his thumb back and forth over her slippery clit. Continued his forceful strokes into her body.

A wash of tingles broke over her, and she groaned again,

louder. She started to think she could. She would.

"Come for me, sweetheart. Before I lose all semblance of my control." He stroked her again, leaned over to kiss her with passion before he recommenced his hard, deep thrusts.

This time, her release was gentler, sweeter. It swept over her as she stared deep into Josh's eyes.

"That's it," he growled. "God, your eyes go darker when you come. That pretty flush on your cheeks, your breasts." He plunged into her, and she felt her channel ripple around his cock. "But most of all, I love the way your pussy cradles me so sweetly. It's a taste of heaven."

He shuttled in and out, going faster and faster, then he stilled sheathed deep and let out a sexy growl.

"Yes," he whispered, his expression all hard-edged warrior. His lashes fluttered, but he forced his eyes to remain open, the entire time watching her. He let her see inside him, let her glimpse his softer, vulnerable side as he surrendered to his release.

11

NOT SCARED ENOUGH

SHE WASN'T SCARED ENOUGH. Hadn't experienced the same terror as he had. The pain. The aching loss.

It was harder to get to her now. People everywhere. Damn bodyguards, although he'd managed to shoot the boyfriend. The fiancé. That must have caused a few tears. She was a hard bitch. Made out she was soft and that he was the bully.

She'd started this train ride.

He intended to end it.

There had to be a way to peel back her layers of security, make her nervous until she faltered. Made a mistake.

He paced through the empty house, glad to be alone for a while instead of cozying up with his lover.

While he couldn't see a way of getting to her, he could still niggle. Behave like that little Jack Russell that lived next door. Bark and harry. Snap at her heels. Get her to start looking over her shoulder again.

The radio broadcast in the background caught his attention. He hated the damn thing and tuned it out, but his lover liked to keep up with the play, harbored an interest in politics.

"...and in the latest poll results, Ashley Townsend has taken the lead for the first time, surging ahead of the incumbent National party. Her brand of honesty and her stance on bullying plus her other social policies have struck a note with the voting public. It will be interesting to see what the results are in the next poll.

"And in other news, the teachers' union is warning of strike action if their demands are ignored..."

He cursed under his breath. How could she be ahead in the polls? His social media posts had taken off. People had commented on them, shared them. The fuckin' things had gone viral in some cases. Yet, somehow, she'd still managed to swing the public in her favor.

Well.

He strode through the empty house in another fast circuit. He itched to break something, to grab a knife and slam it into her soft flesh. Instead, he stomped into his bedroom, his hand pressing to his temple in an attempt to will away the aching throb in his head. He spotted the bag of soft toys meant for the local Hospice charity store after their cleanup. He grabbed the bag and heaved it at the bed, desperate for a physical release.

Stuffed bears, a lone doll, a woolen lamb spewed from the plastic carrier bag.

At the end of his control, he grabbed the nearest stuffed

animal and wrenched off its head. The act took energy. A surprising amount. The soft fabric ripped, and he ended up with a dog's head in one hand and the stuffing-filled body in the other.

A dog.

He stared at the pink tongue that flopped from the toy's open mouth, his eyes filling with furious tears.

It wasn't right.

This wasn't right.

Ashley Townsend needed to suffer as he'd suffered. She shouldn't escape punishment.

He refused to let her.

Determined, he retrieved the plastic bag and shoved the discarded toys back into their temporary home. He'd deliver the bag to the charity store as he'd promised. Once he did that, he'd return to the West Coast beach—his private hideaway. He'd walk barefooted along the warm black sand, and he'd think. He'd plan.

He'd formulate a strategy to end this stalemate.

Sweet revenge.

Once he achieved what he wanted, the voices in his head would fade, sated by his success.

He'd have a clean slate. Start over.

A chuckle escaped him as muscle memory walked him through the house around the circuit he traveled so frequently.

Once he succeeded, he'd move to Australia. Maybe he'd travel farther afield and hit the tourist spots that'd tickled his curiosity. Although he'd gone overseas, most of his experience was in war zones. Sandpits.

He barked out another laugh. He'd been happy in the sand. Seemed he had an affinity.

The beach it was since he always did his best thinking in the sea air while he listened to the surf rumble into shore.

And meantime...

Yes, that would work.

When his footsteps took him back to the bedroom, he plucked the head and the torso of the dog off the floor. He found an old shoebox, destined for the rubbish and placed the dog inside. On the way to the beach, he'd stop at a post office. He'd courier the package to the woman and put her on notice. His smile twisted as another thought occurred.

Even better.

He'd lay a false trail and send the cops on a fruitless chase. Let them think they had their man.

It might make Ashley relax and give him an opportunity to strike. It'd solve his other problem too.

Win-win.

12

SOARING IN THE POLLS

ASHLEY ENTERED HER OFFICE just after seven-thirty the next morning. Today, she wore a dress that skimmed her figure without stepping into tacky. It was a forest-green with cream polka dots, and she could hardly wait for the press reaction.

"Great news in the latest poll," Robert said, a spring in his step.

"I heard. Geoffrey rang me," Ashley said. "We have a fighting chance of winning now."

"I'll admit I worried when the party decided you should lead us. I know you're efficient and capable. It wasn't that. You're young compared to other leaders we've had in the past. You don't have the experience of the other candidates."

"I have experienced advisors," Ashley countered, having heard these same comments earlier in the week. "I think voters—some at least—are hungry for new ideas or twists on the policies and ideals we've counted on before." She checked the time. "I'd better get moving with the correspondence. I have a full day today."

"For two weeks."

Ashley smiled. "I'll certainly need sleep by the time we get to election day. Fifteen days to go." She entered her office and set her handbag and laptop near her desk. "Anything interesting in the correspondence?"

"Just the usual. The campaign manager has finalized your itinerary. I'll print it out for you so you can check it during the drive to the Waikato. Call if you need clarification. I'm going to book airline tickets to Wellington and for your few days in the South Island. Will your fiancé be going with you?"

"Yes. Charge me for Josh's tickets and expenses. Oh, and print out three extra copies of the itinerary. Nelson and Gerry will want to know what we're doing during the upcoming weeks."

"Will do," Robert said.

Ashley's hand shook as she reached for the first letter in her pile, but today, nothing loitered there to scare her.

A tap on her door half an hour later announced Josh's arrival. He filled the doorway. "We're ready when you are."

She picked up her handbag and rifled through until she found her bright pink purse. "Can you give my credit card to Robert for me? I'm paying for personal expenses."

"Sure."

"Another ten minutes. I won't be much longer than that," Ashley promised, and she doubled down on her correspondence pile.

Josh closed the door behind him, confident Ashley was safe since Gerry stood guard outside her office. He prowled over to Robert's desk, intent on prizing information from the taciturn man.

"Ashley asked me to give you her credit card. She said she needed to pay personal expenses."

"Yes, for your flights."

"My flights?" Josh sat on one of the two seats arranged in front of Robert's desk. "Am I going somewhere?"

"Wellington, Christchurch, Dunedin, and Invercargill. You'll hire a car from Dunedin and drive to several of the southern towns including Invercargill."

"Huh." Although Ashley had mentioned travel, Josh hadn't understood exactly how much was involved. "Do you attend the meetings and functions?"

"If Ashley needs me. I attended more before you arrived." Robert raised his head. "Sorry. That sounded as if I resent your presence. I'm not interested in Ashley in that way. We're friends. Have been for a long time."

"Are you married?"

Robert hesitated, his gaze falling to his desk before he replied. "Divorced. Dating now."

Hmm, a touchy subject. Ashley had told him Robert was gay. Perhaps that was it? "Do you live locally or do you fight your way through Auckland traffic every day?"

"I live in Conifer Grove. My place is only ten minutes away, but getting past the motorway on-ramps can be a nightmare, especially with the roadworks."

"I hear you," Josh said. "I grew up in Eketahuna. It took me a while to get used to the traffic up here."

"A country boy," Robert said, friendlier than when they'd met on earlier occasions.

"I haven't lived at home for a while, but I'm still a country boy at heart."

Ashley emerged from her office before Josh could gather more information from Robert. He already had the basics but intended to dig more in-depth.

Robert picked up the credit card and noted the details before handing it back to Ashley. "Thanks. I should have the flights firmed up by this afternoon."

"Excellent. I'll grab the details tomorrow morning when I'm in the office."

"I'll email you everything as well," Robert said.

"The car is ready," Gerry called.

"Okay. Robert, ring or text me if you need anything while I'm out of the office."

Josh moved to the door and waited for Ashley.

"I'll get the door," Gerry said.

Josh nodded. They'd perfected the speed of getting Ashley in and out of venues by working between the three of them.

Once they were in the car and on the motorway driving south to Matamata and Hobbiton, the site of their first meeting, Josh asked about Robert.

"How long has Robert been working for you?"

Ashley glanced heavenward, her exasperation clear. "Surely, you don't *still* suspect him?"

"I didn't say that, but our clues are pitifully small. We're digging deeper in all areas and combing through the info again," Josh said.

"Josh is right," Nelson said. "We haven't found anything useful. We're going over everything again. This man or woman—we still don't know for certain, but let's call him a man—upped the ante when they shot Josh. It wasn't an accident. It was a cool, deliberate attempt to murder him. We're digging into the personal lives of everyone who works or volunteers for you again since we've hit a wall with everyone in your past."

"Oh. Well. I trust Robert implicitly. We met at a meeting of the Young Labor party. I was twenty and Robert twenty-four."

"Did he not want to stand for a seat?" Gerry asked. "I thought that was the goal of all youngsters."

"Yes, but the senior party officials award the positions to those they consider have the best shot of winning. Robert is steady and reliable, but he can be standoffish with those he doesn't know well. He says himself he prefers to stay behind the scenes. We work well together, and I couldn't run a successful campaign without him." Shock filled Ashley's expression. "I can't believe he'd harm me or upset the campaign. He's blunt. If he has a problem with something I do or say, he tells me to my face. What he wouldn't do is skulk in the shadows or use violence."

"Do you know his boyfriend?" Josh asked.

"No," Ashley said.

"Did he give a name?" Nelson demanded, fingers poised over his phone.

"No," Josh said.

"We need to check out the partner. Especially since Ashley hasn't met him. It's the sort of thing workmates share between each other. Partners come to parties and other social functions, no?" Nelson turned to glance at Ashley.

"Not if the relationship is new," she said. "I hadn't mentioned Josh to anyone, mainly because he was in the military and he couldn't attend because he was overseas. With me, it was a security matter, yet none of you are looking into Josh's background."

The pulsing silence had Josh barking out a laugh. "They have checked me out, sweetheart."

"You did?"

"He appeared suddenly in your life." Nelson shrugged his unconcern.

"Because I was with the New Zealand Special Air Service," Josh said. "As is Ashley's older brother. That's how Ashley and I met."

"You checked out," Nelson said.

"I can't believe you suspected Josh," Ashley said hotly. "Did you check on me as well? Did you wonder if I was making up this stuff?"

"It's standard procedure." Nelson's rumbly voice remained even and non-judgmental.

"That's so wrong. As a public figure, I get that all the time. It's part of the job description, but Josh shouldn't have to put up with this crap." Ashley heaved out a hard sigh. "I get it. I do. You're trying to do your job and stop the threat, but you're investigating my life, and it feels intrusive."

"Robert was cagey about his relationship. Oh, he was polite, and I was asking nosey questions, but something in his manner... It was off. Maybe he isn't sure of his partner, or perhaps they'd fought this morning," Josh said.

"We'll dig deeper," Gerry said.

Nelson picked up his phone again and rang someone. He rattled off the particulars and issued instructions.

"Where are we going today?" Josh asked.

"We're visiting the Hobbits." Ashley wiggled on her seat, enthusiasm digging a deep grin into her face. "Where they filmed some of the scenes for Lord of the Rings. I adored the movies, and I've wanted to visit Hobbiton for ages. A perk of the job."

Hobbits, as it turned out, lived in holes, but their places of residence were cute. The entire village was set on farmland in Matamata, and instead of destroying the filmset after the movie was done, the farm owner and Sir Peter Jackson had turned it into a tourist attraction and created jobs for some of the locals.

Along with Ashley, Gerry, Nelson, and their guide, they trod the paths between the Hobbit holes and listened to stories relating to the filming and the various actors. They learned about making the set and what it took to keep it in pristine condition for visitors.

The attention to detail at each of the Hobbit homes amazed Josh. The baker had loaves of bread for sale at his gate. The fisherman's drying racks for his fish sat outside for all to see. Even the beekeeper's house fascinated Josh with its hive and the pots of honey.

Ashley spoke to workers, the site owners, gardeners,

and fellow tourists. The isolation of the fastest growing tourist attraction in New Zealand allowed Josh, Nelson, and Gerry to relax their guard a tad. Entrance to the site was controlled, and visitors were bused to the area, which lessened his worry of a shooter.

Josh snapped photos, including some of Ashley, which he figured her office could use. Nope. He might as well admit the truth to himself. The images of Ashley were for him. In them, she was relaxed and laughing, and when this was over, and their engagement ended, he'd have a way of remembering her.

His throat tightened. Walking away was the last thing he wanted, but he'd promised Frog. Josh was a man of his word.

Except, he'd slipped.

He'd made love to Ashley, and not even the guilt pressing on him was enough to make him sorry they'd carved out a slice of heaven for themselves last night. In a short time, he'd come to care for her.

Josh ambled along the gravel path, following the guide who was showing them around. The grass on the hills in the village and beyond was the same dazzling green he saw each time he visited home. Flowers bloomed in the gardens set around the Hobbit holes, and pumpkins and other winter vegetables awaited harvest in the produce garden while pears still hung on a nearby tree. It was apparent to him—a country boy—how much work went on behind the scenes.

And that thought led to another. What the hell was he going to do with his life?

Straight out of school, he'd not hesitated to join the army. But after Dillon had left, Josh had started to reassess too. He'd seen enough to suffer nightmares, done his bit for his country, and determined he was ready to shift to the next phase. While he had no regrets leaving instead of re-upping, he wished the hell he could get a grip on his future.

"Hey," Ashley murmured. "Are you okay?"

"Heavy thoughts," he replied, keeping his voice low. "Stand over there and let me take a photo."

Ashley complied, and he took several.

"Isn't this place amazing? The entire region of Matamata has benefited from Hobbiton. Jobs created for adults who normally need to leave the area to find work. The related fields of accommodation and food have prospered. We need more similar projects. Not necessarily related to a movie, but people thinking outside the box and looking to the future." Enthusiasm bubbled from her, and she'd never looked so beautiful with the sun glinting on her golden hair, her brown eyes sparkling.

His gaze wandered to her lips, his need to kiss her a fever in his veins. He took half a step toward her before his promise to Frog had him screeching to a halt. Too many lines crossed. If Frog discovered the truth, he'd thump Josh. Hell, Josh would deserve the beating.

So instead of kissing Ashley as he wanted, he gave her a quick hug. She'd given him an idea. Somehow, he needed to find a project or service that played to his strengths. Tonight, while Ashley was busy with her reading and preparations for the following day, he'd do an honest assessment of his skills and see if he could come up with *his* Hobbiton.

It was nine at night and dark by the time Nelson drove up her drive. A long day for all of them. Ashley covered her yawn with her hand and opened the car door.

"No," Josh snapped, reaching over to stay her with a hand. "The security light hasn't come on."

Ashley froze. *Stupid!* She hadn't even noticed. Nelson and Gerry had. Their swift exchange of glances and the tension in their muscular bodies told her that clearly. She mentally kicked herself for failing this hurdle. Matt's lectures about staying aware of her surroundings had faded because of her fatigue. *Epic fail.*

"I'll go," Nelson said.

"I have a torch in the glove-box if that's any help," Ashley said.

Gerry pulled out the torch and switched it on to test the batteries. "Good job."

His quiet praise stifled the inadequacies plaguing her mind.

Nelson left the vehicle, and Ashley peered after him until she could no longer see the bob of the torchlight.

"What's the problem?" Ashley could think of dozens of reasons and none of them reassured her or relieved her of the angst preying on her mind.

"Power cut," Josh said.

Ashley grimaced at the house belonging to her nearest neighbor. It was ablaze with light, probably because her neighbor's teenage boys never turned off lights when they left a room. Her neighbor had complained and shook her head over her sons' lack of awareness only two weeks ago when they'd chatted over their boundary fence.

Nelson returned and climbed back into the car. "I can't see anything out of place. The house is secure, and the alarm is still activated. It's just the security lights that are off. It might be a fault."

Ashley caught Josh's frown. The fear she'd corralled to manageable portions during their trip south swaggered back into prominence. Chill bumps prickled along Ashley's arms and legs.

"This isn't a big deal," she said, her voice small and lacking her usual confidence. Weak, because she didn't honestly believe her assertion, not with the men's protective reactions. "The house is secure. The alarm isn't wailing. Those are both good things. Right?"

"There is a package at the door," Nelson said.

"A package?" Ashley asked. "What sort of package?" *Don't say bomb. Don't say a bomb.* "D-did it tick?" This was New Zealand. A peaceful country of mainly law-abiding citizens. Of course, it didn't tick. Reading thrillers—she'd stop that right away. Find a nice romance instead.

"I didn't pick it up," Nelson said. "It's a courier parcel."

"Something campaign-related," Ashley decided aloud.

"Are you expecting a delivery?" Josh asked.

"No." She frowned, worry gnawing at the oddity. "Most of the stuff goes to my office. I don't publicize my residential address. I mean, it's easy enough for someone to discover it. Wait, this is silly. We're overthinking this situation."

"It's not ridiculous if it keeps you alive," Josh growled. "I'll check out the parcel and turn off the alarm. We'll relax once we can see with the lights. We can make a decision on what to do next then."

"All right," Nelson said. "Shout if anything is weird. Do you want a torch?"

"No. I'll rely on my night vision." Josh slid out of the vehicle, leaving a taut silence behind him.

"Will he be all right?" she asked. His wound was still healing, and she'd hate him to get injured again. He—his safety and wellbeing mattered to her.

"He's a highly trained soldier," Gerry said. "Try not to worry."

The tension within the vehicle remained, and Ashley clenched her hands together. She bit her inner cheek to contain her urge to scream. She'd never enjoyed horror movies and this... This was like living in the midst of one.

Lights flicked on inside her house. Nelson's phone buzzed.

"It's Josh," Nelson said. "He says the package is a courier parcel. He says Robert sent it."

The tautness released from Ashley's shoulders. "If it's from Robert, it'll be related to the campaign."

Gerry eased in front. "Let's go. Ashley, I'll lead. You walk behind me, and Nelson will guard your back."

Ashley opened her mouth to argue, then hesitated. They were the security experts, and she'd be an idiot if she second-guessed their every decision. No one could accuse her of idiocy.

Five minutes later, they were inside the house, the door

locked behind them.

Josh was speaking to the friend who'd installed the security lights while she, Gerry, and Nelson observed the courier package. The size of a shoebox, it appeared innocuous enough.

"Try to call Robert again," Nelson said.

Ashley put through the call. After ringing several times, it went through to voicemail. She left a message. "That's unusual," she said. "He always answers his calls, especially if they're from me. What do we do? Do we open the parcel or not?"

13

THE DATE WITH MR. RIGHT

Robert heard the firm knock on the office door and smiled, anticipation dancing through him. Dinner had arrived.

With eager steps, he hurried to answer. A peek through the security peephole had his smile widening. He unlocked the door, beaming, and not even attempting to hide his emotions from the man who stood in the doorway. "Stephen. Hey!"

His lover winked at him, a sunny smile in place. "Dinner is served. I fancied fish and chips tonight. Is that okay with you?" He stepped inside, his hands full of parcels wrapped in newspaper.

"Perfect brain food," Robert said, after closing the door. "Let's eat now." He led the way to a small room holding a table and six mismatched chairs. "I'm starving and could do with a break. I've been working on Ashley's program for the run-up to the election. So many details to finesse. You should meet her. You'll like her. Most people do."

"What I need is a kiss." Stephen set down the parcels.

Robert walked into his arms without hesitation, but a small part of him wondered at the smile that didn't quite reach his lover's pretty eyes. His man had a temper, although thankfully he didn't lose it often. And the makeup sex—well, it was worth the harsh words and the bruises on his upper arms.

Firm lips mastered his while strong muscles cradled his less conditioned ones. Every day he had to pinch himself at his luck in meeting Stephen. The man had an easy-going charm that had enticed Robert, seduced him during that first meeting while running in the park near his home.

He'd thought Stephen wanted a fling and had been game enough, interested enough, dazzled enough to break his rules regarding one-night stands.

Stephen had surprised him though, turning up at his home the following evening with a bunch of tulips. Robert's favorite flower. The next week Stephen had moved in with him, giving up his cheap digs when Robert had argued he had room.

"Hey," Stephen said. "Where did you go? Are you falling for another guy and want me gone?"

"Never." Robert moved closer and squeezed Stephen's brawny biceps. "If I'm falling for anyone, it's for you. This has happened so fast between us." He grinned. "A fairy tale."

Stephen leaned forward and stole a quick kiss. "Why don't you sit and I'll feed you? You've worked a long day.

You must be tired."

"A little," Robert conceded. "But it will be worth it come election day. At first, I didn't think the Labor party had a chance, but with Ashley at the helm, things have changed for the better."

"Hey, no more talk of work. This is a break and a romantic dinner. Sit. Close your eyes and let your mind rest while I get things organized."

Robert reached for Stephen's hand and squeezed. "You're too good to me." He closed his eyes, focusing on the small sounds Stephen made as he prepared. His phone rang in the outer office. His eyes flicked open. "I'd better get that. It might be important."

"Stay." Stephen softened the command with a smile. "If it's important, they'll leave a message. You deserve a break to rest and eat your dinner."

Robert stared at the china plates Stephen had produced, the single candle. As Robert smiled, touched by the thoughtful gesture, Stephen produced a lighter and lit the candle. Oh, brilliant. *Someone was going to get lucky tonight once they arrived home.*

The phone rang once more, but this time, Robert didn't move a muscle. The Six Tenors sang in the background. Stephen had turned out the light, and the flickering candle offered the only illumination. Slowly, Robert relaxed, even though guilt cut through him when the phone rang yet again. This time, the caller left a message. He'd make the call his priority as soon as they ate dinner.

Stephen produced a bottle of wine from his bag. Condensation beaded on the glass neck, and Robert saw it was another of his favorites.

"You spoil me," he murmured, his heart pulsing extra fast for a few beats. Not even during his ill-fated marriage had he experienced this—the caring. The simple things like curling up against a lover throughout the night. Breakfast in bed. Dinner ready when he dragged himself through the door after a long day. And sex. Regular sex. He enjoyed that part too. "Not too big a glass. I promised to finish a report before I leave the office."

"I'll drive us home," Stephen said, his brown eyes serious. "You deserve time out to relax. If you want my opinion, you're better to take time for yourself and recharge." He scowled. "Your boss works you way too hard."

"Stephen." Robert sighed because he'd explained this before. Several times. "When the election is done, my days will be much shorter. Normal days. Weekends. We'll be able to take a vacation. How does lying out in the sun with a cocktail sound?"

Stephen refused to meet Ashley. Reckoned he couldn't be polite to her after seeing the social media posts. It was the only sore point in their relationship. He avoided the mistake of mentioning it because he hated to spoil this intimate moment.

Stephen handed him a glass of wine. "Is it the one you prefer?"

"It is." Robert took a sip of the crisp, fruity Sauvignon blanc. "Perfect."

His lover served the fish and chips, produced slices of lemon, a bottle of vinegar, and a small dish of tartare sauce.

Stephen's insistence on taking care of details amused him, but in cases like this, the quirk truly worked.

"Thank you," Robert said when Stephen joined him at the rickety table. "I promise to return the favor one day soon."

"I'm not keeping score," Stephen said. "I enjoy doing things for you."

The weird note in Stephen's voice claimed Robert's attention since the man was normally so controlled. Apart from in bed. As a lover, the intensity and focus to detail produced spectacular results.

"The girl suggested the blue cod." Stephen moaned around a mouthful of fish. "This is delicious. The batter is crisp while the fish is tender."

Watching the man eat and hearing his growls of appreciation pushed Robert's buttons. With a trembling hand, he took a big sip of wine. It tasted different. He frowned before deciding the deep-fried food had probably coated his taste buds. He took another sip. Tasted fine.

Halfway through his meal, Robert yawned. His eyes had become heavy.

Stephen caught him with his eyes closed. "You're exhausted. I was right. That bitch is working you to the bone."

"No," Robert protested, his tongue thick and the word coming out garbled.

"That does it," Stephen said. "I'm taking you home right now."

Robert didn't offer a protest. His head swam, and his limbs trembled. He remained seated while Stephen hastily packed up everything.

"Your computer. Do you turn it off too?"

"Yes," Robert murmured. "I'll do it." He tried to stand, and his legs failed him.

"I'll tend to everything," Stephen said. "Let's get you into the car first. Then I'll do a quick cleanup here. We don't want your office stinking of fried food."

Stephen helped him to stand and supported him during the walk to the car. He'd been fine. Robert couldn't understand what was wrong with him. He'd worked long hours before. Perhaps the late nights were catching up on him, and Stephen was right. He wanted the Labor party in power again. The long hours were worth it if he could be a part of that happening. Ashley—she was a marvel. She'd swung the polls and was handling the press with grace and ease. She was blooming before his eyes. When her fiancé had turned up, he'd worried the man might split her focus. Robert's fears had never realized, and he was starting to admire the man. It took a special someone to wait in the background.

Stephen.

Robert smiled as Stephen settled him in the passenger seat. He thought he might've found his exceptional home support too. Stephen would be perfect once he got over his strange dislike of Ashley.

14

BOOBY TRAP

"You're certain that's your assistant's writing on the parcel?" Nelson asked.

"Positive. I'd recognize his scrawl and distinctive loops anywhere. Look, this is stupid. It's probably campaign stuff he wanted me to have on hand. I told him I might not make it to the office in the morning." Ashley brushed past Nelson. "I'll open it. You've confirmed there's no suspicious ticking."

"Wait," Josh said. "Let me cut the tape. Then, you can lift the lid and retreat if something is odd."

Ashley huffed. "You're behaving like a bunch of old women."

"That's our job," Gerry said drily. "To keep you alive."

"I'll say *I told you* so once I prove the parcel is harmless."

Josh sent her a look reminiscent of one Matt might give her. A wave of shame engulfed her.

"I'm sorry. I'm acting like a brat. It won't happen again. Josh, do your thing and open it for me. I'll stand back here."

Josh collected a sharp knife from the kitchen. With a steady hand, he sliced the tape. After setting the blade aside, he lifted the lid off the box and peered at the contents.

Unable to stand the suspense, Ashley edged closer. "What is it?" she asked.

Josh straightened. "You're right. It's political brochures."

Ashley frowned and edged close enough to see. "That's strange. Why would Robert send me these?" She plucked the top bundle out to study them. Something burst from inside the box and flew at her. She screamed and jerked as a hard object struck her head. Liquid streamed into her eyes.

Josh seized her and pulled her away to safety.

The DPS officers converged on the box to survey the contents.

"Hold still," Josh ordered. "Let me check your head."

"W-what hit me?"

"It's a soft toy," Nelson said, his voice harsh and controlled. "Bastard chopped off its head. Ashley, are you all right?"

"No injuries," Josh confirmed.

"What is the red stuff?" Gerry asked.

"I think it's dye." Josh wiped at it with his hand. "Crap, it's gonna stain your hair. I'll get her in the shower."

Josh hustled her to their bedroom and into the en suite. He turned on the shower. "Quick, sweetheart."

Shocked and shaking, Ashley pulled off her jacket and stared at the red splotches. It was one of her favorites, and it was ruined. Her fingers trembled so much, the buttons became a chore.

Josh brushed her hands aside. "Let me."

Seconds later, he shunted her into the shower. As soon as the water hit her, red liquid sluiced over her face and torso. She shuddered, staring at the swirling red. *Blood-red*.

"Rinse your hair," Josh said.

She let water pour over her head, and his scowl deepened. "What?"

"It's not washing off. Try shampoo while I check with Gerry and Nelson."

Josh hurried back to the kitchen. "What else was in the box?"

"The other half of the toy plus a note," Gerry said.

Nelson was busy taking photos.

"What did the note say?" Josh asked.

"*You have blood on your hands*," Gerry said, his tone as grim as his face. "Ashley okay?"

"She's shocked, and the red dye has stained her hair." Josh had a thought and rang his sister.

"Do you know what fuckin' time it is?" Nikolai growled. "If you've woken Sam expect a fist in your face, the next time I see you."

"I'm sorry," Josh said sincerely. "I didn't realize it was so late. We've had a scare, and I need Summer's help. I'll tell you what. After the election, I'll look after Sam for a night, and you and Summer can have private time."

"Is Ashley okay?" Nikolai asked, his tone shifting to concern. "You? The security detail?"

"We're okay, but Ashley's hair is covered with red dye. I need Summer's advice."

When Summer took control of the phone, he explained the problem.

"I have an idea," Summer said. "If Ashley agrees. I'll ask Mac to look after Sam for a few hours. She won't mind. I'll be there tomorrow morning at seven."

"No!" Josh snapped. "It's too risky to come here."

"This stalker has seen me at Ashley's house," Summer said. "I'll bring Nikolai. He mentioned helping Louie to recheck your security lights."

"Keep your wits about you and come straight inside. I'll let Nelson and Gerry know to expect you."

Josh returned to Ashley and found her sitting on the corner of her bed, crying.

"Sweetheart," he murmured, going to her, hauling her onto his knee. She was typically so strong, and he hated to see her weep.

"My hair is terrible. How am I going to explain this? I have a meeting at nine tomorrow morning." She gave a hoarse laugh. "At least it's Labor colors. It would've been tragic if my hair turned blue."

Josh grinned, imagining the political cartoonist for the Herald making a big deal if Ashley's hair took on National party colors. "Positive spin. Perfect. Summer will arrive tomorrow morning at seven. She says she has a plan."

"The obvious thing is to go to a hairdresser and have them dye it blonde. It's such a vibrant red. I'm not sure if blonde will cover it."

"Go with the political statement and wear a red dress or suit tomorrow. Do you have anything suitable?"

"I do," Ashley said, straightening, her mettle returning. "You're right. If I can explain away the social media rubbish, I can do this without breaking a sweat."

"You give 'em hell." Ever-present pride in her squeezed his heart. "You should rest. Get in bed while I check with Nelson and Gerry again? I'll fill you in when I get back."

"You know what the worst thing is," Ashley asked, standing.

"What?"

"That Robert is involved in this prank. I trusted him, and it hurts knowing someone close to me holds me in such contempt."

Josh settled Ashley and left a bedside lamp on before he sought out Nelson and Gerry.

"She okay?"

"Yes." Josh chuckled, recalling her words. "Told me he did her a favor by pelting her with the Labor-party-red. Would've been unfortunate if it'd been National-party-blue."

Gerry barked out a laugh. "She's gutsy."

"She is," Josh agreed. "Do we have anything?"

"We asked a patrol car to drop by Robert's home and take him in for questioning. His house is empty. Guy isn't home. His vehicle isn't there."

Josh checked his watch. "Ashley told me he works long hours, but even he couldn't still be at the electoral office."

"I've asked them to check." Gerry rubbed his chin and

yawned.

"What do you make of this stalker?" Josh asked.

Nelson scowled, the bags under his eyes showing his fatigue. "The guy is dangerous. Unpredictable. He's not afraid to injure or worse. Ashley speaks at public locations. What's stopping him from planting a bomb or pulling out a gun and taking out everyone? It's difficult to focus on every aspect when the crowds and the press clamor for her."

"Yeah." Concern for Ashley and their inability to keep her safe had Josh's shoulders slumping. "My conclusion too. Could Robert be the culprit?"

Nelson shifted his rugby-player body as if he fought the urge to pace. "It's starting to look that way, but why do it in this manner? He could get to Ashley at the electoral office. She trusts him."

"I've got nothing," Josh said. "We'll understand more when we find Robert."

Nelson's phone rang, and Josh stiffened, wondering if the cops had found Robert.

"Yes," Nelson barked after glancing at the screen. "Crap." He paused to listen. "Okay, let me know if you learn anything else."

"Problem?" Gerry asked.

"Someone trashed Ashley's electoral office and sprayed red dye everywhere. The officers arriving at the scene thought it was blood at first."

"Anyone there? See anything?" Josh asked.

"They spoke to a homeless guy. He told them two men were inside. When they left, one man appeared drunk.

They got into a vehicle and drove away. The guy didn't hear much. Nothing out of the ordinary."

"Did he see their faces?" Gerry asked.

"No." Nelson's voice held concern. "He was too far away. He stays out of sight because the man who works there always calls the cops to move him on."

"Did he recognize Robert?"

"Not with certainty, although he says the pair drove out in Robert's car," Nelson said. "This situation stinks. What I don't get is if Robert is responsible, then why has he waited until now to act? I hate puzzles that make no sense."

Josh stood and shrugged. "After thinking about it, the only motivation I can see is jealousy. Robert isn't advancing while Ashley is the party's shining star. But given the accusations this stalker posted on the internet, the jealousy angle doesn't jibe. He stated Ashley is a murderer."

"No one in the Webster family blames Ashley for the death of their daughter," Nelson said. "We've spoken to the remaining family members. Not one of them criticized Ashley for the crash, and each of them called it an unfortunate accident, even Jo. They told us Jessica suffered from mood swings and rebelled against parental control. In hindsight, her mother says she thinks her daughter suffered from depression."

"I'm going to bed. See you in the morning," Josh said.

Nelson nodded. "Goodnight."

"Night." Gerry stood and stretched his arms above his head. "I'll do a circuit of the house before I hit the sheets.

My spidey senses are clanging."

"Mine too," Josh said in a grim voice before he left to join Ashley.

Ashley woke within Josh's arms. Keeping her eyes closed, she shoved Matt's warning from her mind and savored Josh's embrace. It was scary how fast she'd become used to Josh's presence.

The alarm on her phone played several bars of a classic rock ballad, and with an inaudible groan, she silenced the din.

"What time is it?"

"Six-thirty," Ashley said. "Lots to do. Find Robert and demand answers, for one," she added, clenching and unclenching her hands. "I don't understand why he'd do this or what he hopes to gain by calling me a murderer. I trusted him, dammit."

"Shush." Josh drew her close again. "We have time for a kiss and a cuddle."

"Morning breath is a thing," she stated in a prissy tone.

Josh pushed his lower body against her, making her aware of his erection. "So is morning wood, but you don't hear me complaining."

He didn't give her a chance for another protest before he kissed her. It was an unhurried kiss, but one that signaled passion and caring, and it pushed Ashley's mind to skirt thoughts of love. No, she couldn't fall for him. *She mustn't.* But Ashley kept right on kissing him back and would've continued if Nelson hadn't banged on their door.

"Josh, your sister is here with her husband."

Josh's arms stiffened around her. "Spoilsports," he mumbled before calling out to Nelson. "We'll be out in a few minutes." His embrace loosened. "We'd better move because Summer is likely to barge in here without warning. She'd enjoy that."

Ashley grinned and gave him a quick consolation kiss.

"You think I'm joking. After the crap we gave her dates, she owes Dillon and me payback." Josh slid out of bed and pulled on jeans.

A thump on the bedroom door had Ashley jumping. "Hurry in there. Ashley, put on something old that you don't mind getting dirty."

Ashley rolled to her feet and shot Josh a frown. "What is Summer intending to do to me?"

"I don't know, but if she has a plan, you can bet it'll be solid. My sister is smart."

"Josh!" Summer yelled.

Josh hastened to the door and yanked it open. "You'd better have coffee started."

"Oh, you're awake." Summer's mouth twitched as she held back her amusement.

Josh bared his teeth. "Coffee."

Summer backed up, her hands held high in surrender. "Time to get a move-on. Ashley, are you ready? I have Ella waiting on Skype to offer advice. Ooh! You're a scarlet woman."

"Is my hair that bad?" Ashley asked, her hand gliding over her head.

"That's what Ella and I are aiming to fix." Summer gave

off positive vibes. "I'm confident my plan will work."

· ♥ · ♥ · ♥ · ♥ · ♥ ·

STEPHEN THREW THE REMOTE at the television and took pleasure in the way the screen cracked, and the control broke apart as it struck the tile floor.

"Fuckin' Ashley Townsend," he growled.

He'd wanted to cause her stress, to get under her skin.

Instead, everyone was raving about her new, trendy hairstyle. Her fashionable wardrobe. Her political success. On the internet news sites, social media, the radio, the television. Newspapers. He couldn't escape the bloody woman, not even in this beachside cottage. His haven.

She'd destroyed his family.

She'd destroyed his peace, his mental sanity.

Ashley Townsend had destroyed his life, and for that, the woman was gonna pay.

But first...

Stephen turned to Robert. He'd drugged the man a second time to shut him the hell up, although he should wake soon. He'd give Robert one more opportunity to tell him the best way to get to Ashley, the perfect way to make the woman hurt as he suffered.

Stephen squatted beside the man who slumped in the corner of his tiny kitchen. He slapped his face. When Robert didn't react, he hit him again. Harder, this time.

"Robert. Robert!"

Slap. Slap. Slap.

"Come on, old chap. It's time to wake."

15

A Rainbow Success

Later that night

"I owe Summer and Ella big time." Ashley hugged Josh then bounced up and down on her toes, beaming. "Today went *so* much better than I'd expected. The swell of support has the senior party members and our campaign manager ecstatic." Her smile faded as she considered the policies her party wanted to focus on this campaign. They were important, but many of the reporters preferred to discuss her sunset hair and why she'd gone for the color change, or they asked about Josh and their wedding date. She'd shrugged and given a vague answer before steering back to campaign-appropriate material, but the personal attention frustrated her.

"What's wrong?" Josh asked.

"I wish the press paid more attention to our policies. I entered politics because I wanted every New Zealander to have a full life with opportunities to thrive. The campaign manager tells me any publicity is good publicity, and I shouldn't worry."

"I imagine the opposition parties are gritting their teeth," Josh said.

"I had one candidate accuse me of making up my stalker." Ashley shuddered, her top lip curling in disgust. "If she'd experienced the numbing fear I have, she might cut me slack."

"What did you tell her?"

"That I'd pay her to take my stalker. The sad thing was she told me yes, to sign her up. Then, when I spluttered and coughed, she told me she'd suspected the stalker was a fabrication."

"The voters don't need her in charge of your electorate," Josh said. "The woman is an idiot. How about this? Tomorrow, when they ask personal questions, give them a deal. Say you'll answer one personal question—within reason—for every three political or policy questions they ask. If they ignore that. Ask yourself a question and answer it."

"Huh! I bet that doesn't work."

"You're on." He held out his hand. "Ten dollars."

"We have the leader's debate tonight," she said, sealing the bet with a firm handshake. Her stomach curled at his touch, and she had to force herself to release her grip. "At least I'll get sensible questions with the focus on politics, the economy, and our other policies. I'm nervous because it's important to show well." She peeked at her phone. "On that note, I'd better get ready."

"Do you fancy something to eat?"

"I might have a sandwich or a cup of soup, so my stomach doesn't rumble on live television. I'll eat dinner afterward."

Ashley marched to her bedroom and studied the two outfits Summer had suggested she could wear for the debate. In the end, she chose a slim-line black dress with the ruby-red trim on the hem and pockets. She showered, did her hair in a French braid, and moisturized her skin. Her contact had told her not to bother with makeup since they had studio artists to do that for them.

She drank the cup of soup Josh had prepared and ate a toasted cheese sandwich before hitting the road.

The first question, when it came, concerned her changed appearance. "Don't you think your new look will be too trendy for the older voters?" the man chairing the debate asked. Mike was an experienced journalist and known for his hard-hitting questions.

"Perhaps," Ashley said, instinct leading her to tell the truth. "Last night, what I thought was a courier package from my office turned out to be a prank. When I opened it, the head of a soft toy flew out and splattered me with red dye. I could throw out my clothes, but the ink stained my hair. I could've gone to a hairdresser to get my hair dyed back to the original color, but I'm busy with the campaign. The last thing I want is to cancel and disappoint people, so on the advice of a friend, I decided to display Labor party colors *and* fix my hair."

"You made lemonade out of lemons. What sort of toy

was it?"

"That is correct, Mike. It was a dog. Is it time to discuss policies now? I'm eager to hear what my fellow politicians have to say." She smiled at each of the men. The man standing nearest to her had clenched his teeth, and his return smile held strain.

"Quite so," Mike said, and he launched the first real question of the debate.

When it was over, Ashley thanked Mike and the producer before walking over to join Josh, Nelson, and Gerry. "How did I do?"

Josh entwined their fingers and kissed her knuckles. The sizzle of heat no longer took her by surprise, but the parallel yearning gave her pause.

"Great job," Josh said. "It was an even debate—at least between you and the National leader. All that matters is you answered the questions while sounding informed and intelligent."

"Are you ready to leave?" Nelson asked.

"Yes."

"Gerry will get the car and collect us outside at the front door," Nelson said.

"What do you fancy for dinner?" Josh asked.

"I've been craving a cheese omelet and salad. Something that isn't too heavy."

"I'm terrible at omelets," Josh said. "My last attempt turned into a burned, watery mass of rubber."

"Then we're lucky I'm the champion of all things egg." Ashley wiggled her brows. "If you want to help, you can make the salad. Did you hear two New Zealand students won the World egg-throwing contest yesterday? They did a throw of sixty meters to beat the Canadian team."

"You're kidding," Josh said.

"Nope. According to the students, they took a crack at it." She laughed at her egg pun while Josh groaned.

Even staid Nelson's lips twitched. His phone rang, his smile vanished, and he answered in his usual abrupt manner. "Yes." He listened. "Car okay?" He paused. "Yeah, I'll bring Ashley out now."

"Something wrong?" Ashley asked.

"Someone tagged your vehicle while we were in here."

Ashley closed her eyes, took a deep breath, but it didn't halt the snakes of fear from writhing through her chest. "Let me guess. *Murderer* or something along those lines."

"Not sure of the exact wording," Nelson said.

"At least it's dark and not many will see us on the way home." Josh embraced her in silent comfort.

Ashley shivered, her feel-good mood dispersed with the call. "I wish I knew what I'd done to deserve this harassment. Have the police located Robert yet?"

Gerry pulled up outside the door.

Ashley grimaced at the blue paint and the slogan that said *Vote National*. "Charming. I should've kept my mouth shut about my hair color."

Josh ushered her into the vehicle. "Two reporters heading this way, Ashley. Keep your head lowered, so they don't get the money shot."

"This is the part of politics I loathe," she muttered as Josh joined her in the back. She ducked and pressed her face against Josh's chest.

"You're shivering," he murmured.

"Yes." His chest muffled her reply.

"Are both sides of the vehicle tagged?" Josh asked.

"Yes," Nelson replied once Gerry moved off.

Ashley stiffened, anger pumping through her veins. She detested this helplessness bearing down on her. None of this situation was fair, and it was impossible to fight an invisible villain who forced her to react instead of taking action. And Robert. What was up with his disappearing act? He was making himself appear guilty. She'd known Robert for years, and in that time, he'd never missed a day of work. She'd relied on him to run the office, and now everything was falling apart.

If Robert didn't turn up soon, she'd have to replace him. The campaign manager might suggest a suitable candidate, but a replacement wouldn't possess Robert's knowledge or experience.

No! She couldn't believe Robert was her stalker.

The car stopped, and she straightened. "Oh, we're home."

"Wait until Gerry checks around the house," Josh murmured, his body tensing as his gaze swept the area the security lights illuminated.

After five minutes, Gerry returned and opened the vehicle door for her. The lights gleamed off his bald head. "Everything looks normal."

"What, no parcels?" Ashley asked as she slid from the car.

Gerry offered a faint smile. "Not this evening."

"Give me your keys," Josh demanded, holding out her

hand. "I'd prefer to enter your house first. Wait with Nelson and Gerry."

"I hate this." Ashley clenched her hands at her sides. "Have you checked with Robert's parents? Last I heard, they still live in Taupo."

Ashley's shivers had ceased during the journey home, but now a chill prickled her limbs. A someone-walking-over-her-grave sensation, according to her grandmother.

"I'll pass on the info," Nelson said.

"Clear." Josh stood in the doorway. "Let's cook that dinner."

"If Robert doesn't turn up with credible explanations, I need help in the office. I don't have time to vet a suitable candidate."

"Won't the party have someone who could help?"

Ashley set down her handbag. "Yes, but I have a certain way I prefer things done. I want a loyal assistant. Someone who can tell me to pull in my head if I need checking. The party candidate might be experienced, but they'll be set in their ways." She wrinkled her nose. "I don't want traditional. I want someone younger with initiative. Gah! I'm not making sense."

"Is it possible to do the work from home?" Josh asked.

"I don't see why not. As long as the information remains secure. Some is sensitive."

"Summer might help you on a short-term basis. At least get you through until election day. I mean, Robert might turn up with a reasonable excuse."

"Summer... Hmm, that might work," she said.

"Disappearing—this is unlike Robert. I mean, why would he do this? I thought Summer intended to visit your parents in Eketahuna?"

"Against my advice, she and Nikolai had a rethink and decided to stay. I'll start dinner," Josh said. "Why don't you talk to Summer?"

Ashley wandered to her bedroom and rang Josh's sister.

"I'd love to," Summer said. "The library has received a funding cut, and they've decreased my hours to the point where the pay barely covers my fuel costs. What tasks did you have in mind for me? I'm happy to sign a non-disclosure document if you require one, but remember I intend to vote for the opposition."

"I haven't forgotten. It's not as if you'll have access to top secret info. I just need someone to keep me on track. I figure my future sister-in-law can do that."

"And you're paying me for my loyalty," Summer said, her tone cheeky.

"There is that." Ashley grinned as she explained Summer's duties and ended the call, her mood more positive. She'd give Summer a chance, and if the situation didn't work out, she could always get the campaign manager to suggest someone. She changed into an old pair of jeans and a T-shirt and removed the heavier studio makeup before joining Josh in the kitchen.

"Your omelet is served." Josh slid a plate across the breakfast bar.

It held a perfect omelet and a side salad.

"But is it edible?"

"Gerry supervised me." Josh studied the golden omelet

with pride. "It looks ten times better than mine, so we're ahead already."

The enticing cheesy scent wafting toward her settled the matter. While Josh made another one, she attacked her meal.

"Well?" Josh asked.

"I doubt I could've made it better myself," Ashley said. "Gerry is an excellent teacher. Nelson, is that permanent paint on my car? Will it clean off?"

"No," Nelson said. "I've arranged for us to use a department vehicle. We might swap vehicles every day to keep your stalker guessing."

"I hate this." Moodily, Ashley finished her meal and stood to help clear the kitchen.

"I'll stack the dishwasher," Gerry said. "Watch television or catch up on your rest."

"Thanks, we appreciate it." Josh wrapped his arm around Ashley's waist and urged her down the passage.

"I feel like a kid being sent to bed for misbehavior," Ashley complained, balking at her bedroom door.

"I didn't have anything childish on my mind." Josh tugged on her braid. "I was thinking of something more adult, and the bedroom is the perfect place. Sex is an excellent stress release."

Heat bloomed low in her belly. A sizzle of anticipation. "Misbehavior. I love your idea." She grasped his forearm and yanked him into her room. With the door shut behind them, she advanced on the sexy, enticing man. "Shirt off," she ordered, nimble fingers already slipping the buttons from the holes. "Give me skin."

Josh dragged off his shirt and didn't stop there. He stripped off footwear and his black trousers. His upper arm still bore a light dressing, but thankfully, the injury hadn't slowed him.

"Someone is happy to see me," she whispered, her gaze roving his broad chest, his lickable abs and settling on the erection tenting his black boxer-briefs.

"Always," he whispered, his blue eyes full of sensual heat.

Ashley melted inside. This man... He did it for her. She'd never met a man who meshed so well with her life. He hadn't once complained about the constant waiting, and he made her feel safe. Happy, despite everything else going on in her life.

She sashayed closer and slid her hands over his muscular back. When her hand met the band of his underwear, she slipped her fingers beneath and squeezed his buttocks.

"Nice," she said with appreciation.

She backed him toward the bed, laughing at the second of surprise in his expression when he toppled to the mattress. Ashley followed him down and tugged off his last garment. "My turn. I've been wanting to explore."

"Have at it," Josh murmured. "I'm all yours."

Ashley leaned over him to snatch a quick kiss then pulled back to strip off her outer clothes. His appreciative gaze warmed her again, and the stress of the day slid away. Grinning, she traced a finger along his length and settled in to have some fun.

16

SEX TAPES AND SHENANIGANS

A PHONE WOKE ASHLEY from a deep sleep. She rubbed her face.

"Is that your phone?" Josh rumbled, his voice thick with sleep.

"Yes, it's becoming a habit. A bad one." She sat up and grabbed her phone. "Hello."

"Ashley, have you been online this morning?" Summer asked, her tone urgent.

"No, you woke me. I didn't set the alarm."

"Boss, someone posted a sex tape of you," Summer said.

"What?" Ashley shrieked. "I've never. I haven't!"

The sound of clicks and mutters sounded on the line. "Oh my god!" Summer cried. "It's you and Josh. I thought this—"

Josh took the phone from Ashley. "Summer, it's Josh. Tell me everything right now."

Ashley sat frozen, her arms wrapped around her waist. *A sex tape*. She hadn't. *They hadn't*. She rose and pulled on a wrap. She needed coffee to deal with this—cluster-fuck.

A coffee-scent floated in her direction before she reached the kitchen. Nelson and Gerry sat at the breakfast bar, cups in hand while they whispered their conversation. They fell silent when they spotted her.

"I have never, ever made a sex-tape in my life. *Never*," she added with emphasis. "I need coffee." She stomped to the coffeemaker and poured herself a cup. "I don't understand any of this."

Josh appeared in the kitchen wearing jeans and nothing else. "Bastard had a camera in our bedroom," he snapped. "I've disabled it now, but Summer said the video has spread over the web. Thank god, it was pictures only and not audio too."

That was good news? Ashley moaned, her stomach roiling. Pictures were bad enough. "What am I going to do?"

"You will get ahead of this shit-fest before it rolls downhill," Josh stated and set her phone on the counter beside her. "Summer is drafting a press release for you to approve. Ring your campaign manager and tell him what has happened. Make a public statement detailing everything the stalker has done to you. Be as honest as you can."

"Josh is right," Nelson said. "Where is the camera? I suppose it has your fingerprints on it now."

"Probably," Josh said, unrepentant. "There was no need to give the guy more entertainment than necessary."

Ashley's phone rang, and she scowled. "So it begins." She answered the call. "Geoffrey, how can I help you?"

"We need someone to search every room for more cameras," Josh said to Nelson. "Are we any closer to finding Robert?"

"The local cops spoke to his parents last night. They haven't heard from him, but it wasn't unusual to go a week between calls. They have no idea where he is or might have gone. According to them, he lived for his work and is loyal to Ashley. Neither of them had heard him speak negatively about her. As far as they knew, he was dedicated and thought she had a good chance of winning her seat."

"Another dead end," Josh said.

Nelson shrugged. "He'll make a mistake soon. Get sloppy. Whoever the stalker is, he's angry and vindictive. Someone will see him."

Josh dragged a hand through his hair. "Summer informed me I'm in the video, toward the end. Ashley's brother is gonna kill me. What a fuckin' mess."

Ashley jumped into damage control, and during her first engagement of the day, she read her statement. Her voice remained steady, she kept her head held high, and she didn't flinch when the press pounced and asked questions.

"My stalker is deluded and wrong in his or her assertions. I am a law-abiding citizen who has become a victim of these increasingly serious pranks. He shot at my fiancé, and it was only pure luck that saved Josh from a worse injury."

"What about the sex tapes?" someone called from the

back.

"As I told you," Ashley said in a frosty voice. "I have never and will never make a sex tape. My stalker planted a camera in my bedroom, where one assumes a measure of privacy. I'm engaged to Josh. What we do in the privacy of our bedroom is our business, and this stalker has broken the law by filming us. It is a breach of privacy, and when the police discover this person's identity, they will charge him to the fullest extent of the law. Thank you."

"I don't believe you," a man's voice called from the rear. "Hand me the popcorn. I think you're using drama to make the public sorry for you. You're not a suitable candidate, and you've concocted this plan to win votes."

Josh relocated toward the man hurling accusations at Ashley. Surely the press would see through this bullshit. The bullet graze on his arm had gushed enough blood to show the stalker was real and not a figment of Ashley's imagination. Josh pushed past two men and a woman reporter. The speaker was in his sights but retreating. Josh thought back to the night Ashley's car had broken down. From memory, she'd mentioned a man who'd asked her if she had secrets. She'd intimated he looked like a homeless man.

He'd make a safe bet that Ashley's stalker was hiring people to harass her and put her off stride. With his gaze on his quarry's black beanie, Josh closed in. He glimpsed two policemen approaching the man from the other side.

The man spotted them and turned toward Josh, his long black coat flapping as the man swung around, intent on escape.

Josh planted himself in front of the man and braced for contact.

"Get out of my way," the man shouted.

"I believe the police wish to speak with you." Josh swiveled and blocked the man when he attempted to duck around Josh.

"This is harassment."

Around them, reporters started to pay attention. Josh stayed the man enough for the police to grab him.

"You can't arrest me. I have done nothing wrong," the man shouted.

"We'll take it from here," a policeman told Josh.

"This is false arrest!"

"We're not arresting you, sir," a third policeman, a female officer, said. "But we want a chat with you. Once we talk, you can go on your way. Deal?"

"You're not arresting me?"

"No, sir," the female officer said. "We just want a chat."

Once he was confident the cops had the situation under control, Josh drifted through the groups of bystanders and press to stand nearer to Ashley. She'd completed the speech part of the informal meeting at The Viaduct in central Auckland and was now speaking one-on-one with the locals.

"Who chooses your wardrobe each day?" an elderly woman asked.

Ashley smiled. "I do, but I also get advice from my female friends."

"I don't hold with hair dye and cosmetics. You should be satisfied with what God gave you." Her querulous voice carried to everyone in the vicinity.

Josh flinched on Ashley's behalf.

"Don't listen to Grandma," a teenager whispered to Ashley. "Your hair is rad. I'd do something similar to mine if I got the chance."

Ashley smiled. "Thank you. I appreciate the compliment." She leaned closer to the teenager, but Josh was near enough to overhear. "I like it. Every time I look in the mirror, seeing the blaze of sunset colors makes me happy."

"Does your boyfriend like your hair?"

"He does," Josh said. "Very much."

The teenager giggled while Ashley sent him a broad smile. His heart flip-flopped, pleasure surging through him at the shared moment. Then, he thought of the sex tapes emblazoned over social media. While most had been removed, he could imagine Frog's reaction. Not that he regretted making love with Ashley. He'd do it again in a heartbeat, but he hated lies. He and Ashley needed to talk, to decide how to handle their fake engagement. The way he saw it, no matter what they did, they'd face backlash.

From Frog or from the public and perhaps Ashley's work colleagues.

His gut clenched. Ashley was intelligent and gorgeous, and since meeting her, he'd fallen under her spell. Despite the circumstances, she'd kept going when others would've stumbled or cracked under pressure. He had no doubt, she had an excellent chance of winning the election, but he couldn't figure out how he might fit into her life permanently.

He was a soldier. One without a job.

Their political beliefs were different.

Yet when it was just them, they synced.

It was only when the outside world intruded that the doubts crept into his brain.

He trailed Ashley, gaze scanning the faces in the crowds who waited to meet her. A faint breeze blew in off the harbor, ruffling her sunset hair. Overhead a seagull sat atop the roof of a restaurant, squawking at the intruders while its beady eyes scanned for tidbits of food.

Ashley spoke to men, women, and children. Some asked for policy details, one woman asked the location of the restrooms while others had comments about her personal life. Josh had no idea how she remained smiling and pleasant.

At precisely eleven, they moved on to their next engagement. A new business had started up in the city—a cat café. Josh was a dog person himself, so he sat at a table with Nelson and sipped his coffee while Ashley spoke with the owners, the employees, and the other patrons. She stroked a purring cat while she discussed policies for businesses and the Labor party's thoughts on shifting the minimum wage. Ashley visibly relaxed, opening Josh's eyes to the purpose of the café.

His phone buzzed, indicating an incoming message. A groan escaped him as he saw Frog's name.

"I need to make a phone call," he said to Nelson. "Won't be long."

"No problem. If you see Gerry, tell him to grab sandwiches for lunch. I'm starving." Gerry had received a pass on this visit because of his allergies.

"I'll get something. Nothing you dislike?" Josh asked.

"We'll both eat anything," Nelson replied.

Josh left and jogged down the stairs. The cat café was off Queen Street, the main shopping street, and he found Gerry loitering at the nearby coffee shop.

"I don't think they'll be much longer. Nelson asked me to buy sandwiches."

"Not in there," Gerry said. "They've sold out."

"No problem. I'll find something." Before he left, he messaged Frog. *Will ring in a few.*

Now came Frog's instant reply.

Josh sighed, found a quiet spot out of the way of the pedestrian traffic, and dialed his friend. No doubt, if Frog had his way, it'd be ex-friend. His own damn fault. Josh shouldn't have crossed the line.

"What the fuck is going on over there?" Frog roared. "Sex tapes? What the fuck, man? I trusted you to protect Ashley. Instead, you think with your dick and make a sex tape."

"You gonna let me speak?" Josh asked before Frog started again.

"Speak!" Frog roared.

"Ashley's stalker placed a hidden camera in her bedroom."

"Which doesn't explain why your pasty white arse is in the movie. The thing about a fake engagement is that it remains a pretense. No sex." Frog's voice grew in volume. "What part of *no sex* don't you get? If you screw Ashley's chance to follow her dream because of sex, I'll come home, and your problems will be worse than one stupid stalker. Where is Ashley? You tell her to call me," Frog ordered.

"No, I won't do that. Ashley is coping with the situation. She doesn't need you shouting at her."

"You slept with my sister," Frog said, this time in a scarily quiet voice.

"It was consensual," Josh snapped. "Ashley has enough to deal with now. I'll tell her you're concerned and want to lecture her. But don't you dare upset her. If that's all, I have to buy sandwiches, so Ashley gets to eat before her next gig."

"Keep your hands off my sister." Frog hung up before Josh could reply.

Josh cursed and shoved his phone in his pocket. Dammit, he hated arguing with Frog. Worse, he loathed being the meat in a sibling sandwich. No matter what he did, what he said, he'd be in the wrong. He'd thought this job would help him—give him space to make decisions.

Now, he'd fucked everything up and fallen for Ashley, a woman who was too damn good for him.

17

PUTTING OUT FIRES

The next two days passed, and Ashley felt as if she was putting out fires in every direction. Overseas news agencies had picked up the sex tape story, although thankfully, the social media companies had hastened to remove the videos.

She couldn't go anywhere without Nelson, Gerry, or Josh following her. Her protection squad. Although she appreciated their presence, the lack of freedom to do something as simple as visiting the restroom frustrated her.

Next up, her parents were concerned while Matt had sent a terse email demanding to know why she was putting the career she wanted above all else in jeopardy by jumping into bed with Josh.

Which led to her final problem.

Josh Williams.

Since the day of the sex tape and Matt's call, he'd

distanced himself. They'd shared a bed, but each kept to their respective sides. While in public, they were friendly and polite, but Ashley hated the widening gap between them. She couldn't discuss this with any of her political friends since as far as they knew, the engagement was real. Summer was the next logical choice, but it didn't seem right to discuss Josh with his sister—not with private things. Ashley scowled and twirled the engagement ring on her finger.

As she saw it, she had one final solution. She swallowed her last mouthful of tea. Ugh! Cold. She rinsed the cup and placed it in the dishwasher before turning to Josh.

"Josh, are you busy? We need to have a discussion."

"Can it wait until I finish watching this movie?" Josh didn't take his eyes off the screen.

"I'll be in our bedroom," Ashley said and stalked off. She'd do paperwork, check for correspondence from Summer, and decide what she'd wear tomorrow night to the next political debate.

Ashley picked a red pants suit, deciding to pair it with a cream blouse and black heels. Next up, she checked her email and opened one from Summer with full details of the program for the following day, and the policies she should discuss, given the opportunity.

Summer had written, *you haven't mentioned the middle New Zealander. None of your policies address this.*

Ashley grinned at Summer's extra input. It was helpful to have someone who voted for the other main party to see through flaws in her program. Summer managed it in such a way as to not cause offense. Josh's sister was proving her worth, and Ashley had quickly come to appreciate and trust her. Summer bore the same solid honor as Josh.

Integrity was worthy in its place, but when it became a block sitting between her and Josh, their situation had to change.

When Josh didn't arrive, Ashley prepared for bed. The man intended to wait until she'd fallen asleep. She had plenty of busywork, correspondence to write. No problem. She set her jaw with determination.

Game on.

"Interested in watching another movie?" Josh asked.

"I'm knackered," Nelson said. "I'll do a walk around the property and retire for the night."

"Yeah, I'm heading to bed too," Gerry said. "My spidey senses are tingling."

Josh understood. Getting Ashley to and from her meetings was becoming logistically complicated. Not only did they have to watch for the bad guy, but the reporters reminded him of a pack of marauding dogs, and the public wanted their piece of her too. Her popularity caused difficulties.

The two men left, and Josh turned off the television. Sighing, he stood and switched off the light. Hopefully, his plan had worked. Frog's fist lay in his future. His fault. He'd crossed a line. He should've kept his hands off Ashley.

Josh padded along the passage and opened the bedroom door. It squeaked, and he winced. He paused a beat before entering.

"Josh."

Oh-oh. The note in her voice reminded him strongly of his mother. It was the tone he'd heard whenever he'd misbehaved or stepped into trouble.

He strove for apologetic. "Sorry. Did I wake you?"

"No, I've been waiting for you. Part of me is surprised you didn't sleep on the couch." Ashley sat up and switched on the bedside lamp.

A glow suffused the room, and his gaze jumped to her loose hair. The yellow, orange, and different shades of red shimmered with sunset vibrancy. His fingers itched to touch and test the strands. His gaze lifted to her features. Her frown.

"I contemplated it, but I didn't want Nelson or Gerry to speculate."

She snorted. "As if they and every New Zealander aren't poking their nose into our business. Matt included. Sit. I have something to say, and it's difficult to concentrate when you're hovering. You look as if you intend a swift retreat."

"Considering it," he said with total honesty.

"I thought you were a big, brave military man." She crooked her finger and beckoned him closer. "I promise not to bite. *Much.*"

Josh felt his eyes widen. Her expression gave him nothing. Her words, however... He edged nearer and perched on the corner of the bed.

"I'm going with gut honesty here." Ashley straightened her shoulders. "I like you, Josh. A lot. Making love with you, sharing my life with you—I'd love our arrangement to become real. Not the engagement part because we're still getting to know one another, but I have feelings for you. Could we give what we have between us a chance—if you're agreeable? If you're not on the same page, I understand and ask you to please keep the pretense until the election is done."

Josh stared at Ashley, frozen, and scarcely breathing. Frog had spoken to her too, and instead of listening to her brother, she wanted him. She was willing to fight for him. His chest went rigid, his throat tighter.

He'd thought Frog...

"Josh? Do you intend to say something? Anything?"

Josh swallowed hard, the emotions in him tangling to do a number on his language skills.

Ashley sighed, pulled a face. "I didn't mean to make you uncomfortable, but I thought you'd prefer honesty instead of guessing. My life is too busy for games. I'll back off and try not to make the situation too awkward. After the election, I'll announce the pressure on our relationship—"

"No!" At long last, his brain kicked into gear. He jumped to his feet and prowled toward Ashley. He hauled her from the bed and wrapped her in an embrace. "I..." He swallowed to lubricate his throat. His brain wasn't functioning right. The words to make this right weren't at the tip of his tongue as usual. "Please." He stared into her brown eyes, every single piece of experience deserting him.

A furrow formed between her brows. Damn, he was losing it, losing her.

"I want the same thing," he growled, desperation helping him to get out the words.

The tiny frown didn't shift, and he did the only thing

he could. He kissed her, pouring every emotion into it. Hopefully, he'd manage the words once the fear of losing her wasn't paralyzing him. After Frog had reamed him out and lectured Ashley, he'd figured any chance they'd had of something real had detonated.

Her arms came around his shoulders, gripping him in a possessive manner. Her action penetrated the tension in his gut, his chest, his mind, and he drew back, parting their mouths.

"You're certain?" he croaked.

"One hundred percent."

"What about your brother?"

"He needs to treat me as an adult. If I'm old enough to run a country, I'm capable of a relationship with you. I'm not stupid. I've seen the women come on to you when we're out together. You smile at them. You're polite, but you never flirt with them, not unless they're old enough to be your grandmother. Each day, you look out for me in a dozen little ways. Don't think I haven't noticed. Matt can't do anything except holler from Afghanistan. When he comes home on leave, I'll set him straight."

"Your brother is after my blood. He's threatened me."

"Are you positive about us?" Ashley asked, her gaze direct and unflinching.

"Yes." His throat tightened again. "I-I thought you'd tell me to leave."

"It never entered my mind. Are we positive we found every hidden camera in this room?"

"Yes. We checked the entire house."

"Then, let's go to bed." She scanned the four corners of

her bedroom. "And just to make sure, we'll turn off the lights."

Josh's world tipped again, this time resettling in a place of peace. Happiness.

Laughing, he settled her on the bed. He reached over to switch off the lamp before yanking off his footwear and clothes. Naked, he joined her, determined to give her actions. The words, he'd give her later once his brain rattled back into place.

Ashley wriggled out of her loose T-shirt and panties, firing the garments away instead of tidily folding them as was her standard MO.

He hadn't said no.

When she'd expected rejection, especially given the BS that was her life at present, he'd surprised her. Her pulse still raced, and if she held out her right hand, she suspected it'd tremble.

Josh rolled closer, his hands smoothing over her shoulders. "You're naked."

"I thought it'd be quicker if I stripped too."

A chuckle escaped him, and her world settled onto a more level equilibrium.

Then their mouths connected in the darkness. At first attempt, their teeth clashed but Josh tugged her closer, fit their bodies together, and the kiss settled into perfect.

In the intimate darkness, their lovemaking was fast and furious. Hands stroked roughly as Josh sucked hard on one nipple. Her body bloomed for him, Ashley on board with this, with Josh, with the potential of a future. Desire rippled through her, a certainty in the rightness of her decision.

"Josh," she protested when he separated their bodies.

"Condom," he muttered.

"I'm glad you're thinking," she whispered.

He laughed. "It's a close thing."

"Do you need the light?"

"Nope."

Foil crinkled and Josh shifted his body. "Come on top of me."

Ashley didn't argue. She straddled his big, muscular body and guided his cock to her entrance. Without haste, she sank down and savored the sensual stretch, the decadent glide as she took him deep.

"That feels amazing, sweetheart," he whispered. His voice sounded thicker than usual, and the depth of his passion filled her heart with warmth.

She rose and fell, letting her body guide her.

"Ashley, you're gorgeous," he whispered. "You are a goddess."

His compliment filled her cheeks with a delighted blush. "It's dark. You can't see me."

"Excellent night vision," he countered.

He gripped her hips and lifted to meet her downward slide with an upward one of his own. When she couldn't quite get the friction she wanted, she stroked her clit.

"That's it." Josh encouraged her. "Take what you want."

A streak of pleasure shot through her, and she closed her eyes, grabbing onto passion and sensation and straining for more. Then it was there, claiming her. She caressed her nub more gently now, to prolong the blissful sensations. The pleasure spread, a moan of delight escaping her as her orgasm shimmered, gradually growing bigger, better.

"I can feel you tightening around my cock," Josh murmured. "So good."

She leaned forward to kiss him, and without warning, he rolled. She laughed up at him, barely making out his features in the dark.

He surged into her, filling her again. Ashley gripped his shoulders and savored his unleashed power as he invaded and retreated. His strokes quickened then he stilled, balls-deep inside her.

Their lips met, and in that perfect moment, Ashley felt so close to Josh her heart ached. Yes. She intended to fight for Josh, fight for their fledgling relationship, fight for a future. Because, despite her brother's opinion, Ashley thought they had a chance, and that was worth fighting for.

18

THINGS GET MUCH, MUCH WORSE

THE NEXT MORNING, ASHLEY let Josh take the first shower while she checked her email. One stood out, and her hand trembled as she clicked on it.

You were warned. This is your fault.

The email was a throwaway fake address, but she sent the email to her printer to give to Nelson.

"Something wrong?" Josh strode into the bedroom, naked apart from the towel wrapped around his waist.

"A love letter from my stalker," Ashley said. "I'm printing it now."

Josh retrieved the single page and frowned as he read the message.

"He's done something else." Ashley's gut tangled in knots. "I'm so over this."

"Take a shower. Get ready for your day. We'll worry about things when we meet them." Josh claimed a slow kiss, giving her comfort and diverting her mind, for an instant, to more enticing, enjoyable topics. "Nelson, Gerry, and I have your back."

"I know. Thanks."

"Any preference for breakfast?"

"Toast and cereal. Coffee."

"The usual," he teased.

"Please."

"The coffee will be ready when you are," Josh promised.

"Thanks. I won't be long."

A short time later, Ashley walked into the kitchen. Today, in deference to the overcast weather, she'd chosen a charcoal gray pants suit with a buttercup-yellow silk blouse beneath the jacket. She'd left her hair loose and wondered what the press would make of that.

"Are we nearer to discovering this guy?" she asked Nelson. "The publicity might make the senior Labor party management happy, but I'm over it. It'd be nice if Josh and I could walk on the beach or have a coffee at the local café without the logistics. I want my life back. Right now, even a supermarket shop would thrill me."

"Understandable. We're still searching for Robert. The guy has your personal email, right?"

"Yes."

"And, he'd know bits and pieces of your private life," Nelson said.

"Well, we're not BFFs, but we do work together. He doesn't share every detail of my life, but anything party-related—yes."

Josh set a piece of toast in front of her, along with a mug

of coffee. He'd added milk already. She cupped her hands around the mug and savored the scent before taking her first sip. She closed her eyes and inhaled. Perfect.

"But Robert opens the correspondence that arrives at the office?" Nelson continued.

"Which would give him a chance to add pieces without causing suspicion," Gerry said.

"Yes, that's true." Ashley frowned and nibbled on her toast. "I don't buy this theory of yours. Robert and I have worked together for years. We've known each other even longer. If he was envious of me or bore a grudge, why wait this long for payback?"

"Stakes are higher now," Josh said. "You've been promoted, and now there's a chance you might become the next prime minister. Perhaps Robert saw the way your popularity was increasing and snapped."

"This started before my promotion."

"True, but maybe he wanted to cause you pain. Make you appear in a bad light to the voters."

"According to Matt, it was your pasty backside the voters saw," Ashley said.

"My backside isn't pasty," Josh snapped.

Gerry let out a guffaw, and both of them glared at him. Ashley finished the second half of her toast and downed the last of her coffee.

"Hustle, men. Hustle," Ashley said. "More hands to shake, babies to kiss, policy to expound on."

Gerry finished his coffee and stood. "I'll back up the car." He stacked his mug inside the dishwasher, plucked a ring of keys from his pocket, and sauntered to the rear door.

"Ashley, do you want a travel mug? You haven't eaten much today," Josh said.

Warmth burned away her residual grumpiness. Josh cared for her in so many little ways. "Thanks. There are spare travel mugs in the pantry if Nelson and Gerry or you want one too."

"Nelson!" Gerry roared. "Call the cops. We have a body."

Nelson picked up his phone and dialed even as he ran from the house.

Josh grasped Ashley's upper arm and tugged her to a halt when she tried to follow. "No. Your stalker might be outside. Stay here out of sight."

"But I need to know what is going on." Ashley's pulse raced. She needed to move. Couldn't stand still. Doing nothing didn't sit right. "This is my house."

A siren wailed, rapidly drawing nearer.

"That was quick," Josh commented.

"Please, Josh. If someone has left a body in my garden, I want details. Answers."

"Once the local cops are here, I'll check things out for you. But you have to promise you'll stay inside out of harm's way."

"I promise."

Nelson entered the house before Josh could exit.

"Is it a body?" Ashley asked.

"It's Robert Giles," Nelson said.

"Robert? Are you sure? I want to see," Ashley said. "Please."

Nelson glanced at Josh, who gave a curt nod.

"Right," Nelson said. "Walk between Josh and me. You're not to touch anything, and if you think you might be sick, tell us."

"Is it bad?" she whispered, fear slithering down her spine along with an icy chill.

"Yes."

Josh tangled their fingers and squeezed in silent comfort. Numb, she exited her house, walking between the two men. A police car blocked her driveway, and bright yellow crime scene tape formed a barrier around the spot where a still form lay. As they moved closer, her steps slowed. A harsh groan rammed its way up her throat as she stared at Robert's swollen and bloody face. Because it *was* Robert. His white business shirt was red with blood and hung loose. At some stage, he'd loosened his tie, and her gaze darted to his mottled neck. The bruises.

Ashley couldn't bear it any longer. She turned toward Josh and buried her face in his chest. Tears formed in her eyes while Robert's bloated visage replayed through her mind in a loop. Josh's arms wrapped her in a comforting embrace.

"Are you okay?" he murmured.

"No. This is crazy. Nothing makes sense. I'll call our campaign manager and cancel my meetings for this morning at least. I can't... I didn't... I told you Robert wasn't responsible for this nastiness."

She remained in Josh's arms but eavesdropped on the chatter between the cops.

"...tortured. Poor bastard."

Gerry strode over to Nelson, and they had a hurried discussion before footsteps on the gravel told her one or both of them were approaching her and Josh.

"The local boys have things in hand," Nelson said. "We can go now."

"I can't," Ashley said. "Robert died because of me, and I don't understand why." She swiped away a tear and stood taller. "It's too late to cancel the meeting at the agricultural show."

"Call Summer. Get her to cancel your engagements for today," Josh said.

Ashley turned to Nelson and Gerry. "Do we know anything?"

"Not yet," Nelson said. "But we will catch him."

"Should I give a press conference and appeal for help from the public?" Ashley asked.

"Let me speak with our boss." Nelson's brown eyes held approval.

Ashley nodded. Robert had been proud of her and approved of the way the campaign was going. She'd do this for Robert. She raised her chin. "Let's do this."

Keeping busy helped. Ashley spoke to various farmers, suppliers, and farmers' wives during her visit to the agricultural show. She assisted judges in picking the best sponge cake and chose a winner for the children's decorated sand saucer.

The entire time, reporters dogged her heels and fired questions at her regarding Robert's death. She told the first ones she intended to hold a news conference at four in the afternoon, but the information didn't appease them.

After that, Nelson, Gerry, and Josh kept the reporters at a distance, and Nelson called in uniformed officers to bolster security.

"Excellent job," Josh said. "Although you picked the wrong winner in the kids' floral saucer contest. That red-haired boy had the best arrangement."

Gerry snorted, although when Ashley glanced his way, he wore a poker face.

"The judge's decision is final," she stated. "Let me say my goodbyes and we'll head to the factory opening."

By four, fatigue clung to Ashley. Smiling and chatting and keeping up a happy appearance took more energy than one supposed.

The press conference took place outside her electorate office in Manurewa. The detective in charge of Robert's murder investigation spoke first before handing over to Ashley.

"First, I want to offer my condolences to Robert's family and friends. I've known Robert Giles for many years after meeting him at a young Labor party conference. He has been essential to my career, and I couldn't have reached the position I'm in without his counsel and hard work. He was not only my colleague but also a dear friend. His murder is a senseless act, and I am cooperating with the police in every way I can to bring his murderer to justice.

"If you have witnessed anything, no matter how small or have knowledge that might help the police catch Robert's murderer, please come forward. Contact the police, so Robert, his family, and friends get justice. Thank you very much."

Ashley ignored the flurry of questions and retreated into her electoral office.

"Where to now?" Nelson asked.

"I rescheduled tonight's meeting in Mangere, so we can head home early," Ashley said. "Tomorrow, it's back to the grind."

Nelson's phone buzzed. "Can you wait while I take this call?"

"I'll be in my office." Ashley had given her staff the day off, and the day's mail waited for her. "Want to help me with the mail?" she asked Josh.

Inside her office, Josh dragged the pile of unopened envelopes toward him. "I'll open, and you deal with the contents."

Ashley sensed her smile appeared shaky at the edges and appreciated Josh's offer. "Thanks."

They set to work and had opened and sorted everything by the time Nelson tapped on the door. No nasty surprises, which helped to settle her nerves.

Nelson opened the door. "We have news," he said. "Robert scheduled photos to post on his social media page. We have a name for the other man seen with him. Ready to move? I'll show you once we're in the car."

Later, she and Josh studied the man photographed with Robert. A selfie, judging by the angle. The brown-haired man stared straight at the camera, unsmiling, his face harsh with slashing eyebrows. In contrast, Robert beamed happiness.

"Did you recover Robert's phone?" Josh asked.

"It was on him," Gerry said. "If he'd taken photos,

someone deleted them and the texts he'd sent. If this man deleted the photos, he wouldn't have known Robert had scheduled a post. Our guys are looking at the call log and will contact the telephone company for more information."

"Fingerprints?" Josh asked.

"None. Wiped clean," Nelson said.

"This guy gives off a military vibe," Ashley commented. "It's his stance. His tough-guy look."

"Have you found Robert's car?" Josh asked.

"Not yet, but we will," Nelson said. "You don't recognize this guy?"

"No," Ashley said. "He's not familiar."

Josh scratched his chin. "I think he was the heckler during your waterfront visit last week. He had stubble then and wore a beanie. Old clothes, but I'm certain it was him."

"You should show this photo to the homeless guy who hangs out around my electoral office," Ashley said. "He'd be able to confirm seeing this guy with Robert."

"Already on it," Nelson said. "We're closer to catching him."

What he didn't say, but Ashley was intelligent enough to read between the lines, was that her stalker had escalated. He'd murdered Robert, and she'd be next on his list if he caught her alone.

19

A Clue

A TAP SOUNDED ON the door of Ashley's bedroom. Josh glanced at her, but she didn't stir. He climbed out of bed and padded to the door, glad of his impulse to retain his boxer-briefs instead of going with his usual naked self.

He cracked open the door. "Ashley's asleep."

"We have news," Gerry said.

Josh slid from the room and followed Gerry to the lounge. Eleven-thirty. "What have you got?"

"Members of the public reported seeing Robert's car. We got lucky with fingerprints. We have a full name. Stephen Blackwood."

"Who is he?"

"He lived in the same country town as Ashley but moved to Australia with his mother when he was ten. He's lived there ever since, joining the Australian army out of school before going into the special forces."

"The man is more dangerous than you thought." Josh read between the lines, saw Gerry's worry.

"Yes," Gerry agreed.

"Is it possible for me to have a temporary permit to carry a firearm?"

"Nelson and I will speak to our boss."

"What's stopping him from taking her out? If he's ex-special forces, he possesses the expertise," Josh said. "Why hasn't he shot her?"

"We're wondering the same thing," Nelson said, coming in on the end of their conversation.

"The only reason that makes sense is he wants to scare her, wants her to wonder what he'll do next," Josh said. "It's polling day next Saturday. The party has planned every hour of her day, and the details are available to the public and the media. How the hell are we going to keep Ashley safe?"

A door opened and closed, and soft footsteps sounded in the hall. Seconds later, Ashley appeared in the doorway.

"Are you meeting without me?" she asked.

Her sunset hair was loose and tangled around her shoulders, and she bore a sleepy expression while she'd wrapped up in a thick navy-blue robe.

"The cops found Robert's car and have identified your stalker," Josh said.

"Who?" Ashley demanded.

"Stephen Blackwood."

Ashley appeared blank. "Should I know him?"

"He spent time at Onewhero. Attended the same school as you," Gerry said.

"It's a country school and not that big. I should remember him then, but the name isn't familiar. Neither is his face."

"We'll keep investigating," Nelson promised.

Every news broadcast the following day, every current event television show, every social media feed contained details of Stephen Blackwood, his photo, and a plea from the New Zealand Police for the public to report any sightings of the man to them. The public was not to approach since the police considered him dangerous.

Stephen snorted, having lain low for a few days. Few people walked along the beach as far as his isolated property. He'd remain safe here. The cops wouldn't find his name attached to the ownership records.

A sharp spike of pain pierced his concentration, jerking him from his thoughts, his plan of attack. He reached for a painkiller and swallowed one dry. Probably wouldn't even take the edge off, but damn if he'd take the medication the doctor had prescribed.

Soon, it wouldn't matter.

One last big hurrah and it'd be over.

20

ELECTION NIGHT

"Each day I leave my house wondering if this will be the day Stephen Blackwood strikes again," Ashley murmured.

She and Josh were sitting in a black SUV after leaving a cocktail party at the Auckland city council.

"We're as frustrated as you," Nelson said from the front passenger seat. "No one has seen him for days. We've checked out every rumored sighting. Not one has come to anything."

"My gut is telling me this radio silence should alarm me. My guess is he'll do his worst on election day. I hope innocent people don't get in his way." Ashley pushed out a frustrated sigh. "Then there's the campaign. I have no idea how the voting will swing tomorrow. And it's infuriating that this election run-up has been about me rather than the policies. I've attracted this publicity and none of it for the right reasons."

"You've discussed your policies," Josh reminded her. "Nelson, Gerry, and I could quote your Labor party policies verbatim."

"If the voting goes our way tomorrow, it won't feel right. Satisfying." Ashley gave an irritable shrug. "And I sound like a whiny ten-year-old. Sorry."

Josh reached for her hand. "We understand. I heard several of the National party candidates, and one from the Green party interviewed yesterday. They're complaining this entire campaign has focused on you, and none of them are receiving any coverage. I believe the leader of the New Zealand First Party harangued a reporter this morning for daring to ask questions about you."

Nelson snorted. "He makes a hobby out of berating reporters."

Ashley laughed because Nelson spoke the truth. She hoped if her Labor party did well in the results tomorrow night that they received enough votes to govern on their own. She'd prefer to govern from a position of strength without the necessity to form alliances with any smaller parties who gained five percent or more of the vote.

"So many headaches." Her dream shimmered within her grasp. *Concentrate on the prize. Push these petty annoyances aside.* "Not only do I have a stalker in the wind. I have fellow politicians snapping at my heels, and the press bombarding me with nosy personal questions. Hopefully, my life will settle post-election."

"Your people have vetted the guest list of those who'll be at Labor party headquarters." Gerry pulled into her driveway. "We'll have a large police presence. You've agreed to wait until nine before you arrive, which will allow us to double-check security. We'll get through this."

"I wanted to thank you and Nelson now." Ashley leaned between the front seats, sincere in her thanks. The pair had made a horrid situation a little lighter. "You've done a stellar job looking after my security, and I appreciate it. I'm sure you both have a personal life, friends, and family who you haven't seen because of your duties with me."

"We're doing our job," Nelson said.

"While that's true, I bet your duties rarely contain as much drama and excitement. No matter what happens tomorrow, I wanted you both to know how much I value your help."

"You're welcome." Gerry caught her gaze in the rearview mirror. "We've enjoyed the challenge."

"True that." Nelson turned in his seat to watch her and chuckled. "You've added a layer of excitement to the job."

Ashley sent her gaze skyward, and the three men chortled.

"If this Stephen hurts any of these pre-school children during our next visit, I might take him out myself. I hate this uncertainty. I hate the way I've started to jump at every noise. And most of all, I hate not knowing why Stephen Blackwood is fixated on me."

"His obsession might not be for a tangible reason." Nelson's big shoulders shrugged, and Ashley got the feeling he spoke from experience with a previous case. "You shouldn't stress about the motive behind Blackwood's decisions."

"You concentrate on your job, and we'll focus on catching Blackwood," Gerry said.

Josh drew her near and pressed a kiss to her temple. "They're right, sweetheart. You've come this far, worked so hard to win this election. You can't falter now."

· ♥ · ♥ · ♥ · ♥ · ♥ ·

Election night

Stephen Blackwood studied the grimy photo then his reflection in the square mirror on his bedroom wall. He'd pass inspection by any security Awful Ashley set in place since he'd used his initiative to acquire an invitation. Thankfully, no one had discovered the body yet. If his luck held, no one would check for days since the man was a loner.

He straightened his tie and plucked a piece of lint off his pristine white shirt. Courtesy of the army, he'd learned how to dress and, more importantly, the skills required to protect and kill.

The constant low-level pain in his head surged in a spike that forced a groan up his throat. His knees buckled briefly before he forced them to hold his weight, to maintain his upright stance. He breathed through the pain with even, incremental breaths. Once the levels became manageable, Stephen checked the time. The attendees had received notification they must arrive and pass through security before nine. They could leave when they wished, but re-entry into the hotel venue was impossible.

Entering with a weapon might prove difficult,

but Stephen remained confident in his abilities. The Australian army had taught him to use his ingenuity under fire to overcome unseen obstacles. With a grin, he picked up the carved wooden stick from where he'd set it against the wall. Then, sliding into character, he made a final check on his wallet, invitation, identification, concealed weapon. Yes, the necessities were in order. He limped to the vehicle he'd appropriated.

Time to finish this game and gain payback for everything Ashley Townsend had taken from him and his family.

· ♥ · ♥ · ♥ · ♥ · ♥ ·

Ashley dressed with care for her final public appearance before the election results started to come through. After consulting with Summer, whose opinion she valued, she'd decided on a knee-length yellow-and-black dress with long sleeves. It skimmed her figure and gave her a feminine air without tipping into overtly sexy. She wore ankle boots to project a fashionable edge and left her sunset-colored hair loose to fall in soft waves around her shoulders. As was her norm, she'd kept her makeup subtle, although for the evening, she'd gone with a smoky eye.

Josh entered the bedroom, dressed in a dark suit. This evening, the police had given him special permission to carry a weapon, although she had no idea where he'd concealed his handgun. Like most men, a suit looked good on him, but Ashley knew the excellent cut of the garment hid strong muscles rather than a body gone soft from too many business lunches.

Her heart twisted, and it wasn't only the knowledge her stalker might make his move tonight that bothered her. Now that the election was over, save for counting the votes, how would things play out between her and Josh? She cared for him, and the thought of not seeing him every day hurt. In the past, she might've sucked it up and gone with the original plan. Not now. Tonight, she intended to follow gut instinct.

"Josh, what happens after today? With our engagement, I mean." She held up a hand when he turned to her and opened his mouth to speak. "I wanted to say something first."

He nodded, and tension slid through her. Her hands bunched and relaxed while she sought the right words. Ashley cleared her throat and fixed her gaze on his handsome yet serious face. For once, his eyes didn't dance with mischief while he waited for her to speak.

"All along, I've tried to remind myself our arrangement is temporary. You took this position as a favor to Matt. The thing is I like and admire you. No, that's not the truth." She inhaled and started again. "I've fallen for you, Josh. I want... I want to wake up next to you in the morning. To go to sleep beside you at night. And in between spend time with you. If you're not of the same mind, I'll understand, but the truth is you'll be a hard act to follow, Josh Williams. You've spoiled me for other men."

With her heart pounding, Ashley stopped talking. She

fidgeted, her gaze fastening on his face. Why wasn't he saying something? Anything. Disappointment seared her while the backs of her eyes stung.

He didn't feel the same way.

"I'm sorry. I shouldn't have mentioned it. Put you in this position." How the devil had she misjudged the situation? Her gaze shot to her toes. When it came to body language, she had talent. Her expertise had become an asset in her job and allowed her to read people and act. Maybe Josh had broken her skills, and this time she'd wandered off course. About to retreat, she took one last peek at his face.

A slow smile bloomed on his lips and mischief sparkled in those eyes of his. He intended to tease her. Disappointment filled her. Regret. Letting him go would hurt, but at least she could bury herself in work.

"Frog will have words. He threatened to rearrange my face."

"This has nothing to do with my brother. This is you and me."

"Yes."

"Matt needs to butt out of my personal life. I'm an adult, and he has a cheek telling me what and what not to do," Ashley said, on a roll now. She was in the mood to send her nosy brother a sharply worded email or blast him during a succinct phone call.

"Yes." Josh's smile was broader, and it lit up his blue eyes, drawing her in, stealing her breath.

"What?" Ashley asked.

"Yes, I want you in my life. I still have no clue what to

do job-wise, but having you as my wife—that I'm certain about. Ashley Townsend, will you marry me?"

"Are you sure?" Ashley barely breathed, every part of her focused on Josh and his answer.

"Yes. It didn't take me long to fall for you. You're not only sexy and smart, but your determination and work ethic got me. You consider other people, care for them, and even though we might be on opposite sides of the political spectrum, I admire you. Whenever I think of you, I can't imagine a time when you're not at my side."

"And my political career? If the Labor party gets voted into power, I'll be the next prime minister. We'd have to live in Wellington for part of the year and Auckland the rest. We'd have to travel, and when foreign dignitaries visit New Zealand, you'd have to stand at my side."

"It sounds as if you're trying to put me off."

"I'm not. Walking away from you would hurt, but you must understand what you'd be signing up for by marrying me. Yes, I'd love children, but not immediately. I've had my eye on the prime minister job since I was a kid. If I fail this time, I'll try again. Giving up isn't part of my vocabulary."

"Since we've been together, I've had a taste of the future. I understand a little of what I might face. Yes to the children, but we have time to plan a family. Things will calm once the cops catch your stalker. I want this, Ashley. I want you."

Josh closed the distance between them, and Ashley met him halfway. He wrapped his arms around her shoulders and brought her flush with his hard frame. Their lips met, and he kissed her. Softly at first, then with growing passion.

A knock at the door interrupted. "We need to leave now," Nelson called.

"Coming," Josh replied. "Are you nervous about the results?"

"No, I did the best job I could. If I didn't swing the voters around my way, I'll try again in three years at the next election. I'll wish the leader of the National party well, congratulate him and his party on their win, and move on. That's all I can do."

Josh stroked her cheek. "One thing, before you go. I love you, and your brother will be difficult. What do you say we get married during your first free weekend? We'll zap up to Fiji for a long weekend and make our relationship official."

Ashley considered his suggestion for all of five seconds. Her mother had turned into Bridezilla's mother during her older sister's wedding. "Yes. I'll have Summer block out time in my schedule."

"I owe Nikolai a favor and promised to babysit my nephew to allow him and Summer a special night. What if I arrange a babysitter and ask them to come to Fiji as our witnesses? Would you be okay with that?"

"Done deal. I'll speak to Summer and tell her it's my treat for stepping in and helping me with the campaign. We'll spring the wedding surprise on them once we arrive in Fiji."

"I'll arrange the wedding part," Josh said. "I'll have plenty of time to sort out licenses and hotels. The flights."

"Ashley. Josh." Nelson pounded on the door again.

Josh brushed his lips over hers and clasped her hand. "Let's get this show on the road."

"We're gonna be late." Nelson narrowed his brown gaze on them.

"We were having an important discussion," Josh said. "Couldn't wait."

"Right." Nelson's tone edged toward a growl. "Normal procedure. Gerry will back up the car and give us an all-clear then Josh and I will escort you to the door."

"Thank you, Nelson." Ashley forced a smile. Tension simmered in the man, which ratcheted up her own anxiety.

They performed the maneuver they'd perfected over the weeks and were soon driving toward the hotel where the Labor party intended to celebrate or commiserate over the election results. Although tempted, Ashley had refrained from checking the early results.

"Are you worried you might lose your Manurewa seat?" Josh murmured.

"No. I've worked hard for my electorate, and I'm confident of retaining my majority vote. There is always the possibility of a surprise. That's what makes this career so fascinating."

"Not much job security," Josh said.

"I figured I'd go into office administration if I'm ever ousted." Ashley tilted her chin. She'd consider it a new challenge. A chance to grow. "That's my backup plan. I'm skilled at scheduling, communication, most computer programs. I figure I could cope."

"Okay," Josh said. "What about me? Help me decide what to do next."

"You're good at security, have a cool head and don't panic," Nelson said from behind the wheel. "You could always train to be a cop."

"I don't think Ashley will need her Plan B, which means I'll be shuttling back and forth between Wellington and Auckland for the next three years."

"Personal trainer," Gerry suggested. "Self-defense classes too. Or you could run classes to prep youngsters wanting to join the army."

"You could write a book, the topic being the first lady of New Zealand politics," Ashley chirped.

Their laughter provided an escape from the growing tension.

"Thanks." Josh groaned. "I can imagine the teasing now. My brother and sister and my mates won't let me forget this."

"You can always change your mind and walk away," Ashley whispered.

"Not a chance, sweetheart. You. Me. A Fijian beach. Count on it."

Ashley prayed Josh was right because she wasn't worried about the election results. It was the damage Stephen Blackwood might exact that nagged at her most.

· ♥ · ♥ · ♥ · ♥ · ♥ ·

STEPHEN FOUND IT LAUGHABLY easy to enter the hotel ballroom. He limped to the security line and waited his turn. His walking stick *tap-tap-tapped* on the hardwood floor. Kind of like slow-motion rifle fire. A man waved a

JOSH'S FAKE FIANCEE

wand over his person, and as Stephen had expected, the equipment didn't issue a single beep.

Next, a perky brunette, dressed in black trousers and a white shirt bearing a Labor party badge, examined his invitation and compared it to her list. An older man scanned the pilfered driver's license that Stephen handed over along with his invitation. The man's gaze studied his face then the photo on the driver's license before giving both back.

"Enjoy your evening, Mr. Landish."

"Thank you." Stephen intended to enjoy the hell out of his attendance. In fact, he'd take a safe wager he'd make this gathering memorable for everyone.

· ♥ · ♥ · ♥ · ♥ · ♥ ·

Nelson's phone buzzed, signaling an incoming call. A second later, Gerry's phone played a riff from a popular song. Ashley exchanged a glance with Josh.

Gerry answered. "Wakefield. What? Yes. Keep us informed." He hung up. "They've discovered a beachside property, formerly owned by Stephen Blackwood's paternal grandmother. The surname on the property title is different, which is why initial searches showed nothing. We have a team checking. They'll let us know what they find."

"So this might be over soon?" Ashley asked.

"We should still stay alert," Josh said. "It's not over until Stephen Blackwood is in custody."

Ashley nodded even as her stomach muscles tightened.

This was the biggest day of her life, and Stephen Blackwood was spoiling it for her. A beat later, guilt struck. Robert was dead, and here she was having a pity party. Not cool. She lifted her chin a fraction, her woe-is-me attitude replaced with anger on Robert's behalf. He had deserved none of this. He'd been so happy, thought he'd found his one.

Her phone rang from the depths of her clutch, and she fumbled with the clasp to get the call before it diverted to voicemail.

"Ashley Townsend," she said.

"It's Geoffrey." Her political colleague heaved out a breath.

"Geoffrey, what's wrong? Are you okay?"

He gasped in another audible breath before he pushed out slow and unsteady words. "I'm at Allen Landish's house. I'd told him I'd pick him up to take him to the hotel tonight. He's d-dead."

"How?" Ashley's breath caught, her throat tightening as tension slid through her. Allen had helped her during her younger days as a fresh-faced politician. A blunt man who didn't suffer fools, but one who held such knowledge and wisdom.

"Gunshot to the h-head." Geoffrey's voice trembled and he swallowed hard. "I've called the police. They're on their way."

"Just a moment, Geoffrey. I'll mention it to my DPS officers." As she spoke, she lifted her head to Gerry. "Geoffrey is at the house of one of our long-term supporters. Allen is dead. Geoffrey has called the police.

He's waiting for them now."

"Let me speak to him," Gerry said.

Numb, Ashley handed over her phone. Another dead. This had to be the work of Stephen Blackwood. "Tell the police to search for Allen's invitation to our Labor party function. It might be a home invasion or robbery, but if the invitation is missing, it's more likely Stephen Blackwood."

Call finished, Gerry handed back her phone and got busy on his own. "I want you to check the guest list," he barked. "Tell me if Allen Landish has arrived. I'll wait while you check. Make sure you're discreet. I'd hate to cause any alarm."

Ashley's heart raced as she waited.

"He's there." Gerry's powerful jaw clenched. "He's used the invitation to enter your function."

"But it's after nine," Ashley said. "We invited three hundred people. We think Stephen Blackwood has killed two people. If the police barge into that ballroom, it'll place everyone in danger."

21

DANGER STALKS INTO THE CELEBRATION

"WHAT ARE WE GOING to do?" Ashley whispered. "Won't it agitate the man if I don't arrive at the celebration?"

Josh cursed softly and with creativity. "Ashley is right. He'll get suspicious if she doesn't appear soon. He's unpredictable."

"We need plain-clothes cops in there. If Blackwood has used Landish's invitation, he would've had to show identification and go through the security line. He has changed his appearance enough to pass for Landish." Nelson pulled up to the curb. "Ring the boss, Gerry. Ask for instructions."

Ashley glanced out the window. They weren't far from the hotel. A blaze of lights illuminated the forecourt and the two couples having a strident discussion with a policeman.

"Do we have a photo of this Allen Landish?" Gerry asked.

"He's—was—in his sixties. Blond. Blue eyes. Glasses. He had several pairs so I was never confident of which frames he'd wear. He was in a car accident and walked with a limp. His left leg. He carried a walking stick in his left hand." Ashley paused to clear the croak from her voice, her heart heavy. This had happened because of her. "He dresses—dressed—well and wore a charcoal-gray suit. I mean, he would've if it was really him."

Gerry passed on the information.

Ashley's phone rang. "Mum."

"You won your seat with an increased majority. Ashley, your father and I are so proud of you. The voters are ready for a change. You've done it. My baby. Running the country. I'm so proud I could burst."

"Thanks, Mum," Ashley said. "I can't talk now, but I'll ring you tomorrow, okay?"

"I understand. You must be very busy. Talk to you tomorrow, sweetheart. The prime minister. I can't believe it," her mother murmured.

Ashley disconnected. "I won my seat. It sounds as if the Labor party is ahead. I should make an appearance."

"No," Josh protested. "It's too dangerous."

"What if we announce supper earlier than we'd planned?" Ashley asked. "At the very least, it should get most of my guests to safety. I could also enter and speak with people one-on-one. Get them out of the main ballroom. That might make it easier to spot Stephen Blackwood amongst the crowd."

"I don't like this," Josh said. "It's too risky."

"He's killed two people. What's stopping him from taking out more innocents? He's unpredictable. What if he shoots or stabs guests inside the ballroom? We know he's clever. Capable. This is my fault. It's me he wants."

"It's not your fault," Josh snapped. "We don't know why he's doing this or what he wants."

"Ashley is right. She must make an appearance soon," Nelson said. "It's nine-thirty already."

"I have to do this, Josh. I'll never forgive myself if someone else dies because I didn't act."

"You won't do this country any good if you get killed."

"We have plain-clothes policemen inside." Gerry's expression remained calm yet watchful. "Ten with more on the way."

"I have to get inside the ballroom," Ashley repeated. "This is a celebration. Everyone on my team has worked hard to make this day a reality. I owe it to Robert and to Allen Landish."

Gerry and Nelson exchanged a glance.

"She's right," Nelson said. "And bigger picture—if we're to have any chance of getting this guy, we'll have to play his game."

Josh stared at each of the men and finally rested his gaze on Ashley. A military man, he'd gone on ops, followed orders, kept people safe, but it was different now. Ashley meant something to him. She'd crept into his heart and made him want to be a better person. *For her*. He couldn't lose her. Yet, if they didn't catch Stephen Blackwood tonight, she'd always be looking over her shoulder, wondering if today was the day her stalker ended her life.

It couldn't be easy for Ashley either.

He sighed, understanding her need to end this situation and regain control over her life.

"What's the plan?" he asked.

"We'll go in with Ashley. The three of us," Nelson said. "We flank her at all times while she does her thing. The officers inside have seen photos of both Blackwood and Landish. They'll be watching for him."

"What will happen when you find him?" Ashley asked.

"We'll arrest his arse." Gerry's mouth set with determination. "Don't worry. Do whatever you deem necessary and celebrate your night."

"I'm nervous," Ashley confessed, and the vulnerability in her face had Josh's protectiveness coming to the fore.

No one hurt his woman.

"You'd be an idiot if you weren't anxious," Nelson stated in his blunt way. "Blackwood and the election result."

Josh reached for Ashley's hand. "We're engaged." He forced himself to wink at her. "That means we're allowed to hold hands. I'm terrified," he added. "The physical contact will help me conquer my fear."

A snort came from Gerry, but Ashley beamed at him, and something in Josh softened for an instant. Then, he snapped back to his military training because he could do nothing else if he wanted to keep his woman safe.

With their decision made, Nelson started the vehicle and drove the short distance into the hotel forecourt. Josh squeezed her hand before releasing it and exiting the car. Nelson and Gerry climbed out, and Nelson handed over the car keys to a man who he appeared to know. A plain-clothes policeman, Josh decided.

"We'll ring you when we want the car again." The cop nodded and drove away. "Ready?" Nelson asked.

"Yes." Josh opened the door for Ashley.

Like when he'd been on a mission, his focus narrowed to the essential things. Ashley and those who stood in his peripheral vision. He reached for Ashley's hand, her touch bringing a rush of pleasure. Although they hadn't been together for long, he was confident she was his one. All he had to do was keep her safe.

Now a well-practiced team he, Nelson, and Gerry flanked Ashley and strode into the foyer. They turned right toward the ballroom the Labor party had hired. At the room entrance, they paused. The chatter faded as party supporters recognized and acknowledged Ashley's arrival.

An elegant arrangement comprised of red flowers sat on a pedestal just inside the door. Bunches of red and white balloons and other decorations, predominantly in Labor red festooned the room. Overhead a chandelier glittered while on a noticeboard attached to the wall on their left held a display of candid photos from the campaign. Background music played. Instrumental but with a New Zealand flavor.

Tension radiated through Josh. He scanned faces. Charles stood chatting with Geoffrey and another man.

His lip curled on noticing Ashley as if he'd smelled something nasty. *Moron*. No one fit Landish's description. "I don't see him."

On spotting them, Geoffrey strode forward, a microphone in his right hand and a broad beam of satisfaction on his visage. "Ladies and gentlemen, please welcome Ashley Townsend, the leader of the Labor party."

When Ashley stepped past the threshold, Josh moved with her, keeping their hands linked. A full and happy smile curved her lips, but her hand in his communicated rigidity and hinted at her apprehension. *Excellent*. Complacency would get them killed.

"With the way the results are going, she'll be the next prime minister," a masculine voice shouted from the back.

Cheers and applause rang out, and Ashley released Josh's hand to hug Geoffrey. The instant Geoffrey stepped back, Josh reclaimed his position at Ashley's side. Nelson and Gerry moved into their protective formation.

"Speech!" a woman to their right called.

Josh continued to scan faces, searching for Blackwood. He didn't see him, but every instinct screamed he was here. A preternatural sense that only appeared during times of danger shrieked at Josh, upping his level of alertness.

If the bastard had somehow sneaked a weapon inside, they'd be in trouble. No security was infallible, and although Nelson had assured Josh they'd scan every attendee with a wand, there were workarounds. As a special ops military man, Blackwood was as highly trained as him. Anything might happen. Those spidey senses of his wailed. Josh ran his gaze over faces, bodies.

Where the hell was the bastard?

Geoffrey handed Ashley the microphone.

"Well," she said. "It's been a busy night, and I haven't caught up on the results. I spoke with my mother ten minutes ago. She told me we're doing okay." Ashley beamed at the ensuing shouts and cheers. "Seriously though," she said once silence fell again. "I'd like to thank every one of you for your support and your enthusiasm. My fellow candidates and I couldn't have done our job without you."

"Got him," Josh murmured to Nelson who stood to his left. "Ten o'clock."

"I see him," Nelson replied. He plucked his phone from his pocket, dialed a number and spoke in a low voice, issuing directions and updating information.

"As a small way of showing my appreciation, I've organized supper in the adjoining Blue room. If you're like me, you were too nervous for dinner, so you'll welcome something to eat now. Go ahead, before more of the final results come through. I'm sure we'll talk again soon. Go," she urged. "Grab some food. Get another drink. Enjoy!"

Half a dozen people bolted from the main ballroom, and soon a slow trickle of attendees wandered through the door. Not enough. Not fast enough to escape trouble.

Josh kept his attention on Blackwood. He'd dyed his hair to match Landish's, but he'd given up on maintaining the older man's posture. Blackwood stood tall and still, his gaze not moving from Ashley. Hate etched into his features, visible even from this distance.

One glimpse told Josh fury drove the guy. He glared

across the room at Ashley, his mouth flat and determined. He reminded Josh of an unblinking predator watching his prey. His attitude wasn't one of forgiveness. Josh had met men like him before. Blackwood had drawn his line in the sand. He'd refuse to back down.

"I'm going to chat with my guests and urge them to take advantage of the supper." Ashley sounded calm, but because he'd come to know her so well, he heard the faint tremor lacing her voice.

"Veer toward your right," Josh urged.

Ashley never hesitated. She stopped to speak to an elderly lady. "Hello, Mrs. Canon. How are you tonight?"

"I find myself very pleased," Mrs. Canon said. "I've supported the Labor party since I was a teenager and never have I experienced so much optimism for the future."

Mrs. Canon was resplendent in a floor-length pale blue gown and sequins. While she appeared older, her blue eyes held shrewdness. A woman who'd speak with bluntness.

"Thank you," Ashley said. "If you don't head to supper, you'll miss out on the meat savories. I made sure I ordered a few platters of sausage rolls."

Mrs. Canon patted Ashley's arm. "Don't worry, dear. I ate before I left the house. I'm so proud of the way you've turned around the election campaign. The initial results are auspicious. I have a good feeling with this election. Now, introduce me to your young man."

"This is Josh Williams," Ashley said, and the pride in her voice made Josh feel ten-feet tall.

"Are you willing to support Ashley in her political aspirations? If not, step aside. Ashley requires a supportive partner. Forgive me saying this, but I believe you're ex-military. You alpha types never hang back. You prefer action."

Josh felt his eyes widen at the woman's bluntness. "I understand Ashley and support her in everything she does."

"I will not be happy if she gets pregnant."

Ashley leaned closer. "Mrs. Canon. *Please*. Collect your granddaughters Sarah and Trina. Go into the supper-room. You'll be safer there."

"What?" The elderly woman's piercing gaze took in the men flanking Ashley. "Oh. I'll heed your advice. Sarah and Trina are over there."

She indicated two women in their early twenties. One wore a cream dress, accessorized with gold while the other wore pastel blue shot through with silver. All things he'd learned from listening to his sister and Ashley discussing wardrobe choices.

"Thanks." Ashley relaxed, sounding less distressed. She hadn't noticed Blackwood closing in on the two young women.

"Nelson," Josh warned.

"I see him," Nelson gritted out.

Before Nelson could act, Blackwood grabbed the women wearing cream. Her scream rippled through the ballroom, slicing through the chatter and laughter. The woman in blue fell or got pushed in the ensuing scramble.

"Let my sister go!" The young woman in blue picked herself up from the floor.

A man in a black suit grasped her arm and dragged her

a safe distance from Blackwood.

The remaining nearby guests scattered like a colony of disturbed ants. Shouts and screams rang out, then silence fell.

The woman Blackwood had snatched sobbed and struggled to get free. Blackwood held her with ease, the knife at her neck not moving.

Instinctively, Josh stepped in front of Ashley while he studied Blackwood again. The young woman trembled, and tears rolled over her cheeks. Blackwood cared nothing for her distress. Anger still rode his face. A determination that told Josh the man would never surrender.

A reporter and a man carrying a camera started to film until a policeman escorted the protesting pair from the ballroom.

"Let her go," Nelson said. "She has done nothing to you. She's innocent. You can't go anywhere. We have you surrounded."

"Tell your suits to back off. Come any closer, and I'll slit her throat." Blackwood's voice emerged cool, emotionless, and in control as he dragged the woman back two steps for a better view of the surrounding people. He held a knife beneath her chin to ensure the woman's cooperation. Blood ran down her pale throat and merged with the fabric of her dress.

"Oh! Trina. Do something," Mrs. Canon cried.

Two plain-clothes cops were ushering out attendees.

"Mrs. Canon, please go with the others. Sarah needs you. Let Nelson and his team help Trina," Ashley murmured. "Please."

"No, I..." A tear dampened her wrinkled cheek.

"Please, Mrs. Canon. They can't do their job with you here. We will look after Trina. I promise." Josh's gut twisted as he uttered the words because Blackwood showed no guilt or concern for the woman in his arms. She was a tool and tools were disposable.

Finally, Mrs. Canon left at the prompting of her other granddaughter, and only policemen remained.

"Tell your men to back off." He drew Trina closer and exerted pressure on the knife. She croaked, and blood ran down her chest and into her cleavage.

Ashley gasped while Josh stiffened in outrage and squeezed her hand in commiseration. "Let Nelson talk," he whispered.

Nelson gestured for the men to give Blackwood space. "What do you want?"

Stephen Blackwood glared at Nelson before he focused on Ashley. "I want the truth to come out. I want Ashley Townsend to suffer."

Behind him, Ashley mumbled something. Josh didn't take his gaze off Blackwood. Neither did Nelson nor Gerry or the dozen plain-clothes cops.

"Why?" Josh asked. "What has Ashley done to you?"

Blackwood stuck his hand in his pocket, and Josh froze. Before he could draw his weapon, Blackwood pulled something small and black from his pocket. It wasn't a gun.

"Flash drive," Blackwood said, his gaze intent on Ashley. "I want the contents played on the news."

"If we do that, you must do something for us too."

Nelson attempted to negotiate. "Let the girl go."

"Fine. Give me Ashley in exchange." A twisted smile curved Blackwood's mouth. Yep, not an ounce of remorse or hesitation. Just a man set on following a plan.

"No," Josh snarled. He'd seen men like Blackwood before. They'd lost all hope and didn't care what happened to them, had no fear of death.

"She's fooled you too," Blackwood sneered. "You're an idiot."

Ashley dropped Josh's hand and squeezed closer to Nelson to see better. Trina. That poor girl. Heaviness filled her stomach. Fear. Her fists clenched. Anger.

Nothing about Stephen Blackwood cried familiar. She still had no idea what he thought she'd done.

"Before we agree to your conditions, let the girl go," Nelson stated.

Her heart ached for Trina. They couldn't trust Stephen Blackwood to keep his word.

"I think not." He jerked the girl back two steps. "Play this on the news, on the screen up there with the political coverage before I make any deal."

"It will take time to organize," Nelson said.

"I have time." Blackwood adjusted his hold on the girl and pressed the knife more firmly against her pale throat. "I'm not going anywhere." His gaze shot to Ashley, and his mouth curled with a cruel twist.

"Give me the flash drive," Nelson ordered.

In reply, Blackwood tossed it toward one of the surrounding cops who strode over to Nelson.

"Let's go," Nelson murmured.

"Ashley stays," Blackwood barked. "I will kill this girl. She means nothing to me."

Ashley met Trina's terrified gaze and gave a clipped nod. She'd never forgive herself if Blackwood killed Trina.

"I'll be back as soon as I can," Nelson murmured. He gestured at another cop to take his place beside Ashley.

"Five minutes," Blackwood called. "And just to show you I mean business..." He adjusted his hold of Trina, grasped her long hair and hacked it off with his knife. "If you're not back in five minutes, I'll cut off something that won't grow back."

"Trina," Ashley whispered, tears stinging her eyes. This was her fault, and she still had no clue why Blackwood hated her so much.

Nelson hustled from the ballroom, and the door closed behind him with a defining click. Tension spread through her shoulders and slid up her neck. Her head started to ache, and she wondered what the heck she thought she was doing. How could she run the country?

A strident bang rang out. Adrenaline pumped through her, and Josh, Gerry, and the replacement cop surrounded her.

Blackwood's bark of laughter and Trina's strangled scream created confusion in Ashley until she realized a balloon had popped.

"Clock is ticking," Blackwood called out, taunting. "The girl won't look so pretty minus one ear."

Ashley swallowed hard.

The huge television screen flickered. The election

coverage disappeared, and another picture came on screen. It was the female reporter the cop had ushered from the ballroom.

"Turn up the sound," Blackwood ordered.

"Now. While we've split his attention," Josh murmured.

"He'll kill the girl," Gerry objected.

"He's gonna kill her, anyway. There's nothing left for him to lose."

Ashley croaked an objection.

"Shush," Josh snapped in a whisper.

Ashley trembled and pressed her lips together to barricade her objections. She studied the screen, which showed the reporter still talking, then her gaze darted to Blackwood. He was staring at her.

"Turn up the sound!" he shouted again.

A picture of a dog came on the screen, and Ashley blinked, not understanding.

"He'll kill the girl if we don't act," Josh said. "He would've known this was his last stand."

"Tell him I'll let him take me if he releases Trina." Ashley wished she could get her hands on the man. That poor girl. "Then shoot his arse."

"No, I can't lose you," Josh said, his reaction instantaneous, his voice hoarse with emotion.

"She's right. We need to shove him off balance," Gerry agreed. "But Ashley, not with you. He means business. He's got nothing to lose."

"Where is the damn sound?" Blackwood shouted.

"He's rattled." Gerry remained calm and watchful, ready to act given an opportunity. "We won't have a better chance."

"Let's stop mucking around. Stephen!" Ashley shouted. "Trina needs medical attention. Let her go, and you can have me in exchange." She pushed between Josh and Gerry, tension stiffening her limbs, but determination squaring her shoulders. She could do this. She *would* do this.

"If shooting starts, drop and roll to the side," Josh whispered to her. "Don't take risks."

Her legs trembled as she took a step away from her man. Her knees buckled a fraction before she strengthened them and took another shaky step toward Stephen Blackwood. Trina turned pleading eyes in her direction, her oval face so pale Ashley wondered if the girl might faint.

"Why is there no sound?"

Things weren't going the way Blackwood wanted, and it rattled him.

Ashley took another step forward. "I'm not coming any closer until you release Trina."

Blackwood shoved Trina, and the knife clattered to the hardwood floor. He reached in his jacket and pulled out a gun. Behind her, a weapon fired. Instinct had her dropping. *Roll.* Josh had told her to roll. She turned so fast she became dizzy.

Another gun fired. Two sharp barks in succession.

"Stand down," Nelson shouted.

"Quick," a man ordered. "Get behind us."

Ashley crawled on her hands and knees. "What's happening? Is Trina okay?"

"The gunman is down. Girl is okay," the cop said.

"Josh?"

The cop hesitated, and Ashley scrambled to her feet, wanting to see for herself. A cop had helped Trina up and was checking her neck. He pulled out a hanky and pressed it to her throat. Other cops surrounded Stephen Blackwood. They had him under control.

Josh. Where was Josh?

She spotted him on the ground with Gerry at his side. Another cop spoke on his phone. Ashley rushed to Josh.

"Josh! What happened?"

"Ashley. Ashley!" Gerry spoke louder, his words piercing her panic. "He's okay. Blackwood shot him in the shoulder. It's not a fatal shot, but it's worse than last time. We've called an ambulance."

Ashley sank to the ground beside Josh and stroked his face. His eyes flicked open, fierce but pain-filled. "I'm fine, sweetheart. I might have a scar from this one, but I was too pretty, anyway."

Gerry snorted, and Ashley issued a small, relieved laugh.

When Nelson prowled over to them, he scowled at Gerry and shared his displeasure with Josh. "Thanks to you two, I'll have a ton of paperwork."

"He intended to kill Ashley," Josh said.

"I would've done the same thing," Nelson replied quietly. "You took the only possible action."

The doors behind them opened, and two ambulance officers strode inside. Ashley stood, her attention snagged by the dog on the screen. This time, it looked familiar, and things started to click.

22

THE REAL DEAL

SUMMER AND NIKOLAI RUSHED into the waiting room, Nikolai shouldering a cop away from his wife. Ashley sprang to her feet. The uniformed policeman chased them, determined to carry out his duties.

"It's fine." Nelson gestured the cop back to his post. "They're family."

"What happened? Coverage from the Labor party ceased without warning, and no one knew what was happening." Summer gripped Ashley's shoulder and clung, her eyes demanding information. "Then I got your phone call and nothing made sense."

"Josh will make a full recovery, but they needed to dig the bullet out of his shoulder. I told you that," Ashley said.

"I wanted to see for myself."

"You can wait with me." Ashley led Summer to a chair. "The nurse I spoke with told me we'd hear soon."

Summer dropped onto the seat. "But what happened?"

"My stalker. Stephen Blackwood. He took a guest at knifepoint, but she's okay."

"But why?" Summer asked.

"You know the accident I had where my passenger died?"

"Yes." Summer turned her head on hearing approaching footsteps.

A nurse appeared at the door. "Mr. Williams is awake now. Two visitors at a time. No more."

"Thank you," Ashley said.

"Follow me." The nurse hustled down the corridor.

Summer gave Ashley a quick hug. "Congratulations."

"Why?" Josh had almost died. Again. Because of her. Trina would bear a scar for the rest of her life.

"The Labor party won by a majority of ten seats. You have enough seats to form a government on your own," Summer said.

"We won?" After everything that had happened, the election hadn't seemed important. She'd been more frantic for Josh and Trina.

"Yes, Prime Minister."

Ashley stared after the departing nurse and hurried to catch up with her. "I've wanted this since I was five-years-old. Now, I just feel empty."

Summer fell into step while Nikolai followed.

"This hasn't been a typical day or the usual campaign. Understandably, you feel flat. We had to force our way past dozens of cops at the entrance. There are reporters everywhere, and no one is saying anything. Not even the people at the Labor party function."

Ashley paused in the doorway of Josh's room. His eyes were open, and he gave a crooked smile on seeing her.

"Sweetheart."

Ashley ran to him, kissed him on the lips without concerning herself with their audience.

"They make their relationship look real," Summer whispered.

"That's what I said." Nikolai sounded smug.

For some reason, the nurse had let everyone enter the room. Nelson and Gerry waited outside.

Ashley smiled against Josh's lips.

"Of course it's real," he said. "I'm not stupid enough to let Ashley get away."

"How do you feel?"

"Shoulder is throbbing, but the doctor says I should regain full use soon enough. Not this weekend, but the next. You. Me. Fiji."

"Deal," she whispered. "I'll ask my expert admin aid to get right on that."

"What happened? Why was this Blackwood guy stalking you? He is in police custody, right?" Summer continued with her questions.

"He's dead," Ashley said. "Josh shot him when Blackwood drew his weapon."

"Oh. Will you be in trouble?" Summer asked.

"No," Josh said. "Gerry fired his weapon too. Blackwood never intended to leave the ballroom alive."

"My assessment too." Ashley shook her head at the memory of his twisted face, right before Josh had shot him.

He hadn't cared about anything except revenge.

"But I still don't understand why he stalked you," Summer said. "None of this makes any sense. You mentioned the accident, but it wasn't any of Jess's family stalking you. They were all cleared."

"The accident happened in the first place because a dog ran out on the road. That's why I crashed into the tree. I swerved to miss it, but I never saw the dog again. It ran away. According to documents they found on the flash drive, the dog was a valuable, champion stud. It was worth twenty thousand dollars. Although the dog ran off, it succumbed to its injuries. Stephen Blackwood's father lost his job. According to Stephen, he lost everything because that dog died. His parents divorced. His father committed suicide. His mother dragged him off to Australia, away from his friends."

"All this because of a dog?" Summer said. "Why didn't he do something sooner? I mean, what set him off?"

"I don't think we'll ever know the full truth," Josh said. "It could've festered over the years until everything bubbled over, and he snapped. It might've been a news item regarding Ashley that pushed him, or it might've been something to do with his military career."

"You're saying he might have suffered from post-traumatic stress?" Summer asked.

"It could've been any of those factors or a combination," Nikolai commented.

Ashley sighed. "From what we have, it was clear Stephen loved and admired his father. After his father's suicide, his life changed. He hated school. He hated living in

Australia."

"Returning to New Zealand didn't make him happy either," Summer pointed out.

"No, but he had a mission. He wanted to punish you and make you realize how your actions changed his life for the worse," Josh said.

Ashley swallowed hard. "I had no idea. Jess's death hit me hard, and the fact I'd been driving the vehicle was ghastly. I told the police there was a dog, but I don't think any of them believed me."

"What happens now?" Summer asked.

"I'll reach out to Stephen's mother and speak with her," Ashley said. "Tell her how sorry I am."

"Then you'll whip New Zealand into shape, right?" Summer winked at Josh.

Ashley smiled. "I'll sort out my cabinet, formerly take office when the Governor-General swears me in as Prime Minister, and then whip the country into shape. That should take about two weeks. I thought I might have a long weekend in Fiji after those two weeks."

"That sounds heavenly, and I'm envious." Summer sighed. "I wish we could take a break."

Josh winked at Ashley. "We might offer an incentive."

Ashley grinned. "What Josh said." She glanced toward the door where Nelson and Gerry kept guard. Then, she leaned closer to Summer and Nikolai. "Here's what we were thinking."

23

ELOPING TO FIJI

THE SUN SHONE OVERHEAD, bringing out a jewel-like sparkle in the fine white sand. Ashley followed the waves with her eyes as they sounded a gentle whoosh of advance and retreat. A warm breeze rattled the nearby coconut palms while the floral scent of the air screamed tropical island.

Fiji, and her wedding day.

Ashley stepped beneath a flower-decorated pagoda at The Ocean Resort Hotel, her hands linked with Josh's. She grinned, her gaze becoming enmeshed with Josh's as a tall Fijian marriage celebrant spoke in a deep voice and started their wedding vows. Euphoria and excitement tugged at her, and she'd never been more certain of a decision.

"The rings," the marriage celebrant said.

Seconds later, Josh pushed a golden wedding band onto

her finger, and she repeated the action a few minutes later, claiming him with her own ring. *Mine*, she thought. *My man.* Happiness filled her, and she wondered if she might burst with anticipation and delight.

"I now pronounce you man and wife. You may kiss your bride."

Josh took her in his arms and kissed her. Glee bubbled through her. Contentment.

"That's enough of the kissing," Summer chided from behind them. "Some of us want to offer congratulations."

They pulled apart with reluctance.

"Later," Josh promised with a wink.

"Welcome to the family." Summer offered Ashley a heartfelt hug. Summer turned to Josh and embraced him too. "You realize Mum will have a strong opinion regarding this secret wedding."

"So will Frog." Josh's grin dimmed a fraction.

Ashley smiled. "I don't care. We're married. Besides, I'm the Prime Minister of New Zealand. I must have *some* authority."

"And I'm married to the PM." Josh beamed at her, the love in his gaze making her breath stall. "We have our own security guys." He waved at Gerry and Nelson who stood at a distance, but close enough to witness their vows too. Both wore a casual uniform of cotton shirts and shorts. "Want to go for a walk? A paddle in the sea?"

"We're coming too," Summer said. "I'm the official photographer. We'll take casual shots of the beach. I take a great photo. Besides, I could sell one or two to a ladies' magazine and put our kid through university with the proceeds."

"He's not even two yet," Josh protested.

"Pre-planning never hurt," Summer said.

"Excellent strategy, sweetheart." Nikolai chuckled. "Having an in with the prime minister might prove beneficial."

"Bah! You're all talk," Ashley said. "But we'd love photos to share. I have to put something on my social media page. After we call the parental units, I mean."

Ashley toed off her shoes, took Josh's hand, and meandered along the beach. The fine sand massaged the soles of her feet while a local waved and cried, "*Bula*."

"*Bula!*" Ashley returned the traditional Fijian greeting, a multi-purpose word used to say hello.

Summer snapped photos during their walk—informal and full of smiles.

"You've made me very happy, Prime Minister." Josh cradled her face and stared into her eyes. Her heart beat extra fast, and confidence settled over her plus excitement for the future. In the background, the click and whir of Summer's camera continued.

"Don't go formal on me," Ashley said. "That's work. This is you and me. Ashley and Josh. The couple who eloped to avoid a huge, fussy wedding. We're the wild ones."

"I love you, Ashley."

"I know." Her voice thickened with emotion. This attractive *he-man* loved her and showed her in a dozen little ways each day. She'd been so wrong in restricting her dating pool to intellectual men. She cleared her throat.

"What say we drink champagne, eat delicious food, ring our parents then celebrate in private?"

"Works for me." Josh swung her into his arms and spun them around.

Later that evening, after they'd rung their parents and confessed their elopement plus promised a family party soon, they settled into their room, showered and relaxed.

"Josh, I'm so happy. Before you charged into my life, I lived by schedules and lists. The accident changed me—made me wary and over-controlling of what I did and didn't do. I prefer how I am now—a mix of the two Ashleys. More relaxed because I'm not at war with myself. I can be myself with no apologies. You helped me blossom."

"You're too hard on yourself, sweetheart. The accident was simply that. An accident. A set of unfortunate events that created havoc for Jess's family, for Stephen Blackwood and his family, and for you. You were as much a victim as the others."

"My head knows this, but it's so sad. His pain. Suicide rates are climbing amongst young people," Ashley said.

"Use your power for good. Make it one of your priorities or part of your particular portfolio of responsibilities. You could even name your plan or scheme or whatever you parliament types call them after Blackwood. Make him matter."

"Something to consider when we arrive home," Ashley said.

"Enough talk." Josh stood and strolled over to her, his gaze remaining fixed on her face. Her pulse jumped until it raced, then he gripped her hips to hold her in place. He kissed her and slipped off her robe, leaving her naked. "Better." His eyes glowed with love and emotion as he ran his hands over her shoulders and down her arms. He scooped her off her feet and lowered her onto the bed.

He grinned at her—a wide and devastating grin—while yanking off his boxer-briefs. It made her glad she was lying down because her knees would've failed her for sure. "Ready to celebrate?"

"Bring it," Ashley said with an answering laugh. He made seduction fun, and she was eager to sample more of his expertise, his teasing, his touch.

He leaped at her with a mock growl, trapping her within his arms while smothering her face with kisses. Gradually, the kisses deepened, and his hands wandered. He shaped her breasts and nibbled her neck. Ashley sighed against his mouth, allowing her tongue to tangle with his and thought how lucky she was to have this strong, wonderful man in her life. Her power didn't threaten him or cause resentment, and she treasured his support. She tried to show him with touch, with actions, and later, she'd confirm it in words, so he'd know she valued him and his contribution to her mental wellbeing.

Ashley nipped a spot low on his neck and soothed the sting with her tongue. He growled, and she smiled so wide, her facial muscles protested. And when he parted her legs and filled her, she rocked with him, her heart full of joy. She watched him as pleasure darkened his eyes.

"I love you, Ashley."

"I love you right back, Josh." She shuddered and

surrendered to the passion storming her body. "My husband."

She fell asleep with his scent surrounding her, the taste of him on her mouth, and her happiness overflowing.

The next morning, after lazy sex, the phone rang. Josh reached out for the cell phone and answered it.

"Yeah." Sleep wove through his husky voice, and she suffered a similar lethargy. Then, he stiffened. "Frog."

"What are you doing answering Ashley's phone?" Matt roared loud enough for Ashley to hear.

She plucked her phone from Josh's hand. "Why are you ringing me at this time of the morning?"

"What are you doing with Josh? He sounded sleepy. Are you in bed together?" Matt's voice filled their hotel room. "I told you not to get involved—"

"Matt," Ashley interrupted in a stern voice. "Shut up and listen to me. I *am* the prime minister. I am not your little sister or someone for you to order around with that bossy military tone."

"Where are you?"

"Fiji. I wanted to take a long weekend break after the drama at home," Ashley said. "We'll be home tomorrow afternoon."

"Flight?"

Ashley gave her brother the details, and he disconnected. She pulled a face at her phone. "That went well. He's become bossy in his old age."

"Never mind your brother. We'll talk to him when we get home. We have the entire day to relax and have fun. I vote for snorkeling and swimming and a picnic lunch."

"He mustn't have talked to Mum and Dad yet. He always arrives home without telling anyone." Ashley slid out of bed. "I'm hungry. Breakfast then swimming and snorkeling."

"And a sexy bikini?"

"I might have one of those."

· ♥ · ♥ · ♥ · ♥ · ♥ ·

Almost twenty-four hours later, their commercial flight landed in Auckland. They'd sat in business class for the three-hour flight from Fiji and were the first to disembark. Progress through the airport was speedy. Frog wasn't at the airport, but several members of the public did a double-take with some stopping to converse with Ashley and tell her they'd voted for her.

They piled into a large vehicle with Nikolai, Summer, and the two DPS officers and headed to Ashley's house in South Auckland.

A lone figure climbed from a rental car when Nelson parked in the driveway.

"Ah, there he is," Josh said.

"Summer and I are heading to Louie's place to pick up Sam." Nikolai grabbed their hand luggage.

"Can't you wait for ten minutes?" Josh asked.

"Worried Frog will break you and you'll lose your manly mystique?" Nikolai countered.

"Stop acting like babies." Summer picked up a bag of duty-free purchases. "There will be no physical stuff. Nelson and Gerry won't allow it."

"We'll only intervene if Ashley is in danger." Nelson's mouth twitched with suppressed humor.

Josh snorted. "Let's do this, Ashley. Together."

"Matt won't punch you," Ashley said.

"You didn't hear his succinct threats."

"Baby," Summer taunted. "Maybe I'll take photos of this too."

"Summer." Nikolai urged her toward the vehicle they'd left parked at Ashley's place.

"I haven't received enough payback yet," Summer protested. "Josh owes me."

"Matt!" Ashley ran at her brother.

He wrapped his beefy arms around her, as always making her feel safe. She pulled back and patted his stubbled cheek. "How long are you back in New Zealand?"

"Two weeks," Matt said, his gaze hard as he glowered at Josh. "You were in bed with my sister. I meant this to be a pretend engagement to help keep Ashley safe. I told you she was off-bounds, but did you listen? No."

Ashley narrowed her eyes at her big brother. She'd seen him angry, and this wasn't it. A thought popped into her mind. She tested it, and enlightenment poured through her. *The dirty rat.* "You might have warned Josh not to step over the line with me, but have you considered that none of this was his fault? I seduced him."

Someone standing behind her and Josh made a scoffing sound. Ashley ignored the interruption from their audience.

"It's true. I jumped him and seduced him before he had

a chance."

"You're wearing rings. Both of you." Matt cocked his head, his eyes narrowing. "You're married?"

"We are," Josh confirmed. "I love your sister."

Matt let out a loud cheer and pumped his fist in the air. "Yes! Yes! My plan worked."

Ashley clicked her fingers and leaned into Josh. "Huh! I knew something was suspicious as soon as I saw you. You set us up."

Matt's grin was broad and toothy. "I've always thought you and Josh would work together, but I knew if I suggested it you'd both turn your backs. When I heard you were having trouble, I decided this was the perfect way to get you together. I figured if I warned you away from each other, it'd raise your curiosity and allow nature to take its course." Matt held out his hand. "Welcome to the family, Josh."

Slightly bemused, Josh accepted Matt's handshake.

"Well-played," Summer said as Ashley did the introductions.

"Nikolai, great to see you again." Matt clapped him over the back. "I'm heading to the parents' place. I'll catch up with you tomorrow. Congratulations to both of you." He grinned. "I'm an excellent matchmaker if I say so myself. You'll have a party. I'll sing."

Ashley booed and waved him away.

Josh narrowed his eyes at his departing mate. "We'll have to burst his bubble."

"Yes," Ashley said. "Matt might've been right, but I hate being manipulated."

"You want me to post a few pictures on your official social media page? Make it an announcement?" Summer asked.

"Yes, please," Ashley said. "I trust you not to embarrass me. I'll contact Geoffrey and the senior members myself, so they're not blindsided."

Nikolai and Summer left not long after Matt.

Josh hugged her. "I can't believe Frog—Matt—was setting us up."

"I'm glad he did," Ashley said. "Although I'll never admit it to him."

Josh unlocked the front door. "Wait there." He darted inside to turn off the alarm.

On his return, he lifted her and carried her over the threshold. Ashley laughed but appreciated their adhering to the old ritual. Their relationship had held little in the way of tradition, and she welcomed the return of normalcy.

Nelson and Gerry applauded them and like the discreet men they were, neither commented on Matt's revelations of a fake engagement.

"I can't wait to share this adventure with you," Josh whispered as he set her on her feet.

Ashley gave her new husband a swift kiss. "Me too," she said, her happiness almost too big for her body to contain. "Let the adventure begin."

·❤·❤·❤·❤·❤·

THANK YOU FOR READING **Josh's Fake Fiancée**. How

did you enjoy Ashley's and Josh's romance and the taste of New Zealand politics? I'd love to learn what you thought so please consider leaving a review at your favorite online bookstore, Goodreads, or Bookbub. A review would make my day!

Next up is Frog's story. He meets one tough lady who shouts at him when he lands in the middle of her flower garden. **Operation Flower Petal** is available now.

I write several contemporary romance series. Please turn the page for an excerpt from ***Protection***, the first book in the *Fancy Free* series plus an excerpt from ***Enemy Lovers***, part of my *Friendship Chronicles* series. Both series are set in my home country of New Zealand.

If you'd like to keep up with my releases check out my newsletter (https://shelleymunro.com/newsletter)

EXCERPT – PROTECTION

A SMALL COUNTRY TOWN.
An out-of-the-box condom company.
Fun, laughter and suspense.
Let the romance begin!
Book #1 in the Fancy Free series.

Warning: *Condoms were tested and a few harmed during the writing of this story.*

·♥·♥·♥·♥·♥·

JAMES FROZE, THE RUB of her luscious breasts against his chest felt like a kind of torture. For the second time she'd implied he had way too much experience. He studied her innocent expression and let his indignation go. For the moment. He traced his fingers around the base of one breast before following the feathering of veins beneath the surface. No freckles, but instead, skin the color of rich cream with not a blemish. Her breast quivered at his touch, her pretty pink nipple pulling tight. The soft sound of pleasure that whispered from her lips made his cock twitch.

Hell, she was beautiful, from her full, creamy breasts to her slim waist and flaring hips. Not exactly fashionable, but her body would make any red-blooded man howl with joy. His affronted feelings subsided even more when he concentrated on her. He trailed his hand across her collarbone, savoring the petal-soft skin. Touching her. Desire filled him plus the need to give her pleasure and make her first time with him one she would always remember. Selfishly, he didn't intend to give her another opportunity to say no. He'd tried his best to do the right thing, to warn her. His conscience remained clear.

She was willing.

She wanted him, and knowing that was a powerful aphrodisiac.

"If there's anything you don't enjoy or if something I do hurts, let me know." His voice sounded gritty while his cock tightened with pure need. Fighting the urgency thrumming through his body, he splayed his fingers across her breasts, lightly kneaded and plucked at her nipples.

Alice jerked before stilling, her eyes wide and full of anxiety. The reaction told him she didn't believe she was a treasure worthy of exploration. James bit back a groan. God. He could explore sexuality with this woman for months, for years, and never get tired. A frown surfaced at the oddball notion. He wasn't settling down with anyone.

Damned if he'd stay in Sloan so his mother could sneer at him whenever they met. Fuck, he had no idea why he'd returned to Sloan anyway—some misbegotten idea that he'd be welcomed back into the family fold.

"Is something wrong?" Her voice held anxiety, the emotion underlined in her golden-brown eyes.

James summoned a reassuring grin—hell, it must have been a smirk if her reaction was anything to go by—he leaned over and blew on her nipple. Large, to match her breasts, they puckered even more and colored to a deep pink on contact with the warmth of his breath. James licked around the circumference of her nipple, carefully watching Alice's reaction. She took a hasty breath and held it for long seconds, her golden eyes wide and still unsure.

"You're beautiful," James murmured, the reassurance she needed to gain confidence easy for him to give. "So responsive." He blew on her other nipple and watched her reaction. "See?" Unable to deny himself the treat any longer he leaned closer and drew her nipple into his mouth. Alice jerked and let out a soft moan. James used one hand to tease and tug at a nipple while his tongue swirled over the other one. Another low moan sounded, her hands clamped on his shoulders and fingernails dug into his skin. His mouth quirked into a grin and he let go with an audible pop. "Did you like that?"

Alice seemed to consider her answer before she replied. "Yes."

"What did you feel? And where did you feel it?" A test. James waited to see what she'd say. A test of his willpower too. He kissed and nibbled at her breast while maintaining eye contact, enjoying the shimmer of expression across her face and the way she clamped her bottom lip between her teeth. Suddenly he couldn't wait to see how she'd react when he kissed her intimately. "Alice?" he prompted.

Alice let go of her lip and moistened the curves of her mouth with her tongue. James watched the innocent gesture avidly, his gut jumped with awareness. Innocent but oh-so sexy.

His.

Awe filled him. Possessiveness. Reality followed swiftly.

Ugh, had he just thought that? This—whatever what might be between them—must remain a temporary thing.

Yeah, temporary.

He shook himself to emphasize the fact. "Alice?"

"When you," she paused, her cheeks going pink, "sucked, I felt it all the way down there." She gestured with her hand.

"Show me," he whispered, intent on pushing her out of her comfort zone.

Alice hesitated then seemed to gather her courage. Her pale hand crept from his shoulder and skimmed down her body, across her quivering belly and halted half an inch away from the short curls that guarded her femininity.

"Go on."

Her fingers moved stealthily downward. Her legs parted.

James smiled. Innocent and sexy. That was test enough for her now. He'd take it from here. He slid his hand down her body, following the same path her fingers had taken. But he didn't stop. Instead, he parted her legs, his fingers skimmed across her swollen folds, lightly in an exploration of her moist flesh. Her scent rose, teasing him. James breathed deep and couldn't resist a pass over her clit. The tiny bud peeked from its hood and pulsed beneath his touch. Soon he would thrust into her sweet flesh. His cock jolted at the thought and he thrust lightly against her upper thigh, teasing himself and pushing his need higher.

Alice's hand slid across his shoulders, hesitant and a little shy. Her hand slipped downward and she seemed to gain confidence when he didn't protest. Alice squeezed one buttock and earned a quick kiss. "Please," she whispered, wanting him to hurry before he changed his mind. "Please, I need you."

"Where? Tell me. Describe what you want," he ordered, forgetting for an instant that he'd decided to take control.

She worried her bottom lip between white teeth, her eyes wide and uncertain.

"If you don't tell me, I might do something you hate," he drawled.

Alice hesitated for so long he thought he might have frightened her or pushed her too hard and fast. Finally, she released her bottom lip and the pale column of her throat moved when she swallowed. "I want to explore your body," she whispered. "I want to know what you like." Her warm hand squeezed his ass again, the innocent touch a heated reverberation throughout his entire body.

Giving. So bloody giving. Her first lover must have had rocks in his head. His heart thumped when he rolled off her, an offer of free access to his body and silent permission to explore as she wanted.

Trembling fingers skimmed across his stubble-covered jaw, dipped into his dimple and traced his mouth. James parted his lips a fraction and sucked her forefinger inside. Her gasp was loud. Startled. And it made him want to laugh. Instead, he sucked lightly on her finger and cupped her head. The silky strands of hair tickled his palm, bringing a desire to touch and stroke and soothe her jumpy virginal nerves aside, raising tenderness in him. His tongue smoothed across her fingernail and ran across the delicate skin between fingertip and nail. Alice gasped again, golden glints shining in her eyes. He captured her gaze with his and released her finger. James nipped her earlobe and surprised a yelp out of her.

"Ouch." She pulled away to finger her ear. "I thought I was meant to be the one in charge."

"That can be arranged." After brushing another kiss across her lips, he kissed the tip of one breast and skimmed his hands across her rib cage. James smiled when she finally plucked up the courage to curl her hand around his cock. Her fingers traced the flared head, her curiosity endearing and arousing. She explored his tender balls and wrapped her fingers around his shaft. She pumped, focused so hard her tongue poked between her lips. The innocent exploration dragged a soft curse from him. "Enough," he growled. "This is torture," he added quickly before she put a different interpretation on his words. Discouragement was the last thing he intended.

He took a moment to kiss her again. Good girl. She learned quickly, opening her mouth to him in full participation rather than her previous passive behavior. A quick study. Their tongues tangled lazily. James felt the rapid beat of her heart, saw the flush of rosy arousal on her face and chest. He wanted to go slowly, to arouse her fully, teasing until she throbbed in need, until they both ached for the conclusion.

But it wasn't going down that way. Not today. At least they agreed and wanted the same thing. James thrust one leg between her thighs, silently indicating she should part her legs. So beautiful. So sexy. He dipped his head to nuzzle at her breasts, moving over Alice and guiding his cock to her pussy. Moist warmth met him when he pushed just the tip of his cock into her sexy body.

"Fuck." James froze, a heavy jolt of disbelief coloring his voice. He jerked away from her, horror in his stare.

Through his dismay, James saw her flinch as if he'd struck her. Another abrupt move on his part and she'd run for the hills that surrounded Sloan.

He cleared his throat. "I don't suppose you have a condom?"

A surprised burst of laughter bubbled from her, diluting the alarm he'd seen seconds earlier. "A condom?"

"It's not funny," he said stiffly. His body ached for release. Without a condom, he'd have to take care of the matter himself when he wanted the satisfaction that only the snug feel of a woman's pussy would give. He'd end up with blue balls for hours if he couldn't have her now. His hand just wouldn't be the same.

"You do work for a condom company, right?" She chuckled, her breasts jiggling in a distracting manner. "Manager, isn't it?" She giggled and her brows rose to punctuate the question.

"Give it a rest," he muttered, a tinge of heat at the tips of his ears. A thought occurred. His gaze speared toward her. "If you're offering sex, shouldn't you have condoms?" More than a trace of accusation shaded his words.

"Oh sure. Do you know I've inherited a share in a condom company, and I don't even know what one looks like in the flesh so to speak? All I've seen is the X-100 in all its inflated glory." She giggled, her cute button nose twitching at the same time. "I guess we'll have to do this another time."

Will James finally get his hands on some condoms?
Learn more!
(https://shelleymunro.com/books/protection/)

EXCERPT – ENEMY LOVERS

Friendship Chronicles, #5
Love lurks in enemy territory...
Note: this book can be read without reading the prior romances in the series.

·♥·♥·♥·♥·♥·

Whoa. Dallas O'Grady caught a glimpse of blonde hair seconds before the woman kicked her flat tire. She owned the sexiest arse he'd seen in months. Without another thought, he pulled his truck onto the shoulder and climbed out to offer assistance.

"Problem?"

"My brother is an idiot." Her lyrical voice held the same crisp chill of the wind whistling across the Napier road. She turned, and he caught a friendly smile belying her words. "Thanks for stop— You!"

JOSH'S FAKE FIANCEE

The smile skidded away.

Hard drops of rain fell on Dallas's face, the sleeves of his brown leather jacket, as he eyeballed a very sexy, very grown-up Laura Drummond. His gaze shifted to the gray, washed out clouds, the sky building to dense black on the horizon, then to the rear tire on her late model sedan. "Fine, if you don't want my help, I'll be leaving."

"No, please." Her hand shot out to halt his retreat. "I'm sorry."

"Sorry you're hobnobbing with the enemy?" He spelled out what they were both thinking. Their parents would issue horrendous battle cries if they witnessed this scene, saw the pair inhaling the same air, let alone engaging in something civil like a conversation.

She swept a strand of blonde hair away from her pink lips. "You're not my enemy. I don't know you." She stuffed her hands in her jacket pockets, hunched her shoulders against the rain and stamped her feet. "Look, I'm grouchy. I have a flat. My brother borrowed my spare last week and told me he put it back. My phone is dead, and I'm not going to make Clare in time for my cousin's hen party. My mother will make dolls in my image and stick pins in them."

"My brother said there's a slip partially blocking the road leading into the town, near the Shannon Pass. If it keeps raining, they might close the roads, if they haven't already. You wouldn't make it even if your car was drivable."

"Yep, I'm screwed," she said.

No, she wasn't—not yet, but he'd love to take that

thought to its logical conclusion. While their families might harbor long-standing grudges, his dick wasn't sticking with the program. The skinny Laura Drummond from his vague school-day memories had grown into a classy woman. Her brown eyes glinted with intelligence while her mouth...

Dallas tore his gaze off her because his inappropriate thoughts bore repercussions. For one—a painful hard-on. And two, no way could he cozy up with the enemy.

He cleared his throat. "What do you want to do? I can give you a lift to Clare and hope we'll make it past the slip, or I can ring for a breakdown truck."

The rain was coming down harder now, icy crystal pellets pummeling his cheeks. She caught her bottom lip between her teeth, worried it then nodded a decisive agreement.

"Let me grab my purse and overnight bag," she said. "I'll grab a ride and chance my luck. The slip might have been cleared already."

Dallas told himself not to look, but when she bent over to retrieve her bag, his eyes zeroed in on her arse.

Down boy.

God, he hadn't experienced this sort of reaction to a woman for a long time. He wanted to fuck her. He wanted to fuck her mouth, holding her in place by her hair, and most of all he wanted to tie her to his bed. He wanted the classy Laura Drummond to submit to him while he fucked them both to breath-stealing pleasure.

Shaking the lust away, he accepted her bag and stowed it behind the driver's seat. He straightened, his mind leaping straight to her and sexual desire. Man, he was weak. Giving in to his libido, he watched her lock her sedan and splash through puddles to join him.

"You don't resemble your sisters and brother." They were dark-haired, her sisters both shorter than Laura.

"Nope, everyone says I'm the cuckoo in the nest." She peeled off her wet raincoat and slid her long legs into his vehicle. "Ugh, it's bucketing down out there. I'm lucky you came along."

She was still talking when Dallas climbed behind the wheel. Nervous? He grunted, started his truck and pulled on to the road, trying to ignore the unpleasant sensation of water dripping down his neck.

"I take after my great-grandmother on my mother's side. They say I'm her twin."

Dallas nodded while his mind trotted back to the more pleasant occupation of imagining this woman naked and engaged with him in things carnal. A whoosh of heat replaced the chill of wet clothes.

"What are you going to do if the road is closed?" she asked.

"My cabin is on this side."

"Oh."

"Are you wondering what I'm going to do with you if the road is closed?"

"Please." A strangled laugh emerged from her, tinged with a healthy dose of uncertainty. "I doubt you'd do away with me."

"But you're not too sure?" He set the window wipers to a faster speed and eased up on the accelerator, not taking his attention off the road. "I am one of *those* O'Gradys."

"Positive." She slanted him an ice-princess look, lifted that elegant nose just so. "I'm pretty sure you're not hiding horns under your hair, although you might be concealing a tail. Even so, I'm confident I'll get through this ordeal unscathed. I'll grab a ride back to Napier. There's bound to be someone heading to the city."

Dallas barked out a laugh, amused at her sly humor lurking beneath the hauteur. She didn't act like any Drummond he'd come into contact with in the past. He'd thought he might have consigned himself to an hour of chilly silence—more than an hour in these driving conditions. But she'd tossed his assumptions on their butt, and he found himself wanting to explore her mentally. Ditto the physical.

"What do you do for a job?" He shot her a quick glance, caught the wrinkling of her nose.

"My mother organized a place for me at a charity. I'm working for them at present, but I'd prefer a position with more challenge."

"What sort of employment are you looking for?" Hearsay said Laura's older sisters had never worked in their lives. They'd done the socialite thing, found rich husbands and married. They were now popping out a new generation of Drummonds to heap down hate on the O'Grady family.

"I enjoy organizing things, which makes me a natural in the administration field."

"Are you good with computers?"

"Not bad. Any program I don't know, I can learn. I'm a

quick study." Her chin lifted a fraction as if she expected him to challenge her statement.

Again, he found a smile pushing his lips for escape. He enjoyed a woman who surprised him. "If you weren't a Drummond, I'd offer you a job."

"What sort? What do you do?"

Again, not the reaction he'd expected. "My brothers and I own a couple of Irish bars in Napier, and I have several rental properties. It's getting too much for me to handle the paperwork along with the day-to-day things." The pub where he had his office wasn't in the best part of town. Nah, he couldn't see Laura slumming it at *O'Grady's*. "We're thinking of buying the old pub in Clare."

"The one that closed down due to fire damage?"

"Yeah." Dallas peered through the windshield, not taking his eyes off the road.

"Can I interview for the job?"

Dallas slowed even further until his truck crawled. Closer to the Shannon Pass, the rain slapped the windows, obliterated the scenery. What he could see of the sky was a sullen gray and lightning flashed in the distance, followed by a rumble of thunder. "You want to work in a pub? Maybe I should check *you* for horns and a tail. You have an impish sense of humor."

"I'm not joking," she said, and he felt the weight of her gaze. "But if you want to check me for devilish signs you go right ahead. I might enjoy it."

Dallas opened his mouth, shut it again, risked a swift glance in her direction. A tiny grin played around her luscious lips. Oh yeah. She was pleased with herself.

"I'm an O'Grady, sweetheart. I don't possess the right bloodlines for you."

"My parents want me to marry James Summerville."

Another glance away from the road. Her big brown eyes held silent messages, and it took him an extended second to grasp the stray snippets of gossip and knit them together. His lips pursed in a silent whistle. "Isn't he gay?"

"Yup, but James wants marriage. A… Sorry, you don't want to hear about me." Laura wiped a round circle on the passenger side window. A polite dismissal of the subject. "I don't like the look of this rain. If anything it's getting worse."

"It's not looking promising," he agreed, deciding to let her get away with the change of topic. "Not wedding weather."

"My cousin was set on an early spring wedding. Heck, I picture her stamping her foot and having a full-blown tantrum about the weather. She should've listened to the wedding planner. This time of year is always unpredictable." Wily amusement colored her voice, and Dallas found his lips quirking. He fought the need to fall into a full-out smile of delight. If she'd been anyone else, he'd proposition her, offer her a cozy weekend of hot sex at his cabin.

But that wasn't gonna happen.

She was a Drummond.

How does this Drummond/O'Grady meeting shake down? Learn more here.
(https://shelleymunro.com/books/enemy-lovers/)

ABOUT AUTHOR

USA Today bestselling author Shelley Munro lives in Auckland, the City of Sails, with her husband and a cheeky Jack Russell/mystery breed dog.

Typical New Zealanders, Shelley and her husband left home for their big OE soon after they married (translation of New Zealand speak - big overseas experience). A twelve-month-long adventure lengthened to six years of roaming the world. Enduring memories include being almost sat on by a mountain gorilla in Rwanda, lazing on white sandy beaches in India, whale watching in Alaska, searching for leprechauns in Ireland, and dealing with ghosts in an English pub.

While travel is still a big attraction, these days Shelley is most likely found in front of her computer following another love - that of writing stories of contemporary and paranormal romance and adventure. Other interests include watching rugby (strictly for research purposes), cycling, playing croquet and the ukelele, and curling up with an enjoyable book.

>
> Visit Shelley at her Website
> www.shelleymunro.com
>
> Join Shelley's Newsletter
> www.shelleymunro.com/newsletter

ALSO BY SHELLEY

Military Men
Innocent Next Door
Soldier with Benefits
Safeguarding Sorrel
Stranded with Ella
Josh's Fake Fiancee
Operation Flower Petal
Protecting the Bride

Friendship Chronicles
Secret Lovers
Reunited Lovers
Clandestine Lovers
Part-Time Lovers
Enemy Lovers
Maverick Lovers
Sports Lovers

Fancy Free
Protection
Romp
Buzz
Festive

Single Titles
One Night of Misbehavior
Playing to Win
Reformed Bad Girl

Milton Keynes UK
Ingram Content Group UK Ltd.
UKHW010635290424
441924UK00005B/285